P9-CNC-333

To my wonderful son, Geoffrey

CHAPTER 1

When I walk into Granger's Feed Store early Monday morning, Melvin Granger is up on a ladder shoving big sacks of dog food around. He pauses when he hears my boots on the wood floor and shoots me a look of pure aggravation. "I'll be right with you." The tone of his voice implies he'd just as soon I'd go to hell as be in his store. His old yellow dog, Dusty, is lying on his fluffy brown bed with a long-suffering gloom about him, as if he's been a target, too.

"Don't let me rush you." I'm as irritated as Melvin is.

He goes back to pushing sacks around with a hint of violence. It's hard to see exactly what he's aiming for. But what he gets is one of the sacks plummeting to the floor and breaking wide open. Pellets of dog food scatter everywhere. Dusty heaves himself to his feet with a big sigh, as if to say it's going to be a chore to clean up all that dog food, but he's going to give it his best shot.

"Goddammit! Dusty, get the hell away from that mess!" Melvin clatters down off the ladder, his feet crunching on the pellets. "What do you want?" he says to me.

I'm not taking any of this personally. The whole town is grumpy. For the first time in ten years the Jarrett Creek High School Panthers lost the homecoming football game to the Bobtail Bobcats last Friday night. Coach Eldridge was cursed every which way for keeping the first-string quarterback out of the game in the last ten minutes.

"I came in to get a case of cat food. Is that too much trouble?" In the grumpy department, I can give as good as I get.

Melvin narrows his eyes at me. "I don't know why anybody would keep a cat."

"Same reason you have that flea-bitten hound around here." We stare down at Dusty and he pauses from gobbling up dog food to sneak a nervous look at us.

"Get away from there!" Melvin hooks two fingers under Dusty's collar and hauls him over to his bed, then grabs a broom and starts cleaning up the mess.

I find Zelda's cat food and plunk a case onto the counter. It takes five minutes for Melvin to finish cleaning up the dog food. By then August Nachtway and his son have walked in, looking like they'd like to bite somebody. They nod to me, but don't offer any conversation.

"There's a lot of people don't have a bed as nice as that dog's," I say, while Melvin rings me up.

Dusty thumps his tail, and that's about all the friendliness I get out of the visit.

Back on the highway, I decide to stop by Town Café to listen to Jack Harbin rant about the game, which might be soothing in its own way. Jack was a star quarterback at Jarrett Creek High School and knows the game. His athletic days are over. He joined the army just in time to be swept up into the Gulf War. He was blinded and lost a leg. But he goes to the games every Friday and will talk football all day long, any day. Adversity has left Jack with an unpredictable disposition, but he never lacks for someone to talk to. Like most small towns in Texas, Jarrett Creek holds football in high regard.

Town Café has all the charm of a cow barn. A big tin Quonset hut, it's pockmarked on the outside, as if it was used for target practice in some past life. Bill Schroeder trucked it in about ten years ago and plopped it onto a lot near the railroad tracks. The place has knotty pine walls decorated with random signs advertising beer and farm equipment. Christmas lights are strung all over the place, year-round. But the food is good.

When I walk into the crowded café, Jack isn't at his usual table. Jack's dad, Bob Harbin, brings him to the café every morning from nine to eleven. You get used to certain rhythms in a small town. Jimmy Orozco standing over his barbeque pit outside his stand by seven o'clock every morning, the eight o'clock freight train lumbering down the tracks for twenty minutes. And Jack Harbin parked in the café by nine o'clock.

The waitress, Lurleen, whose droopy brown eyes suggest how hard her life is, says she hasn't heard from Jack, and she's worried. She's too busy with the breakfast crowd to call and find out where he is, so I say I'll do it. She gives me the number and I step into the café's little office to make the call. As I listen to the phone ring, I note that Lurleen knows the number by heart.

No one picks up at the Harbins'. I tell Lurleen that Bob and Jack are probably on their way over right now—most likely they overslept. She's got her hands full of plates of eggs and bacon that look pretty good to me, but her eyes are so anxious that I tell her I'll go over and look in on in them right now and see if everything's okay.

It's already a sultry day. Climbing into my truck I pause and look off to the west. A few puffy clouds are piling up on the horizon, as if deciding whether to collect into something more serious. We could use the rain and a break from the heat.

As I approach Jack's street, I hear a woman screaming, and arrive upon a dreadful sight. Jack Harbin's wheelchair is on its side, Jack spilled out onto the sidewalk, trying to pull himself upright. Bob Harbin lies still on the grass nearby. Their next-door neighbor, Becky Geisenslaw, is standing in her driveway dressed for work in her blue and white Dairy Queen uniform, hands to her cheeks, shrieking. I swerve to the curb and jump out onto the sidewalk so hard that my bad knee almost buckles.

Sprawled on the sidewalk, Jack looks pitiful, his face gaunt, and his shoulders poking out of his T-shirt as sharp as chicken wings. The left leg of his army fatigue pants is pinned up where it's empty. He tried out an artificial leg, but it never worked out. Some kind of chemical in the explosion that crippled him got into the wound and it won't heal properly.

I doubt Jack can hear me over Becky's noise, so I put my hand on his shoulder to get his attention. "Jack, it's Samuel Craddock. I'm going to see about your daddy."

Jack's dark glasses have fallen onto the sidewalk. I pick them up and place them in his hands. It's the first time I've ever seen him without them. His brown eyes are clear, and you wouldn't know anything was wrong, except that the skin surrounding his eyes is pinched and riddled with tiny white scars.

"What's happened to Daddy? Where is he, Mr. Craddock? Daddy!" His voice is harsh with fear.

"Hold on, Jack, just give me a second. Everything's going to be okay." I say that even though a glance at Jack's father tells me I'm probably wrong. He's lying face down in the grass, his head cocked back in an odd way, arms flung out to his sides.

I gesture for Becky to get over here. She shakes her head and hustles to her car faster than a woman her size ought to be able to move.

Ed Hruska comes huffing up the sidewalk to the rescue. He's a burly guy. I ask him to help Jack back into his chair while I see about Bob.

I kneel down and turn Bob over. His face is a meaty color of purple, and his mouth is open as if he was gasping for a last breath. I don't believe he's even sixty, but it looks like a heart attack or a stroke felled him. I feel his carotid artery and there's no pulse, so I start pumping his chest. In the distance I hear a police siren. I hope whoever is on duty has a defibrillator in the car. It will take another twenty minutes for an ambulance to get here from Bobtail.

Ed manages to wrestle Jack into his chair. "I'm going to take you inside Jack," he says. "It's hot as blazes out here."

"What about Daddy? Why isn't he saying anything?" It's painful to watch Jack moving his head from side to side as if he thinks if he can just get in the right position, he'll be able to see for himself.

"Your daddy's unconscious. We'll get the ambulance here and sort things out." I nod for Ed to get Jack out of here.

Rodell Skinner, the town's police chief, pulls up across the street and lets the siren die. For once I'm glad to see him. We've had a reasonable truce since I let him take credit for nabbing a murderer a few months back, but we'll never be bosom buddies. As former police chief, I hold whoever fills the office to a high standard that Rodell stumbles under. He claims to have cut down on his drinking lately, and this early in the morning I'm hoping he'll be sober enough to carry out his duties. He takes his time climbing out of his car and ambling over to join me.

I squint up at him, panting. "You got a defib unit with you?"

He shakes his head. "It's in James Harley's car. You may as well save your energy."

I sigh and sit back on my heels and mop the sweat off my face with my handkerchief. Rodell crouches down and lays his hands on Bob's chest as if he thinks his touch can bring him back to life.

"Yep, he's dead all right." I never have understood Rodell. But he has his supporters—mostly men he drinks with.

When Rodell stands back up I tell him I'm going inside to talk to Jack, thinking he might want to join me. He sends a disinterested glance over in the direction of the house and says he'll wait for the ambulance. I ask him for a hand, it being hard to get up with my bum knee.

"When are you going to get that knee fixed?" he says.

"In my own good time."

I don't like the idea of Bob lying out in the hot sun, uncovered, so I root around in my truck for the blanket I carry around with me. I lay it over Bob, wishing it wasn't so stained.

In the house Ed Hruska is trying to calm Jack down, not always an easy task. When Jack gets a notion in his head, he's sometimes hard to divert.

"Jack, your daddy isn't looking too good," I say. "Rodell has called an ambulance. We need to get somebody in here to stay with you for a while. Do you have anybody in particular for me to call?"

"What do you mean he's not looking too good?" Jack is hyperventilating, with little moans in between breaths.

Ed raises his eyebrows at me and I shrug. I don't want to tell Jack about his daddy, but it doesn't seem right to lie to him. "Jack, I think maybe your daddy has had a heart attack."

"Oh, hellfire!" He beats his fist on the arm of his chair. "Daddy told me this morning he didn't feel good. I said we didn't have to go the café, but he said we ought to go because people would be talking about Friday's game. Goddamn Coach Eldridge!" As if the coach is to blame for Bob's heart attack in addition to losing the game. Jack fumbles in the side pocket of his wheelchair and brings out a pack of cigarettes and a lighter. His hands are shaking so hard that I have to light it for him.

Jack directs me to a list of his friends taped on the refrigerator. Like the living room, the kitchen is spotless. I wonder if I could do what Bob did, turning my whole life over to the long-term care of a son who needs round-the-clock attention.

I reach a friend of Jack's named Walter Dunn. I've seen Dunn with Jack at the café on occasion. He says he'll be there in ten minutes.

Back outside I report to Rodell that Dunn will be here soon. Rodell looks toward Jack's house with a sneer ruffling his brushy mustache. "With his daddy gone, now Jack's really got something to whine about."

I hold back a rush of anger. "The boy's had the devil of a time and it's going to get harder."

Rodell tips the hat back off his forehead, which is slick with sweat. "I guess," he says. After that we stand there in a sour cloud of a mood.

Before long Walter Dunn and another man roar up on motorcycles. The two men are about Jack's age, and dressed like Jack in ratty army fatigues, boots, and T-shirts. Dunn wears his hair in a buzz, while the other man's is in a long ponytail, like Jack's. His faded T-shirt says *Hell on Wheels*.

Dunn walks over, taking off his helmet, and looks down at the covered body. He's a good two inches taller than me, at least six feet four inches, and muscled. His face is rough from a bad case of acne, and his features don't quite come together, with big, flabby lips and little ears. But his blue eyes burn intensely, and I'll bet that's what most people end up remembering about him. He cocks his head at me. "You're Mr. Craddock?"

I nod and we shake hands.

"I appreciate your calling. I guess we'll get on inside to be with Jack. He knows his daddy is dead?"

"I just told him I thought Bob had a heart attack. I felt like it would be better if he had some friends with him when he found out the worst."

Dunn winces and says, "We'll work it out with him."

Rodell watches the men enter Jack's place. "Something tells me they ain't going to wait on Jack hand and foot the way Bob did."

Loretta Singletary's place is right down the street from mine. It's a fine old two-story house, with wood siding painted a handsome gray with white trim. Loretta's a gardener, and this time of year the plants threaten to smother the house. There are hydrangeas with blossoms as big as your head, bushes of purple flowers, and a climbing rose up to the roof. Bees are thick in the air.

I almost don't see Loretta because she's dwarfed by a stand of sun-flowers. She's wearing a big hat and sunglasses and carrying a pair of clippers. The midmorning sun is so bright she has to shade her eyes with her hand to see me. She breaks into a smile and picks her way through the garden to the gate.

"Samuel, I'm glad to see you. It gives me an excuse to get out of this sun. Come on inside and let's have some tea."

She bounds up the steps as if her sixtyish years mean nothing. I feel a nip of envy because I've aggravated my knee with the morning's business, and I'm a little slower following her up the steps.

I'm not one for air-conditioning most of the time, but it feels good right now. My eyes have to adjust to the dim light inside, and I grope my way through her living room back to the kitchen. "What brings you over here?"

I tell her about Bob Harbin. She puts a hand to her neck. "That's a terrible thing! I guess without Bob, Jack will have to go to a veteran's home."

"I don't know what he's going to do. But I was hoping you could get some of the ladies to help him until his situation gets worked out."

She blinks a couple of times and looks toward her telephone, frowning. "There aren't many women who will put up with Jack, so I'll have to get some men. Including you." She jabs a finger at me.

"What about some church ladies who like to do good?"

She smiles. It's a shared joke. Some of the Baptist ladies in town seem hell-bent to get to heaven by good works. "The way that boy carries on, I don't think the Baptist ladies are going to be inclined. I wonder if Marybeth can help?"

"I'll call her, but I doubt if she'll be able to do much."

I'm one of the few people in town who keeps up with Marybeth Harbin, Jack's mother. I feel sorry for her. A year after Jack got home in such bad shape, Marybeth had a nervous collapse and had to spend some time in the hospital. After she got out, she went to live in Bryan–College Station, near enough to visit occasionally. Plenty of folks think badly of her for not being there to help Bob, but they can't blame her any more than she blames herself.

Back home I make a call to the office where Marybeth works and ask to speak to her supervisor. I'd like to tell her what happened to Bob myself, but I don't think it ought to be done on the phone, and she should be told right away. She works as a secretary for some research outfit associated with Texas A&M. The man I talk to sounds a little muddle-headed, but he says he'll break the news to her. I tell him to have her call me if she needs anything.

To settle myself down, I spend some time looking at my Wolf Kahn pastel. If anybody had told me when I was a boy that I would end up with a fine art collection, I would have thought they were crazy. But my wife, Jeanne, grew up with a mother who loved art, and when we were married Jeanne started buying a few pieces, and she dragged me into it. I ended up enjoying it almost as much as she did. Since she died, the pictures we bought together have meant even more to me. I've even bought a couple of new pieces that I think she would have liked.

After a while I make the telephone call I've been putting off, to make an appointment with a surgeon at Texas Orthopedic Hospital in Houston. Rodell hit the nail on the head this morning when he asked when I was going to have my knee fixed. I've been hobbling around ever since one of my heifers accidentally knocked me down and stepped on it. On my last visit, my doc said, "You're going to have to let somebody go in there and put it to rights. Within a few months, you'll be good as new." Months. I don't like the sound of that.

And then there's the question of who's going to take me to the hospital in Houston and bring me back. Loretta will insist, and I'd as soon ride in a car with Jack Harbin at the wheel as Loretta.

The cheerful receptionist makes me an appointment for a couple of weeks off. She apologizes for not being able to fit me in sooner, but later is better than sooner as far as I'm concerned.

Zelda rounds the corner from wherever she's been napping and fixes me with a resentful eye as she meows her way to her dish. "That's two of us feeling sorry for ourselves," I tell her.

CHAPTER 2

Loretta has scheduled me to stay with Jack on Wednesday. I drop by her house on my way, to pick up a bag of her cinnamon rolls.

There are two beefy motorcycles parked in Jack's driveway alongside a giant SUV. At the curb sits an iridescent red pickup with flames painted on the side and plastered with bumper stickers. My favorite says, *Back off! I flunked anger management class*.

The Harbin house is nothing much to look at—a one-story rectangle on concrete piers with vinyl siding, a metal roof, and aluminum windows. A wheelchair ramp leads up to the front door.

I hear voices from around back, and in the backyard I find Jack surrounded by his buddies. Walter Dunn and the other man who showed up at Jack's on Monday are there along with another couple of men, all sprawled in plastic lawn chairs on the concrete patio.

Dunn jumps up to shake hands. "Mornin' Mr. Craddock. You in line to spend some time with Jack today?" There's a sweet smell of marijuana in the air. Seems early for that sort of thing.

"Looking forward to it." I squeeze Jack's shoulder. "Hope that's okay with you."

"I can take it if you can." Jack cranes his head in my direction, his nose working. "Do I smell Loretta's cinnamon rolls?"

"You sure do. She sent over a couple dozen." I open the bag and thrust a roll into Jack's hand. He takes a big bite. I hand the bag to Dunn, who takes one and passes it on.

"Somebody get Mr. Craddock a cup of coffee," Jack says.

Dunn says, "You asking, or ordering?"

Jack snickers. "Just get the damn coffee."

Smirking, Dunn heads for the back door.

"Take a seat, Mr. Craddock," Jack says. I pull up a metal lawn chair with frayed plastic webbing that has faded to a pale gray.

"You boys veterans?" I ask.

They nod. One of them flicks a cigarette butt into the backyard.

"My band of brothers," Jack says, sarcastically.

"Right on." The speaker is a squat man with a shaved head and covered with tattoos. His eyes are so red you can't tell what color they are.

"That's Vic," Jack says. "The rest of you guys introduce yourselves like civilized people.

Johnny B., the one who showed up with Dunn, has a big, knotted scar running along his jaw line. Mike is a slightly built, handsome man with a dark thatch of hair and a shy smile.

"We call Mike 'Pretty Boy,'" Jack says. The way Jack is settled back in his chair tells me he's able to relax with these men.

Dunn comes out with my coffee. "I had to brew a new batch."

Suddenly another man steps out the back door onto the patio. It takes me a second to recognize him. It's Jack's younger brother.

"Well Curtis, I'll be damned."

"Hello, Chief Craddock." He comes over and says for me not to get up, but I do anyway. The hand he offers me to shake is soft and well-manicured. He tells me he drove in late last night. Ramrod straight, he's clean-shaven, his hair cut short and trim, and dressed in slacks and a golf shirt.

I never much cared for Curtis. He was a furtive kid. As soon as he was old enough, he grew a scruffy beard and started going around dressed in old army fatigues. He spent most of his time in the woods, hunting everything from squirrels to snakes. Marybeth used to worry about him because he'd go out camping for several days at a time. Frankly, I was surprised that it was Jack, not Curtis, who signed up for the army. Loretta told me that Curtis hooked up with some kind of survivalist group that lives out in the woods up in East Texas. You wouldn't know it from his soft hands.

The vets go quiet and their stares are cold. "How long are you in town for?" I ask. I wonder if Curtis plans to stay a while and take care of his brother.

"I have to get back to work as soon as the funeral is over. Trying to get His Majesty squared away here in the next couple of days." He nods toward Jack.

Although the words seem nothing more than a mild jibe between siblings, Jack's face twists with anger. "Fuck you, Curtis."

Curtis's face gets red. He forces a laugh, but no one joins in.

"You boys have the funeral arrangements taken care of?" I ask.

"We would if Curtis wasn't such a cheapskate," Jack's voice is belligerent.

Curtis shoots a hard look at Jack. "I'm being realistic about money, Jack. The funeral you've got set up is going to cost a lot. You think you're sitting pretty, but when you have to pay somebody to do everything Daddy did for you, you're going to get a hard dose of the real world." He speaks slowly, as if Jack is not only wounded, but brain-damaged as well.

"What do you know about the real world?"

I break in to ease things. "Curtis, I haven't seen you in a dog's age. You don't get down here too much."

"No, my job and my family keep me pretty busy."

"How many kids you got?"

"Four. Two boys, two girls."

"That would keep you busy all right. What do you do for a living?"

"I manage an outfit that sells at gun shows."

Jack snorts. "Didn't have the guts to go off to war himself, so he's arming for his own private little war."

Jack's friends look at each other and rise as one. "We need to get out of here," Dunn says to me. "Our buddy Eric's at the shop by himself and he's going to be some pissed off if we don't show up pretty soon."

Each man shakes Jack's hand in a kind of solemn ritual. Vic, the one with the heavy tattoos says, "Jack, let's go on over to Coushatta in a couple of weeks. It'll do you good to get out." That's a gambling place just over the Louisiana border.

"I'm going to have to get back to you on that. Got some decisions to make."

The prospect of his friends leaving has Jack clutching the arms of his chair, his hollow-cheeked face vulnerable.

Walter Dunn pauses with his hand on Jack's shoulder before he leaves. "Jackie, I'll come over here every night as long as you need me."

"You don't have to do that," Curtis says. "I'll be in town a couple more days. There's nowhere for you to stay. We just have the two bedrooms."

Dunn gives him a hard look. "I'll bring a tent and set up in the back yard so I won't be in your way."

After they leave, I fumble for a neutral subject to ease the bad atmosphere between the two brothers. "Your wife and kids coming down for the funeral? I wouldn't mind seeing them."

Curtis frowns. "There's no call for Sarah to come. She needs to stay home and take care of my kids."

Jack's jaw is tight. "What do you mean no call for her to come? Daddy was her father-in-law."

"One of the girls is sick. Sarah needs to be there with her."

Jack gropes around in his shirt pocket and yanks out a cigarette. "Christ, Curtis! You are such a jerk!"

Curtis gets up so fast that his lawn chair topples backwards. He grabs it and sets it upright with a clatter. "My family is my concern," he snarls. He starts toward the back door, then pauses and nods to me. "Good to see you, Mr. Craddock."

Jack and I sit quietly for a few minutes, Jack smoking, me sipping my cold coffee. Eventually I say, "You want to talk to me about the funeral arrangements? Maybe I can help you out."

Jack takes a deep drag on the cigarette. "Nothing to talk about. I told Earnest Landau I want the best for Daddy. It's my money. Curtis can't do a damn thing about it. And if he doesn't want to help pay for it, that's his problem."

I nod, but then realize he can't see me. "I know what you mean. It's important to send your loved ones off right."

His face constricts. "I can't believe he's dead. Seems like there's something the paramedics could have done for him."

I tell him about performing CPR. "I tried my best."

"You told me everything was going to be okay. I should have learned by now that when somebody says that, no good is going to come of it. That's what the medic said when he got to me after I'd stepped on the mine that did this to me. He said I'd died and he brought me back, and then he said, 'Everything's going to be okay.' Like hell! Sometimes I wish I had died."

I sigh. "I don't blame you for being mad at me for saying everything was going to be okay, but the fact is with your daddy lying there like that and you on the ground tipped out of your chair, all I could do was stall for time. If I did the wrong thing, I did it with good intentions."

His mouth trembles as if he's struggling not to break down. "I know that. I'm just trapped, that's all." He fumbles around on the table next to his wheelchair, finds the ashtray and grinds out his cigarette. "I wish to God I'd been nicer to Daddy." His voice cracks.

"It's no good thinking that way. Everybody has regrets when someone they care about dies."

I hear someone calling out, and Elva Penning, one of Jack's neighbors, comes around back carrying a tuna casserole. When Jeanne died I found out that tuna casserole was the dish of choice to comfort the bereaved. I haven't had much of a taste for it ever since.

To give them a few minutes to visit, I walk back to Bob's workshop. The house is built on a sizeable piece of land shaded with pecan and post-oak trees, and the workshop is in a shed tucked against the back fence.

The sliding door to the shed is open, and I glance inside. When Bob decided to take care of Jack, he quit his job with a construction company in Bobtail and started doing small appliance repairs. Everybody brought their things to him to repair, and there are lots of things lined up on shelves with tags on them. An ancient radio in a handsome wood cabinet has been pulled apart on the workbench. It would probably be cheaper to buy a new one, but you'd never find one with that art deco style. I slide the door shut to keep out the weather and the varmints, but I crack it open a few inches. People might want to slip in and get their goods without bothering Jack and Curtis.

When Elva is gone, I say to Jack, "What would you think about going over to the café to get some lunch?"

"That would be really good. You think you can push me in my wheelchair?"

"I don't see why not."

In the kitchen, Curtis is on the phone. He shoots us a furtive look as we roll past. It occurs to me that Jack and I ought to have a chat with Earnest Landau, the funeral director, while we're in town, in case Curtis is trying to pull something.

CHAPTER 3

Although it's barely eleven o'clock, Jack and I both order the Mexican special, a plate of enchiladas and tamales made by Johnny Ochoa's wife, Maria. When the food arrives, Lurleen has stripped the cornhusk off the tamales so Jack doesn't have to grope around and do it himself.

Once we're eating, I ask Jack how he's going to get himself taken care of. "Looks like your brother isn't going to be much help."

"That self-righteous son of a bitch. He wants me to sell Daddy's place and go into a veteran's home. That's so he can get half the money from the house."

"He lives somewhere in East Texas, doesn't he?"

"Used to, but now he's in Waco with a bunch of other wackos. Gun nuts. They call themselves survivalists. I'd like to see them survive in a real fight."

Lurleen checks on us. "Jack, you haven't eaten very much. Want me to bring you something else?" Her voice is soft. She touches his arm. She has recently had her hair cut short in little spikes all over her head like a little porcupine. It looks cute on her.

Jack smiles for the first time, tilting his head toward the direction of her voice. Damn, the boy would do well to use that smile a little more freely. "Lurleen, you're always trying to fatten me up. But you know, I don't have much appetite today."

"Shame to waste Maria's Mexican food." Lurleen is one of the good ones. She has continuing trouble with a belligerent ex-husband, but she always has a sweet way about her.

"Okay, here goes. Big bite. See?" Jack stuffs an over-sized chunk of tamale into his mouth.

Margaret E. Heggan Public Library
606 Delsea Drive
Sewell, NJ 08080

"Oh, you're awful!" Lurleen giggles. "You're going to choke, and it will serve you right."

Jack's mouth is too full to reply, but his lips crook into a smile while he chews.

When the meal is cleared away, I circle back to the subject of Jack's prospects.

"Daddy always banked my disability check and we lived on what Daddy made from his business."

"So you've got money put away."

"Yeah, it's a good bit. But Curtis thinks that full time help would run through the money in no time. That's why he's talking about a veteran's home."

Seems to me like it's none of Curtis's business how Jack spends his money. When it's gone, there will be plenty of time to go to a veteran's home. Still, if he went now, at least he'd have company at a vet facility.

"There's one in Temple. Not that far away. Your vet buddies could visit."

Jack kneads his hands, his thin shoulders hunched. "That's going to take some getting used to."

"What do your friends say?"

He snorts. "Those boys are as hare-brained as I am. They all say they'll take care of me, not to worry. But all of them have families, except for Vic."

That takes me by surprise. I had pictured them as loose cannons, as unattached as Jack. "You mean wives and kids?"

"Oh yeah. None of the wives are all that fond of me." He grimaces. "Seems like I can't be trusted to behave like a gentleman around the kids."

"Why am I not surprised?"

That drags a grin out of him.

It's noon and people are drifting into the café. Gabe LoPresto, a football team booster, swaggers over to our table with a couple of his cronies. They pull up chairs and crowd around, LoPresto straddling his chair backwards. He wears black snakeskin boots, a string tie, and a suede hat, but he still looks like a businessman who works in an office, which he is. LoPresto is an arrogant man, and can be annoying, but he provides fresh uniforms for the team every couple of years, which buys him a fair amount of good will.

There's nothing new that can be said about last Friday's football game, but people won't be done rehashing the subject until next Friday's game replaces it. LoPresto kicks off the discussion, declaring in an aggrieved tone that Coach Eldridge was stupid to bench the quarterback for a minor infraction of his rules. "The man's got no sense. There are other ways he could have punished that boy. Instead, he punished the whole damn town."

"That wasn't the only mistake he made. It was one after another the whole game," Harley Lundsford says. He shakes his head in disgust. "I swear! Letting the clock run down too long to get in another play . . ."

LoPresto says, "Jack, I heard you got into it with Eldridge after the game."

That's the first I've heard of it, but LoPresto makes it his business to know pretty much everything people are up to in the football community.

Jack shrugs. "We had a few words."

"I'm glad you spoke out to him. He couldn't have done worse if he threw the game deliberately. Did he ever tell you what his thinking was?"

Jack frowns. "Coach isn't much for explaining himself, but he said he wished he had it to do over, that he made a mistake."

LoPresto perks up. "When was this?"

"He came over Sunday night to smooth things out between us. He brought a nice peace offering—a bottle of Cuervo. We did the bottle some damage."

All the men laugh.

"Well, that says something, I guess," LoPresto says.

"Doesn't change my opinion that he should have handled it different," Jack says.

"Jack, you know your opinion counts for a lot. You're still the finest high school quarterback I ever saw play the game."

We spend some time arguing over the relative merits of the teams from the years since Jack played. LoPresto finally unwinds himself from his chair, brushing off his hat before settling it back on his head. "I'd better be getting back to work. But Jack, I want you to be thinking on this business with Eldridge. Maybe we'd be better off with a different coach."

On the walk back to Jack's place, we stop off at the funeral home. Earnest Landau is busy, but his assistant, Belle, says everything is going the way Jack wants it.

"Did Curtis call over here?" Jack says.

"I think he did." Belle cuts her eyes at me. Belle is about five feet tall and fierce as a banty rooster. I can't see anybody getting the best of her in an argument.

"What did he want?"

"He complained a little bit."

"Belle, don't bullshit me. What did Curtis want?"

Belle picks up a stack of papers and smacks them smartly on the desk to straighten them. "He accused Earnest of pushing you to choose our more expensive line. Don't worry, Earnest set him straight."

"God damn Curtis," Jack says.

"Honey, don't let him rile you up. I see family fights over all kinds of things, and it's not worth getting yourself upset."

"Are they done fixing Daddy up?" Jack says. "I'd like to have some time with him when I can."

"Sugar, I don't think Letitia is finished with the touch-up, but you come on by an hour before visitation tonight and you can sit there with him as long as you like." It's ludicrous to think that Bob needs to look any particular way for Jack, since Jack can't see him anyway. But Belle's word is law.

"There's one more thing." Jack's lip is curled. "I don't want Woody Patterson here tonight. I can't keep him from coming to the funeral, but I don't want him at the visitation."

Belle frowns and squinches up her eyes. "I disagree with you. I think anybody should be allowed in who wants to pay respects, but I'm not going to argue with you."

"Good."

"What about his family? You mind if Laurel comes? Or Woody's daddy?" Her voice is as cold as dry ice.

"I don't have a problem with the rest of them."

When we get back to the house, Jack says he's done in and needs to lie down. I'm glad for the break, and also glad that Curtis isn't around. I help Jack get settled in his bed and head into the kitchen to make myself a cup of coffee. No sooner have I sat down at the dinette table with the coffee when the phone rings. It's Doc Taggart, Bob's doctor, with a verbal report for the boys about the preliminary autopsy report. I jot down the information and take my coffee into the living room.

I jerk awake when Curtis comes in the front door. I sit up and take a deep breath. My neck is stiff from my head flopping backwards onto the back of the chair when I nodded off. I don't usually sleep in the afternoon and I feel stupid with it.

"Don't get up," Curtis says. He's carrying a Dairy Queen sack, which he holds out in an awkward gesture. "Got extra fries, if you want some."

I tell him to go ahead, and about that time Jack calls out for someone to help him get up. I help him into his chair and wheel him into the kitchen where Curtis has his hamburger and French fries set up. Jack lights a cigarette.

Curtis waves his hand in front of his face. "Whole house smells like cigarette smoke."

"There's a perfectly good motel if your delicate nose can't handle it," Jack says. "Besides, think about the advantage to you. I'll probably die faster, so you can inherit what I've got."

"If there's anything left after you burn through it."

"All right boys, you can fight on your own time. There's something I need to tell you." I tell them about the call from Doc Taggart with the preliminary autopsy report. "I hope you don't mind if I took down the particulars."

"Fine with me," Curtis says. "What did Taggart say?"

"Like we all figured, your dad died of a heart attack. I asked the doc if Bob had a history of heart problems and he said no, and the coroner said his heart looked in pretty good shape and it was probably an arrhythmia."

Jack sighs. "I wish that SOB Doc Taggart had kept a better eye on him. He might have needed a pacemaker or something."

"Too late to worry about that now," Curtis says. How did he get to be such a cold-hearted man? Jack sits up and I can see by the set of his mouth that he's about to go off on a tirade.

"Doc Taggart is sometimes a little hard to take," I say. "But he's a good doctor. Smart. Keeps up on things."

There's nothing wrong with my eyesight, so I have no trouble seeing one of those smirks that Curtis passes around so freely. I can't keep my mouth shut. "He took care of my wife, Jeanne when she had cancer, and the doctors in Houston told us he did a good job."

"I know he's a good doctor," Jack says, unaware of the anger at Curtis that has flared up in me. "I'm just wishing for something that can't be. Did he say anything else?"

I look at my notes. "Just that if Bob had lived longer he might have had some prostate problems. And he mentioned alcohol in his system—you told me you two shared a bottle of tequila with Coach Eldridge Sunday night."

"Daddy didn't drink that much, but he had a little to be sociable."

"And he must have been fighting off a cold, because Taggart said he had a fair amount of Benadryl in his system."

"No, that can't be right," Jack says.

"What do you mean that can't be right? Nothing wrong with taking something for a cold." Curtis is talking with his mouth full.

"There's nothing *wrong* with it," Jack says, "except he wouldn't take something like that."

Curtis pops the last French fry and wipes his mouth. "What makes you think you know what daddy would and wouldn't take?"

"He told me he wouldn't ever use any drug that might make him sleep so sound that he wouldn't hear me if I needed him in the night."

Curtis slurps the last of his soft drink. "Well, looks like this time he did."

I recognize the stubborn set of Jack's jaw. "Still," he says, "I'd like to double-check on that autopsy report. If they got it wrong about the Benadryl, they could have gotten other things wrong, too."

About then Dottie Gant comes in to relieve me. She's a retired nurse as big as a linebacker. She won't have any trouble helping Jack in and out of his chair.

On the way home I think about the Benadryl and decide I'll give Taggart a call to make sure I heard it right. Then I brood a little about Jack's insistence that Woody Patterson not attend his dad's visitation. Time was, the two boys were best friends. But that was a long time ago.

CHAPTER 4

"What the hell have you boys gotten yourself up to? You two know how to handle guns! How could you have let this happen?" I'm driving like a bat out of hell toward the county hospital at Bobtail. Jack Harbin is lying in the backseat, groaning, while Woody Patterson leans over the backrest holding a blood-drenched towel onto Jack's foot.

"It just . . . we just . . . ," Woody stutters, sounding like he's going to cry.

Jack groans louder. I've seen men who are hurt a lot worse make not nearly so much noise. You can't accuse the boy of being stoic. "Jack, you got hit every which way on the football field this year. Did you make that much racket every time?"

"This is different, it burns like the fires of hell."

Their story is that they went out to the woods to bag some squirrels and somehow Woody managed to shoot Jack in the foot. Woody drove Jack to the bait shop, but said he was too shook up to drive all the way to the emergency room in Bobtail, so he called me.

There's something fishy about their story. I've known both boys since they were in diapers, and they started learning to shoot as soon as they could hold a gun. How did an accident like this happen? Jeanne told me a while back that these boys both think they are in love with Taylor Brenner. I hope the boys didn't think their rivalry could be solved with rifles. It's a done deal anyway. Woody and Taylor are getting married in a week.

Jack has just finished army boot camp and will be deployed soon. I wonder how this injury is going to affect whether he can rejoin his unit. I almost hope it keeps him back. Rumors are high that there will be war in the Persian Gulf and it wouldn't be the worst thing in the world if Jack was unable to go.

Both the boys signed up for the army fresh out of high school. All the way through school they were big sports heroes—quarterback and receiver, pitcher and catcher. They must have figured the only way they were going to continue to be heroes was to join the service.

And then, out of the blue, the army rejected Woody on account of a knee injury he suffered in his sophomore year. Who would have thought that a boy who broke the school record for yardage gained in his senior year would be judged unfit to serve in the armed forces? Some folks said Taylor was marrying him as a consolation prize.

We screech to a halt at the emergency room, and get chewed out for parking in the driveway until I show them my badge as police chief of Jarrett Creek. Attendants start to haul Jack away, but he stops them. "Chief Craddock, don't tell my folks about this. Please."

"How the hell do you think they're not going to know? It'll be all over town in no time."

"I'll tell them I stepped on a nail or something."

He insists so much that I finally agree to keep quiet. When the attendants take Jack away, I tell Woody to come with me to park the car. After we park, he reaches over to open the door, and I clap him on the shoulder to make him stay put.

"What the hell were you two boys really up to?"

Woody shakes his head.

"Was this on purpose? Is it about Taylor?"

Woody stays quiet.

"All right, you're not telling. It goes down as an accident either way, but I don't like it."

We're stuck in the waiting room for a couple of hours before a grinning nurse comes out to say, "That is one lucky boy! Shot went right through his foot without hitting anything major. Couple of small bones that should be good as new in no time."

"That should make you feel better," I tell Woody.

But he groans and drops his head into his hands, which makes me wonder if he intended worse.

At Woody and Taylor's wedding, Jack serves as best man. He is on crutches with his foot all bound up, but the story that he stepped on a nail seems to have taken hold.

CHAPTER 5

I'm walking up to my front door after leaving Jack's house when a green vintage Buick comes barreling up the street and screeches to a halt in front of my house. I could have told you who was driving with my eyes closed. Laurel Patterson has always driven like the devil is chasing her down the road. She may be married, with two young kids, but that hasn't slowed her down.

I'm hoping she's not coming to see me, as I need a few minutes to unwind, but she jumps out of her car waving at me, and heads my way. Laurel has put on a few pounds and doesn't move as fast outside of the car as she does in it. She's wearing shorts and an over-sized T-shirt, and has her light brown hair pulled back in a ponytail. Up close, I see that her dark eyes are troubled.

"What brings you over this way?"

"Mr. Craddock, I have a favor to ask of you."

"What kind of favor?" She's so serious that I have to hold back a smile.

She plants her hands on her hips. "It's about Woody. Daddy said you could talk sense to almost anybody."

"Come on inside, out of this heat, and tell me why you need me to talk sense to your husband."

We sit down at the kitchen table. Laurel grips her hands together in front of her so hard her knuckles whiten. Her eyes spark fire. "Woody wants to have Jack come and live with us."

"Whoa!" I rear back in my seat. I can't even begin to list how many ways this is a bad idea, the primary one being that the two men haven't spoken a word to each other in twenty-some-odd years. "I sure didn't expect that. I presume it doesn't fit into your plans?"

"That's an understatement! I don't see how Woody can even think about having Jack at our house. He's just an awful man. I mean, I'm sorry what happened to him, but a lot of people say he's made the worst of the situation." She sighs. "That's not fair. I don't know what I'd do if I was in his place, not being able to see or walk."

"Laurel, with his physical problems, even if he was a practicing saint it would still be hard having him live at your house. You'll just have to tell Woody how you feel."

Her smile is tired. "Woody is a good man, but he can be stubborn when he gets something in his head."

It occurs to me that he and Jack are the same that way. "To be honest, I don't think you have anything to worry about. I doubt if Jack would take to the idea anyway."

Her lips go all pinched. "I wouldn't be so sure about that. You have to admit Jack's gotten along fine, being waited on hand and foot by his daddy. And if he thinks he can get Woody to do the same thing, I expect he'll figure out a way to forgive Woody pretty fast."

I'm surprised at the anger in her voice. She's generally even-tempered, if a little impulsive. There must be something else behind the fuss she's putting up. I can't help wondering if Taylor Brenner is in the mix.

Laurel is an attractive enough girl, but nothing special to look at, with a pudgy face and a button nose. Folks were pretty surprised that she ended up with Woody after his divorce from Taylor Brenner. How could Woody go from Taylor, who was about as electric as a girl could be, to steady, plain, easy-going Laurel? But Jeanne told me to wait and see, that she bet it would work out. And sure enough, after he married Laurel, Woody settled down big time, almost as if he was relieved not to have to keep up with Taylor's bright star.

"Why does Woody want to take Jack in, anyway? He's got you and the kids to consider. And doesn't your mamma live with you, too?"

"That's what I told Woody, but he says since he works at home, like

Jack's dad did, he can take care of Jack the way Bob did. And you know good and well who the work would fall to."

"Like I said, why would he want Jack there anyway, the way things are between them?"

She pushes away her untouched coffee and crosses her arms on the table. "You know Woody feels responsible for what happened to Jack. It was his idea for the two of them to sign up for the army."

"I know that's what Woody said at the time. But they were kids. It wasn't Woody's fault the army took Jack and didn't take him."

"Woody says there's more to it. And he won't talk about it."

Okay, so maybe Taylor does figure in there somewhere. But I have a feeling I'm not going to get to the bottom of it right now.

"I still don't think Jack would move in with you all." I tell her about Jack's insistence that Woody not be allowed at the visitation tonight.

Her fine hair has straggled out of its clip, so she undoes it and snatches the hair back up tight and clips it again. "I know it. Belle called the house and told him."

"How did Woody react?"

"He said as long as we can go to the service, that's okay."

"Do you know if Taylor is coming down from Dallas?"

"She's already out at her mamma's. She called this afternoon. She was trying to decide if she ought to go see Jack."

"Why wouldn't she?"

"She doesn't know if Jack would be in the frame of mind to see her."

"You and Taylor get along, do you?"

She shrugs. "We used to get along fine. I don't see much of her these days. When she comes to see her mamma, it's only for the day, so she doesn't have a lot of time for the old crowd."

A neat sidestep to the question I was really asking—if there was any jealousy over Woody.

She looks up at my kitchen clock and bolts out of her chair. "Oh, my Lord, I'm late. I've got to pick up my boys from school." She cocks her head at me. "I hate to ask you, but do you suppose you could talk to Woody about this? He'd listen to you."

I get up and walk to the door with her. "I don't know why he'd listen to me. What about his daddy? Maybe Frank could talk some sense to him."

She pauses at the door. "Sounds like you haven't kept up with Frank. He's gotten to be a hermit since Sissy died. I don't think he's said three sentences to us in the last six months."

"I'm sorry to hear that." I really am. It wouldn't have occurred to me to stop by and see Frank after his wife died, since we don't know one another that well. But it wouldn't have hurt me to call him, having gone through that rough patch myself.

In the late afternoon, I go down to the pasture behind my house to spend a little time with my cows before I go off to Bob's visitation. What Jack said about the Benadryl in Bob's autopsy report is still nagging at me. I make a mental note to call Doc Taggart's office tomorrow to check it out.

CHAPTER 6

Bob Harbin's coffin is a flashy silver-and-chrome affair with dark blue satin lining and outer panels studded with brushed chrome medallions. I imagine it's going to draw some criticism. People in Jarrett Creek are close with a dollar and don't care much for show.

Jack is fitted out in a jacket that swallows his thin frame. His wheelchair is positioned near the coffin for the visitation. A couple of his veteran friends sit in the pew near him. The pungent smell of whiskey floats to me as I bend to speak to Jack. "Your daddy looks good. They did a real fine job with him."

"Yes, sir. Lurleen told me it looks like Daddy could get up out of the coffin and walk out of here."

I pat him on the shoulder and tell him I'll see him at the funeral tomorrow. I only stay twenty minutes before I head off for my weekly date. Ever since my next-door neighbor, Jenny Sandstone, and I made our peace after she saved my art collection from arson, we get together once a week over a bottle of wine. Jenny is a lawyer, and likes taking a break from her work. We stick to gossip and complaints.

Sitting at Jenny's kitchen table over what Jenny claims is a pricey bottle of Pinot Noir, I tell her I'm troubled about what Jack Harbin is going to do now that Bob is gone. "You got any bright ideas? Jack would like to stay put here in Jarrett Creek, but I don't know how he's going to pay for that."

"What happened to Jack's mother?" Jenny is dressed in blue jeans and a white blouse. Her flame-red hair is tied back, with tendrils of it escaping like coiled wire. She's a big woman, around six feet tall and buxom. Jenny made it clear from the get-go that she's not in the market for a man, and that suits me fine. I'm happy to have the occasional company of a smart woman who isn't interested in taking over my wife's position.

I tell her about Marybeth, Jack's mother. "She lives over in Bryan–College Station. She visits every now and then, but she has a hard time with what happened to Jack."

Jenny frowns. "Seems like with his dad passing, she could step up."

I shake my head. "You'd have to know Marybeth. It's not that simple."

"Whatever you say." Jenny doesn't have patience for self-indulgence. "Damn shame for a young man to suffer such grievous wounds."

"You've got that right. He was a pistol when he was young. Best quarterback ever came out of Jarrett Creek High School."

"You mean it would have been okay if he was only good at math?" Jenny can have a sharp tongue at times.

"You know I don't mean that."

"This town and its football!" She doesn't have to elaborate—she has made it clear that she doesn't share the town's obsession with football. She sips her wine. "Only time I've ever seen Jack is down at the café. Hard to imagine him as an athlete."

"He was, though. He could flat-out throw a ball."

"Why didn't he play college ball? Why enlist in the army?"

"Jack and Woody Patterson signed up together. Both of them were after the same girl. That probably had something to do with it. Showing off for her."

"How many times does that tale get told?" Jenny laughs her big laugh and settles back in her chair. "Small town boys and their flirty little girls."

The phrase makes me smile. "Taylor was flirty all right. Those two boys hovered around her like bees around honey. She was partial to the two of them, but she was queen of the school, and everybody loved her."

"Yeah, I knew a few girls like that in high school," Jenny says dryly. "They made the rest of us miserable."

"I believe Taylor was different. Sure, she was pretty and full of piss and vinegar, and smart, too. But Jeanne said all the girls liked her."

"I'd have to see that to believe it. Not casting doubt on your sainted wife, you understand."

I grin. Jenny's the only person with the nerve to poke fun at me about Jeanne. It's been good for me. "Well, you may be right. How am I to know?"

"How did Jeanne know so much about these girls?"

"I'm going to get us some cheese and crackers and I'll tell you about it," I say. Jenny has an aversion to all things involved with the kitchen, so I'm more familiar with her kitchen than she is. I bring the snacks to the table and sit back down. "We found out we weren't going to have children, so Jeanne decided to go to work at the school. She also substitute taught and chaperoned afterschool activities. The girls loved her." I stop for a minute, lost in ghosts of teenagers giggling in the kitchen with Jeanne, and the way her eyes sparkled when they confided in her. "Taylor was her favorite, though."

"I don't recall meeting Taylor. What happened? Did she leave town for the bright lights and big city and the boys were stuck in the army? That sounds about as smart as most small-town Texas boys."

I'm surprised Jenny doesn't know the story. But she grew up in Bobtail, the county seat, and only moved to Jarrett Creek when she found out we needed a lawyer.

"Taylor was set to go off to college in Dallas, but when Woody got rejected by the army, Taylor ended up staying here to marry him."

She frowns. "Is it the same Woody Patterson who lives out east of town?"

"One and the same."

"He came into the office a while back to get something notarized. I thought his wife's name was Laurel."

"That's right. Woody and Taylor didn't even last a year before they called it quits. They divorced right after Jack came back so torn up. Taylor went off to college and now she's married and living in Dallas."

Jenny crosses her long legs out in front of her. She shakes her head. "The way people's lives can turn. Gives you pause."

CHAPTER 7

At Bob's funeral I let my mind wander, as the Methodist pastor drones on about Bob's sacrifice and love of his son, his church attendance and his clean life. Clean life. Something about the phrase tugs at me. I think about the Benadryl again. I didn't call Doc Taggart's office this morning. In the light of day, it seemed insignificant, and likely to get a sharp reply from Taggart. Maybe Bob just forgot what he said to Jack about never taking anything that might cause him to sleep too soundly. I snap out of my reverie when Curtis steps to the podium.

"I could say a lot about how my daddy raised us two boys to stand up for what we thought was right, and how he stood by Jack to the end. But Jack asked me to say a few words for him. And here's what he said." He pulls out a paper, clears his throat, and reads:

"If there was anybody who cared more about his sons than my daddy did, I don't know who it would be. Everybody knows I'm not the easiest person to get along with. I sometimes asked a lot of my daddy. Every Friday night during football season, he was right there, giving me a play-by-play of the action. He kept me in good shape, kept me clean, cooked for me. Even though I won't lie—he wasn't the world's best cook."

A few people chuckle.

"But no matter what kind of grief I gave him, Daddy never once raised his voice to me or complained about what he had to do. I'm not saying he was a saint. You might be surprised how often we laughed and joked and it could get pretty racy."

Curtis pauses and glances toward Marybeth, sitting in the front pew, not far from Jack. Jack has his head bowed. His army buddies are crowded in on both sides of him, and at one point in the reading, Walter Dunn drapes his arm around Jack's shoulders.

"And something else. He never once blamed my mamma for not being here. He'd never hear a thing against her. He said we all have to bear our burdens the best way we can."

By the time Curtis is done reading, everyone's eyes are damp.

Curtis announces that he and Jack are holding a reception at their dad's place after the funeral. Loretta asks me to take her home on my way over there. "I've done my part, going to the funeral. I don't need to see all those people using Bob Harbin's death as an excuse to get drunk." Loretta can be straight-laced at times.

Jack's veteran friends really do have wives, and they have labored to put out a decent spread with sandwiches, chips and salsa, and cold cuts and crackers. I couldn't begin to guess which wife goes with which man. One is a tiny little thing who wears glasses and looks like she'd be at home running a library. Another is tall, with fluffy blonde hair and a ready smile. And there are two who could be sisters, short and plump, bossing each other around.

Loretta was right. Unlike a church reception, there's booze. A lot of it. Bottles of Jack Daniels and Jose Cuervo and cases of beer. After the intensity of the funeral, the reception turns raucous fast. The place is packed, spilling out into the backyard. The hot, humid air is thick with cigarette smoke.

I'm just shaking Jack's hand, when I feel him tense up and he cocks his head in a way that makes me look around to see who he's listening to. Five feet away Woody and Laurel Patterson are talking to Taylor.

"Did I hear Woody Patterson's voice?" Jack squeezes my hand harder and pulls it to him so I can't get away.

"Yes, he's here with Laurel. And Taylor."

Now he shoves my hand away. "Walt!" His voice cuts through the crowd with its ferocious sound, and people pause in mid-conversation.

Walter Dunn appears like a genie at Jack's side. "What do you need, Jack?"

"Woody Patterson is here. I want you to throw him out."

Woody steps forward. He still wears his light hair close-cropped, the way he has ever since high school, now with traces of gray at the temples. He's grown into his rangy body, but his hands still look large for his frame. His suit is a little tight on him, as if he might not have bought a new suit in a while. His eyes are pleading, but his voice is angry. "Now listen, Jack, there's no call for that. I came out of respect for your dad, and . . ."

"Get him out!" Jack snarls.

At Woody's side, Laurel is pale, clutching her purse as if she's protecting her chest. Taylor steps forward. It's been a while since I've seen her. She looks good, but different, tense around the eyes and mouth. She's wearing a gray dress and high heels and her hair is short and crisp. "Jack, cut it out!" Her voice hasn't changed. It's husky, tomboyish. Right now it's raw with emotion.

"Taylor, you stay out of this. It's none of your business."

Taylor steps close in and kneels next to Jack's wheelchair. "Yes, it is my business. You can't keep on blaming Woody. It's as much my fault as it is his."

"Fuck you, Taylor!"

"Tamp it down, son," Walter says, his hand on Jack's shoulder. "We got kids here, and church folks."

"Just get him out of here." Jack's arms shoot out as if he's flinging the whole idea of Woody away from him. He comes close to clipping Woody, who rears his head back just in time. "And her, too."

Taylor glances up at Dunn and a look of some kind of understanding passes between them. Dunn reaches out and offers his hand to help her to her feet. There's something oddly familiar in the gesture, as if they both know Jack so well that they don't have to be introduced to one another.

Woody steps forward. Sweat is beaded on his brow. "Jack, you've got to let me help you!"

Taylor stands up and grabs Woody's arm. "Not now, Woody."

"Let go of me! I need to talk to Jack." Woody has drunk his share of alcohol.

Laurel pulls at Woody's other arm. "Come on now, honey."

"I said no! I need to talk to Jack."

"This isn't a good time!" Taylor's voice is like a whip crack, and Woody deflates. The two women propel Woody past the embarrassed onlookers and out the front door.

"Okay, folks," Jacks yells. "Show's over. Drink up! In honor of my daddy." He takes a long drink of whatever brown whiskey is in his glass.

"Hear, hear! Drink up," his army buddies chorus, and follow his lead. The wives are standing near the table watching. All of them look like they'd give anything to see the last of Jack Harbin.

I look around for Marybeth Harbin, thinking I should say something to her on my way out, but I don't see her anywhere. I'm almost to my car when I look down the street and see Taylor talking to Curtis, face twisted with fury, her fists clenched and her back rigid.

My heart constricts at the sight. Years ago Taylor was a happy, lovely girl. What has put her in such a state? What has she got to talk to Curtis about?

And then I remember that Curtis's wife is Taylor's younger sister. I never knew the sister. Apparently she was a painfully shy girl, the opposite of Taylor. Jeanne told me it was shameful how relieved their mother was to get the younger girl married off—they thought she'd be an old maid. So that is the wife Curtis told me needed to stay home and take care of "his" kids.

Suddenly Taylor draws back her hand and slaps Curtis. He grabs her hand and flings it away so violently that Taylor stumbles and almost loses her balance. I take a step in their direction, but Taylor turns her back on Curtis and strides away, leaving him glaring at her, fists clenched at his sides.

CHAPTER 8

Years ago, Taylor would stop by and say hello when she was in town. I watched her evolve from a giggling, larking teenager to a solemn young wife married to Woody and then divorced. When she went off to college, Jeanne and I saw less of her. Somewhere along the line she lost her teasing, friendly ways and became more serious, even strict. Jeanne worried about her and thought something had happened to take some of the spirit out of her. Since Jeanne's funeral, Taylor hasn't been to see me, which I admit hurt my feelings.

So I'm surprised when I answer the door in the late afternoon the day of the funeral and find her on my steps. She has changed into slacks and a T-shirt and looks more like the girl I once knew.

"Come on into the kitchen, I'm making jelly," I say. "I got some plums the other day and they were yelling to be put up or thrown out."

"Well aren't you a sight in your pretty little apron." She steps inside and hugs me tight.

She might have a few lines around her eyes and a few pounds at her waist, but her eyes are still piercing blue and her body is as compact as a terrier's.

In the kitchen she steps around me to the stove, where the jelly is bubbling. "Mmm, that's smells so good! You picked those yourself?" She opens a drawer, takes out a spoon and dips it into the brew, then waves it around to cool it.

"I'm not that ambitious. Truly Bennett brought me a peck and I figured I'd better do something with it."

She tastes the jam and smacks her lips in approval.

"We're going to have to talk in here. If I leave it too long, it'll set up too hard."

"Samuel, I may not be the world's best cook, but even I know you have to be careful with jelly. My mamma drilled that into me every year when she canned." She grins and a phantom of her outgrown, mischievous self flits across her face. "And every year she'd leave me to watch a batch and the phone would ring or somebody would come by, and next thing you know I'd forget all about it and it would burn. Lord, there'd be hell to pay."

I laugh. "You definitely had other things on your mind when you were a youngster," I say. We're both smiling, enjoying the memories dancing around in the kitchen.

"While I'm finishing up, why don't you tell me about those girls of yours?" She has three little girls who, if Taylor's mother is to be believed, are all raving beauties. Taylor shows me some pictures on her cell phone and tells me something about each of them, although she pauses sometimes as if she has lost her train of thought.

"I'll bet you're a good mother."

"It suits me. My girls make me really happy. I worry about the middle girl, my little Caprice. She reminds me of my sister, Sarah. So shy, and will go along with anyone who's nice to her. The other two, Hannah and Grace . . . ," she grins. "They're more like me. Which may be a problem once they get older. It was fine, me being brought up in a small town. Not as much trouble to get into. But Dallas is a whole different place."

I get her to help me pour the hot jelly into the jars I've got ready, and then we put a film of wax on top and seal the jars. Jeanne was the cook in our household, but somewhere along the line I became the maker of jams and jellies, and I'm pretty proud of what I come up with.

When we're done we take glasses of iced tea out back under the trees to catch a little breeze and to talk. "Something tells me you've got a reason for coming here besides just checking in on me," I say.

Her face flushes. "I'm ashamed that I haven't come to see you since Jeanne died."

"Nothing to be ashamed of. You two were close, I was just an innocent bystander. But I am glad to see you."

She sips tea and sighs heavily as she sets down her glass. "I'm really worried," she says.

"About Jack?"

She frowns. "No. I mean, yes, but that's not what I was talking about. It's my sister, Sarah. I think Curtis has her practically under lock and key. I've tried calling her and she sounds like she's scared to talk to me. You know they're living in one of those religious compounds out near Waco."

"Religious compound? I thought it was a survivalist group."

"It's sort of one-stop shopping. It's all under the umbrella of some religious leader who fashions himself like one of those Mormon offshoots."

Despite the late afternoon heat, a chill passes over me. From the little I've seen of Curtis, and remembering what he was like as a youngster, he strikes me as perfectly capable of holding his wife a virtual prisoner, seeing to it that she takes care of his needs and allowing her no life of her own.

"Have you been to see her?"

She hunches over, looking defeated. "No, she told me not to try to see her. But I'd go anyway if I could get my husband to go with me. He thinks I should keep my nose out of it."

"Remind me what your husband does."

Her look softens. "Alex is a lawyer. He had his own firm, but when the economy went bust, he had to go to work for a big law outfit in Dallas. He's not happy, but we're lucky he has a job."

"And doesn't have much time to worry about Sarah's problems, I imagine."

She shrugs, her expression rueful. "Or anyone else's, really. He works all the time. I tell him he's going to regret not spending time with the girls one day, but he says he'd rather provide them with the things they want."

"I saw you arguing with Curtis this afternoon. Was that about Sarah?"

Her eyes spark fire, her teeth clenched. "I hate him."

I nod. "He and Jack don't have any love lost between them either."

"Oh, Jack," she says. And there's something forlorn in her voice that cuts me.

The sun is going down and the light is soft and quiet. My cows are starting to low in the pasture behind the house. "Let's walk down and see my cows. They expect me this time of day."

A lively noise drifts over from the football stadium up the street. Cars honk long and loud at each other as they pass, engines revving up. In the background the high school band is tuning up.

Taylor glances in that direction. "What's going on?"

"It's Thursday night."

"And?"

"JV football. I'm surprised you don't remember. I don't usually go to junior varsity games, but a lot of people do. Why don't you stay for the varsity game tomorrow night? Jack will be there, and it would be a good time to make amends with him."

She scuffs her shoes in the dirt, but then her head comes up and she's smiling. "Maybe I'll do that. It would be fun. I bet I'd see a lot of people I know. With three girls, I never go to football games." She tucks her arm in mine. "I'll come if I can go with you. You can be my date."

As we make our way down to the pasture, I use my cane to poke ahead of me to warn snakes to get out of the way.

"Why do you use a cane? You have arthritis?"

I tell her about the silly accident where one of my cows knocked me down and stepped on my knee. "I haven't told anybody, but I have to have it cut open and fixed up."

She shudders. "I'm sorry. Is it going to be okay?"

"Doc says yes. I guess I have to believe him. I'd just as soon you keep it quiet for now."

Down at the pasture, Taylor goes right in with the cows, stroking noses and scratching behind ears. I smile, watching her. "You can take the girl out of the farm, but you can't take the farm out of the girl."

"I miss cows. Mamma sold all ours after daddy started failing." She puts her cheek next to one of the young ones. He's usually skittish, but he's instantly in love with her. When she tries to step away, he follows and butts up to her. She laughs. It's a good sound.

When it's too dark to see anymore, we walk back to the house. "I wasn't able to give you much help with your sister," I say.

She looks small, standing on the porch, illuminated just by the light from my front porch. "I have to go see her to settle my mind. Maybe I'll get a girlfriend to go with me." She laughs bitterly. "I guess Curtis isn't going to kill me if I show up with a witness."

"You really think he's that dangerous?"

"I don't know. But I won't feel good until I see my sister."

After I escort her to her car and she drives away, I stand looking at the sky. In the past couple of days the early mornings have been cooler, with high clouds that dissipate by mid-morning, and then the heat comes back in force. But the clouds are piled up in the west this evening. The weather will be changing. I'm ready for the heat to go.

CHAPTER 9

Taylor is as excited as a teenager when she stops by my house to pick me up Friday night. She bounces out of the car wearing a blue jean skirt and a green and gold T-shirt, Jarrett Creek school colors. She has scared up her old cheerleader pom-poms, and waves them around with a jaunty dance. "I'm counting on you to not let me get too wild. I'm a wife and mother now, and it won't do for me to get into trouble."

As soon as we get settled in the stands, people Taylor went to high school with swarm around us. Everyone is chattering, catching up on old times. I don't see Woody and Laurel and I wonder why, since they usually come to the games. I wonder who is going to bring Jack Harbin. Bob always had him here early and they sat right behind the team bench. Bob would keep up a running commentary, and when he ran out of steam, there was always somebody there to pick up where he left off.

It's Walter Dunn who wheels Jack down in front. The team hasn't come out yet. Gabe LoPresto is there, too, and he and Dunn carry Jack up the steps to his seat, and set the wheelchair aside.

You'd get cited for a fire hazard in some stadiums if the wheelchair blocked the aisle, but Panther stadium is made out of local stone. It was built as a WPA project, and is unburnable.

I leave Taylor to her gaggle of friends and go down to spend some time with Jack and his posse. There's no drinking in the stadium, but they're passing around a flask, and I doubt anybody would object.

Walter Dunn scoots over so I can sit down next to Jack. I ask Jack how he's feeling today.

"Okay, I guess. Besides having a hangover, that is. At least Curtis has gone back home. Makes things a little more relaxed."

"With Curtis gone, have you moved into the house?" I ask Dunn. He grimaces. "Struck a little bump in the road on that one."

Jack laughs. "His old lady read him the riot act. Said he had to get his ass back home at night."

"Me and the boys offered to take turns spending the night," Dunn says. "But Miz Gant says she'd just as soon make a little extra money and she's not charging much."

"How's that working out, Jack?"

"I like her," he says. "She doesn't take any shit off me. And she knows how to laugh."

Before I can ask what kind of arrangements he has during the day, the crowd starts to holler as the team trots out of the clubhouse.

"There they come," Dunn says.

"Hanging their heads from last week's loss," somebody behind us comments.

"Hell, it wasn't their fault," LoPresto says, turning around. "They've got nothing to be ashamed of."

I notice Walter Dunn is quiet, and staring at the team, frowning. He leans forward and gets LoPresto's attention and points over at Boone Eldridge. "Is that the coach?"

"That's the SOB that lost the game," LoPresto says.

"Jack," Dunn says, "that coach looks like a regular person. The way everybody talked about him after he lost the game last week, I figured he'd have two heads, horns, and scales."

Everybody laughs. "Might have done a better job if he had two heads," Jack says.

When the game starts, LoPresto takes on the job of announcing the game for Jack's sake, and I have to admit he'd make a good sports announcer. His chatter is lively and accurate. He's seconded by Alvin Carter, a huge black man whose son plays JV quarterback. The boy is rumored to be a shoo-in for varsity next year, even though he'll only be a sophomore.

During halftime, LoPresto and some others sneak off to do some serious drinking to help them through the second half, but I stay with Jack and Walter Dunn. Dunn reaches into the side pouch of Jack's wheelchair and the two of them avail themselves of a flask they've brought.

"Dunn, it looked to me like you recognized the coach when you saw him earlier," I say.

"I may have. Did he drive a Harley?"

"Still does as far as I know. People aren't too happy about it. They complain it isn't a good role model for the boys on the team to see the coach roaring around on it."

"Well I'd argue with them on that," Dunn says. "A motorcycle's a good means of transportation if it's handled right."

"I don't have any dog in that fight," I say. "I'm just telling you what people said."

"Doesn't make any difference anyway," Dunn says. "If it's the same guy, he sold the Harley. He and a college kid from College Station came into the shop a couple of weeks back. Coach was selling the Harley to the kid and the kid wanted us to check it out."

"First I've heard of that," I say.

LoPresto has come in on the tail end of the conversation. "You know how coach is. He buys a car and then sells it before it's been off the lot six months. Then he had to have that motorcycle. Can't seem to make up his mind."

LoPresto is happy to get into an argument with Dunn about the relative merits of motorcycles and automobiles, with Jack chiming in as if he knew anything about it.

I look back up in the stands to see how Taylor's getting on. She's the center of a group having a fine time. As I swing back around, I notice a couple of fellows in the stands that I don't recognize. Not that I always know everyone at the games. But these two are dressed a little different, in crisp khaki slacks and leather jackets. It's too warm to wear something that heavy. In their thirties, they both have dark hair, and they both have a sort of sneering look as if they aren't impressed by what they see.

When Gabe LoPresto comes back, I point out the two strangers to him. LoPresto is in the insurance and real estate business and he knows everybody. "You ever seen those fellows?"

He shakes his head. "Never laid eyes on them."

"You suppose they could be scouting the team?"

"It's a little early in the season for that." He reaches down a row and taps Dilly Bolton's dad on the shoulder and says something. Bolton doesn't hide the ambition he has for his son's chances at a college scholarship.

Bolton cranes his neck to look at the guys. His eyes are alight. He turns back to LoPresto. "I don't know. Maybe they're scouts, but I didn't call them." He wouldn't admit it if he did—that's illegal.

"Here they come." The crowd starts to holler as the team, which is beating poor Burton High School 36-3, rolls back out onto the field.

I glance back once more in time to see the strangers zero in on the team, nudging each other and seeming to take a particular interest.

By the fourth quarter, we're so far ahead that people are straggling out of the stadium. I rejoin Taylor. She makes room for me and puts her arm around my waist.

"You going to talk to Jack?" I ask.

She grimaces. "No. I talked to him last night."

"I'm surprised he was in any shape to have a conversation."

"He wasn't. But he called me after I got home, and I went over there." She turns a forced smile to me.

"He have any idea about how to deal with Curtis?"

"We didn't get around to that." She stands up. "Let's get out of here. I'm tired. Guess I'm too old for this."

CHAPTER 10

I promised Laurel that I'd have a talk with Woody, so I go over Saturday morning. Woody and Laurel live in Laurel's old home place, a sprawling octopus of a house that's been added on to every which way. I make my way through a yard littered with all kinds of kid's conveyances, most of them missing a wheel or two.

My knock on the door generates shrieks inside the house that make me steel myself in case I get tackled. But it's Laurel who answers the door. She's laughing. "Come on in. These boys are about to get sent off to the insane asylum at Rusk; or maybe I'll get sent there for strangling them barehanded."

One of the ruffians in question, a boy of about five, charges up to the door and looks me up and down and bellows, "Howdy Mister!" Then he screams and dashes away.

"I can see your problem," I say.

"If you're looking for Woody, he's out back. I'll throw some hamburgers into these boys, which may give you two time to talk."

"It's a little early for lunch, isn't it?"

"Not when you're up at six. On a school day I have to drag them out of bed, but this is Saturday. They get up at the crack of dawn so they don't miss a minute of it."

She leads me through a minefield of toys to the back door. In some part of the house there's a TV turned on loud, probably Laurel's mother, who lives with them, trying to drown out the racket. I can't even imagine how Laurel's mother would react to having Jack live here.

Out back, Woody is standing in front of his work shed, in the final stages of painting a chest of drawers. He's put a coat of shiny black on the frame and painted the drawers a shade of jade green. I never imagined that Woody would end up making a living refinishing furniture; but turns out he has a knack for it, and he gets orders from as far away as Houston. He's a happy man with a paintbrush in his hand. A couple of scruffy dogs lie in the shade at the side of the shed. They lift their heads to examine me, decide I'm all right, and go back to their nap.

"Chief Craddock, this is a nice surprise. Let me finish this little corner and then I'll be right with you."

He hums along with a country and western song blaring from his portable radio as he finishes up. Then he steps back to admire the work. "What do you think?"

"Looks good to me."

He turns down the radio and disappears into the shed for a few minutes to clean his brushes. He comes back out drying his hands just as Laurel pokes her head out and tells us she's got some coffee ready.

We take our coffee to a rickety wooden table and a couple of chairs out under a pecan tree. It's hot, but the trees give us some shade.

I meant to buttonhole Woody at Bob Harbin's funeral, but with the commotion, I didn't have the opportunity. And now that I'm here, I can't think how to approach him without seeming presumptuous.

"Sounds like Coach Eldridge redeemed himself last night," he says, rescuing me for the moment. "Laurel and I had to go to Bobtail and couldn't make the game."

He takes a sip of his coffee, grimaces, and tosses the rest of it onto the grass. "The day Laurel learns how to make coffee is going to be a red letter day."

I grin. I know what he means, having already tried mine and found it tastes like she waved some coffee grounds over a pot of hot water.

We kick around the ups and downs of the game, and go back over the loss to Bobtail with no new information being imparted on either side.

When we wind down, Woody sits back with a speculative expression. "I'm glad we've had a chance to visit, but it's a little unusual for you to drop by. I expect you're here to talk about Jack Harbin."

I nod. "Laurel came to see me about your idea."

Woody must be over forty, but I can still see the boy in him. Like Laurel, he has thickened up a little at the belly, and he's got a few lines around the eyes. His daddy is practically bald, and Woody's hairline is sneaking backwards. "I know she doesn't like the idea. So she put you up to talking to me?"

"Women have got more sense than men," I say. "It's always been that way. And I have to admit I think she's right on this one. Taking care of Jack would be a big job. A lot of the care will fall to Laurel. You've got your mother-in-law and the two boys to think of."

Woody isn't one to speak on impulse. He takes out a tin of chewing tobacco and tucks a little inside his lower lip, his eyes unfocused. I'd as soon see a man eat mud as chew tobacco.

"She'll come around," he says, finally.

"I think it would help if she knew what was behind it. Obviously Jack has a big problem with you, for whatever reason. Why do you want to stir things up?"

He tightens down the lid of the tobacco tin and slips it into his pocket. "I just think it's time we bury the hatchet." He leans over and spits a stream of tobacco juice on the ground. "Jack blames me for what happened to him, because it was me that wanted to sign up for the army, and he went along with it. And by the time we found out they wouldn't take me, it was too late for him to back out. I don't mind shouldering some of the blame, but some of it was plain old bad luck."

"Taylor said she was as much to blame as you are. What did she mean by that?"

He ponders the question. "I guess Taylor was taken with the idea of us being in uniform. But it's not her fault that Jack got hurt."

"What makes you think Jack is willing to bury the hatchet now?"

"How else is he going to get taken care of? Pay somebody to be around night and day?"

"All I'm saying is, I wouldn't count on getting him to say yes. Have you talked to Taylor about this?"

Woody picks at a spot of paint on his wrist. "She thinks I'm crazy." The lazy grin he's famous for creeps across his face. "Women just don't get how it is between men. Jack and I were as close as brothers, and we can be again."

"Why now? Why not before?"

"Before, he didn't need me."

CHAPTER 11

"Samuel, I'm at Jack Harbin's. I need you to get over here."

It's three o'clock in the morning on Wednesday, the week after Bob Harbin's funeral. The call is from Dottie Gant, the retired nurse hired to take the night shift caring for Jack. The urgency in her voice alarms me. Dottie wouldn't call without good cause. She's as tough as my boots. I tell her I'll be right there.

I slip on jeans and a T-shirt, but when I go outside there's a nip in the night air, so I go back and put on a blue work shirt. When I was chief of police, I was acquainted with the night, but that was some years ago. The intense quiet seems to invite dark thoughts. There's a little wind kicking up, too, and the dull metal smell of rain in the air. I should have heated up a cup of last night's coffee in the microwave.

Dottie's waiting at the door, dressed in slacks and a blouse, her arms hugging her chest. Her gray hair, usually pinned into a neat bun, is tumbling down her back in a wild confusion.

"Jack is dead," she says before I'm even through the front door. "I just found him. Somebody killed him. I've never seen anything like it." She may be tough, but her voice is trembling.

"Killed him how?" A sudden gust of wind swirls into the house and I catch the door before it slams shut.

Dottie gestures toward the bedrooms with a shaking hand. "You better go see for yourself."

I step into the bedroom and find a nightmare scene of blood and turmoil. The front of Jack's T-shirt and the tangled sheets are splotched and spattered with blood from several jagged knife wounds in his chest.

Jack did not die easily. His face is contorted and his head thrown back with his mouth open like he was trying to scream, and there are bruises at his neck. His sightless eyes are damp at the corners, as if tears leaked out as he struggled. In his death throes he flung the covers off and is lying sprawled sideways on the bed. The stump of his missing leg is a horrible thing to see, festered and raw, poking out from the sheets. The air is dense with stale cigarette smoke and the sickly smell of death.

Behind me, Dottie says, "I just can't believe this. I don't know how it happened." She's breathing hard.

I feel suddenly claustrophobic and I step back awkwardly so that my knee gives way and I have to grab the doorframe to keep from stumbling.

"Steady," Dottie says.

"I'm all right," I say. "It's just my damned knee." I turn away and step into the living room. We stare at each other for a few seconds.

"How did you find him? What made you go into his room? Did you hear something?"

Dottie shakes her head. "I get up a couple of times every night to check on him, in case he needs something." Her voice is high and tight. "He's more considerate than you might think. He only calls out if he's in distress. When I checked this time . . ." Her voice falters. "I wanted you to see him like I found him, before I touched anything."

I'm thinking clearer now that the shock has worn off, so I go back into the bedroom to take a closer look at the crime scene. It's hard to escape the sight of Jack's twisted face and body, but I want to fix details in my mind, in case the scene gets contaminated.

I lean over Jack's body and count about half a dozen slits in the T-shirt where a knife went in. I'll leave it to the medical examiner to give me details, but I've seen enough knife wounds to deduce that whoever did this came at Jack with his right hand.

The knife is not in plain sight. Likely whoever did this took it with him. The deep bruises on each side of Jack's Adam's apple mean that whoever killed him grabbed his throat to make sure he wouldn't cry out.

Standing next to me, Dottie reaches for the sheet, as if to cover Jack's body.

"Better leave it," I say. "Have you called Rodell?"

Dottie shakes her head. "I wanted you here first. I'm sorry I got you out of bed." It's surprising the number of people who still call me first when there's a need for the police. I haven't been chief of police for a long time, but that time in my life seems imprinted on folks.

"That's okay. But we'd better call Rodell now and get the wheels turning." Neither of us makes a move to the phone.

"You got a cell phone with a camera on it?"

"Samuel, what would I be doing with something like that?"

"I just know some people have them. Not me." There's probably a camera around here somewhere, but I don't want to go poking around looking for it.

Jack's bedroom is small and not particularly tidy. There's an overflowing ashtray on the bedside stand. "I'm surprised that Jack didn't die from starting a fire in his bed." I'm searching for something to say.

"That smoke is awful. He wouldn't let me open a window in here. I don't see why a man with all his health problems wanted to make it worse. But I've seen that before."

Nudie magazines, veteran's affairs publications, and paperbacks are scattered around the bed, and some have spilled onto the floor in the struggle. His taste in books runs to detective novels with lurid covers, depicting buxom women and guns. Then it strikes me, once again, that Jack couldn't have seen any of these books and magazines.

"Did people read to him?"

"Yes, he liked to be read to."

"And these?" I point to a copy of *Hustler*.

"His friends got great pleasure out of describing the women to him." Her voice borders on the disapproving, but she keeps her expression neutral. Dottie is a devout churchgoer, and she's taken to heart the adage not to cast stones.

The bedside stand is crowded with plastic medicine bottles. I crouch down so I can read the labels without touching them.

"I don't know why he didn't cry out. I'm a light sleeper. I would have heard him."

"Darvocet. Did he take that all the time?"

"Only when he was in pain. But I think he needed a lot of it."

"If he took one of those, he might have been too sound asleep to know anybody was in the room. And by the time he woke up enough, it was too late to cry out." I'm wondering how the killer could see in the dark. The light is on, and Dottie said she didn't touch anything. But it seems strange that someone would risk turning on the light. "Did Jack sleep with a light on?"

"Always. He told me it was so Bob wouldn't have to stumble around in the dark. And I kept it up for the same reason." Dottie gazes at Jack with deep pity. "I don't know how somebody could have been mean enough to do this. What harm could he do anyone?" Her voice breaks and she swipes at her eyes. "He was in a good mood when I put him to bed. We joked. I told him some funny stories about my grandson and he was laughing. Seems like I would have heard something with all this mayhem."

I lay a hand on her arm. "This is not your fault, Dottie. It may have been good that you didn't hear anything, because whoever murdered Jack might have killed you, too."

"Well, I hadn't thought of that."

I go into the kitchen and put on a pot of coffee, and while it drips through, I call down to the police station and rouse James Harley Krueger. He tells me he'll call Rodell and the coroner's office in Bobtail and then he'll come right over.

"No need for the siren," I say, wanting to spare the neighbors. James Harley uses the siren liberally.

When I get off the phone, Dottie has put on a sweater, smoothed her hair into its usual bun, and applied some lipstick, although her face is still deadly pale. I tell her I've called the police, but that I'll wait a couple of hours to call Curtis. "Nothing he can do right now anyway," I say.

"I'm sure he'll appreciate not being bothered," she says. From the sarcasm in her voice, I can tell she shares my opinion of Curtis.

Marybeth should be told what happened, too. But this time I'd better go tell her in person.

I wander into the living room and see that the back door is open an inch. "That's how he got in," I say.

Dottie stares at the door, frowning. "I know I closed that door."

"But was it locked?"

"No, not locked. Jack said he hadn't bothered to lock the doors since his daddy died. I guess for a few days his friend Walter was camping in the backyard and that door was left unlocked in case he wanted to come inside for anything in the night, and Jack didn't get back in the habit of locking up. But I know I closed it."

I turn on the back patio light and step outside. Leaves are skittering across the yard, and I feel a few scattered drops of rain. If there are footprints, the rain will soon obliterate them. And besides, with all the activity here in the last few days, there must be hundreds of footprints.

Dottie and I sit down in the living room to wait for James Harley. I feel both restless and useless, and the change in weather is making my knee throb. In the back of my mind, I'm trying to make some sense out of Jack's death. "Do you know if Jack has had a bad run-in with anybody recently?"

Dottie considers. "I get here at ten o'clock every night, and the other night when I arrived he and his friend Walter were hollering at each other. But by the time he left, they were laughing."

"You know what they were fighting about?"

She sighs, thinks, and then shakes her head. "Something silly. Probably football. That's what usually gets everybody riled up. I remember thinking at the time it was just an excuse to butt up against each other, to keep from getting bored."

"Anything else unusual? Anything that struck you as odd?"

"No more than usual. I always thought Jack was odd. He could have done more for himself, but he seemed more than happy to be taken care of."

"He had bad injuries."

"I've seen worse in my years as a nurse. People who could barely move managed to make a life for themselves. People who wanted to be independent."

"I imagine his was a hard combination. Even if he could get around on crutches, he couldn't see where he was going."

"I'm just saying there are those who wouldn't have taken advantage the way he did."

Even though we are expecting James Harley, his sharp rap on the front door startles us. The first thing I see when I open the door is the barrel of a gun.

"James Harley, put the gun away," I snap.

James Harley is plastered up against the front of the house, to the right of the door. He peeks his head around the side. "Everything okay here?"

"We're not fixing to shoot you, if that's what you're asking."

"Oh, for pity's sake," Dottie says under her breath to me. "That's why I called you."

James Harley edges into the living room, sticking his gun back in his holster. He's Rodell Skinner's favorite lieutenant, being not too bright and inclined to go along with Rodell in most things. He yawns and scratches his considerable belly that seems to get bigger every time I see him. "Chief Craddock, I'll take it from here. I called the ambulance and they should be along after a while. They'll take the body to Bobtail. Then it's T. J.'s problem."

T. J. Sutter is the justice of the peace charged with the duties of the medical examiner. In the instance of a murder, the JP usually calls in an ME from Houston or San Antonio to do the autopsy. But it isn't T. J.'s job to investigate the crime. "Why would it be T. J.'s problem?"

"I just mean he'll have information for us." James Harley speaks in a lofty tone to dismiss my impertinent questions. "Jack back there?" He points toward the hallway. I tell him the body is in the bedroom on the right. James Harley saunters into the bedroom, and I don't hear any movement. When he comes out his expression hasn't changed, as if observing a grisly murder is all in a day's work.

"You going to call in somebody to get forensic evidence?" I ask.

James Harley glares at me. As former chief of police, I know how all this works. And I also know he never would have thought to get evidence if I hadn't mentioned it. "You don't need to worry about that," he says. "We're on it."

"Where is Rodell?" I ask. "Is he on his way?"

"He'll be along."

Somewhere along the line, talking to James Harley always makes me feel testy, and I've just about reached that point. "Well did you talk to him?"

"I said he'll be along. And you two need to vacate the premises." He waves Dottie Gant and me toward the door. "We've got a crime scene here."

I'm reluctant to leave. I'm pretty sure James Harley hasn't reached Rodell. Big surprise. And no telling what James Harley will do left to his own devices. Probably lie down on the couch and sleep until the ambulance arrives, and never bother to call the highway patrol.

"Listen here." I step up toe to toe with him to make my point. "Jack Harbin has been murdered. It's got to be taken seriously. Somebody needs to take pictures and collect evidence."

His face is flushed—he's not happy with my interference. But he goes into the kitchen to contact the Texas Highway Patrol so they can send somebody to help out. When he gets off the phone, things are quiet in the kitchen. Then I hear him dialing the phone again. "This is Deputy James Harley Krueger from the Jarrett Creek Police Department. I just called for an ambulance on a homicide, and, uh, we need to hold off on that. THP will call when they're ready for you."

When I get home, dawn is still a long way off, but the sky is pale gray, light enough to see. I walk down to the pasture and find that the cows are spooked, feeling the change in the weather. There's one who always gets upset at any little thing. She bucks a couple of times when she sees me, to let me know things aren't right. I talk quietly while I feed and water them, but it doesn't help much, with the wind picking up and the scent of rain in the air. It's going to be a long day.

The whole while, I'm thinking, who would stand to gain by killing Jack? Was there an old score that needed settling? That tends in Woody's direction. It's hard to imagine Jack being a threat to anybody, but threats come in all varieties. And something else is bothering me. Bob was barely cold in his grave before Jack was murdered. Is there some connection between Bob's and Jack's deaths? Why did Benadryl show up in Bob's system? Maybe Jack was right and Bob didn't knowingly take it. Maybe somebody slipped it to him to knock him out. Who would be served by having them both out of the way? Curtis comes to mind. Marybeth will probably inherit half of Jack's money, too, but between the two of them, I'd bet on Curtis.

I take a shower to get rid of the smell of death I imagine clinging to me. When I'm dressed, dawn is just tinting the sky. This morning it's a purple and pink sunrise, reflecting off the tower of clouds to the west. While I drink my coffee, I stand in front of a painting that I bought a few months ago. The artist is a young man, a boy really, who loves the land as much as I do, and who captures the deceptive softness of a storm approaching over a sparse field. I have come to appreciate it even more than when I first saw it, and it seems to fit with the storm I know is coming.

CHAPTER 12

Worried that James Harley will leave important things undone, I return to Jack's place to find James Harley out on the sidewalk with a scattering of law enforcement personnel. There's a highway patrol duo and a tall hulk of a man, dressed in khaki pants and shirt with a wide belt and a cowboy hat, with his back to me.

They all turn toward at me as I hobble up. The big man steps forward. "Well, I don't believe my eyes. Samuel Craddock, what the hell are you doing here? I thought you'd retired."

"I might ask you the same thing, Luke." I'm happy to shake hands with Luke Schoppe. The "wheel" badge on his shirt tells me he's still with the Texas Rangers. If he's been brought in to investigate this crime, he'll make short work of it.

Schoppe turns to the patrol duo. "If Samuel is on this, we might as well go home. He'll have it cleared it up in no time."

"Oh, no. Not me. You're right. I retired from law enforcement a long time ago. This is up to you fellows."

Schoppe points to the highway patrolmen. "We're not really assigned to this case. Me and these THP officers have been out since midnight on a big wreck out near Dimebox. We got diverted over here on our way back home." He jerks a thumb in James Harley's direction. "This deputy here says his chief should arrive before too long."

James Harley has his hands on his hips and his legs spread wide, like he's trying to look bigger than he is. His hat is tipped back on his head. "Yeah, Chief Skinner should be coming along any minute now."

The highway patrol contingent looks frazzled. Schoppe throws a worried look my way, and I can see that he's read James Harley Krueger's shortcomings. "I was just telling Deputy Krueger that we've got a big problem. We'll be glad to go in there and take evidence, get photos and what not, but it'll be a while before we can sort out our findings. These budget cuts are killing us. So it might be better if your police officers take the lead."

Getting wind of where this is headed, James Harley says. "Well, I'm going to have to leave you boys to get on with it. I've got some things to see about. Rodell will sort it out with you."

Schoppe straightens even taller and gives James Harley the once-over. He's not a lawman who would think of leaving a crime scene until he was sure it was properly secured. I can see he's about to ask James Harley what's so all-fired important that he has to drop a murder investigation for, when I butt in.

"I'll tell you what, James Harley. I'll stay here until somebody from the department gets here. I promise I won't interfere with your job." I have no intention of waiting around for Rodell or any of his men to show up, but I'm afraid if Schoppe says anything to James Harley, he'll stick around and get in the way.

"I guess that would be all right," he says.

The four of us watch him scurry to his car. Just then a bolt of lightning scatters across the sky and we pause, startled, and wait for the thunder. It takes several seconds, which means the storm is still some distance away. The wind whips up in a flurry and the smell of rain is strong, although it's no more than a promise, and could come to nothing.

"If that doesn't beat everything," Schoppe says as James Harley drives away. "Just leaving us to it."

"I don't want to say too much, but you're not losing a whole lot with him gone," I say.

"No surprise there." Schoppe turns to the highway patrol pair. "Let's get our gear and collect the evidence so we can head on home."

Investigation of capital crimes in small towns in Texas is convoluted. Not that we have all that many murders, but when we do, state authorities have jurisdiction. That can be highway patrol, but more likely Texas Rangers, working with the county sheriff's office.

The medical examiner in the nearest big city also gets involved with the examination of the victim. And sometimes even the FBI gets called on certain cases. But it's not unusual for a good bit of time to pass before much investigation gets done. That is unless it's a serial crime, a mass murder, or some kind of political thing.

I help Schoppe carry in the forensic gear. "How'd you happen by here anyway?" he says.

I tell him how my morning unfolded. "I came back because I had a feeling James Harley wasn't going to take care of business."

"Where's the chief?"

"Likely on a bender."

"Like that, huh?"

In Jack's room Schoppe gets out his fingerprint ID kit. One of the patrolmen begins taking photos, lots of them. Schoppe points to Jack's body, which by now has gone rigid. "You know anything about how this poor boy lost his leg?"

I give Schoppe a sketch of Jack's background, including the fact that not only did he lose a leg, but was also blinded.

"Jesus H. Christ! Who would have done something like this to a busted up war vet?"

They work swiftly. I go in and make a pot of coffee, which they're grateful for. After about ten minutes, we hear doors slamming outside. I look out and see that the ambulance has arrived. I bring the drivers inside and they wait with me in the kitchen until the investigative crew has finished up.

Schoppe hangs back after everybody leaves, and we catch up a little on each other's lives. We're oddly embarrassed to find that we've both lost our wives recently, as if somehow we were careless. But he's got two kids and reports that they're doing well, and he's a grandpa.

Before long he's yawning and gets up to go. "I don't envy those patrolmen. They had a rough night. A four-car pile-up with two teenagers dead and an old boy who's probably not going to make it. He was torn up pretty bad. Crushed. People in the other cars had broken bones and scrapes."

I'd forgotten that Schoppe has a little of the ghoul in him. He relishes going over the worst details of car accidents and crimes. I guess it's his way of dealing with the demons that come with seeing the terrible things people do to themselves and others.

At the door, we shake hands and promise to be in touch, though I doubt we will. "I notice you didn't put up crime scene tape," I say.

"We've got everything we need. I don't know what officer this will be assigned to, or when. Shame, when you consider his sacrifice."

All this has taken a lot less time than it seemed to. It's barely eight o'clock when I call Walter Dunn. Fifteen minutes later I hear his motorcycle pull into the driveway. He tromps into the house and heads straight for Jack's bedroom.

He stays in the room for a long time, and when he comes out his eyes are red. He doesn't seem to know what to do with himself. He looks around, distracted. I know how he feels. "I guess his suffering is over now," he says. Then he smacks the flat of his hand on the wall. "What kind of coward attacks a man who can't fight back?"

"He put up a pretty good fight. Whoever did it not only stabbed him, but strangled him so he'd keep quiet."

"Lord, have mercy." Dunn hangs his head, pinching the bridge of his nose.

I fetch him a cup of coffee. He grabs it with a beefy paw, like it's a lifeline.

"Let's go outside and sit down," I say.

Although the sun is up, it hasn't penetrated the back yard yet, and wisps of mist swirl in the wind, close to the ground under the pecan and post-oak trees. The wind has shifted to come from the north and it's actually chilly, but Dunn, dressed in a T-shirt, seems not to notice.

"How long have you known Jack?" I say.

Dunn runs his hand along his unshaven chin. "Something like fifteen years."

"How did you meet him?"

It takes him several seconds to answer, as if his thoughts are far away. "His dad brought him to a VA meeting I was running over in Bryan." He manages a smile. "Belligerent son of a bitch gave me so much shit, I was ready to throw him out. But after I knew him a while his attitude was what I liked about him." He shakes his head, the smile snuffed out. "Nobody deserves that kind of injury. He always felt that somehow people blamed him. I told him that was ridiculous, but he said the questions people asked him made him feel like that."

"What kind of questions?"

"Oh, like, wasn't there some way of identifying vehicles that had been booby-trapped, or wasn't he wearing body armor. Stuff like that. But what really got to him was people telling him he should trust in God and look on the bright side, and that maybe his wounds were a blessing. What bright side is there to being blind and having a festering wound that won't heal?"

I shake my head. Sometimes people can't imagine someone else's burdens. "Anybody in particular that bothered him?"

Dunn grimaces. "He never mentioned anybody. Probably a good thing. One of us would have had to set them straight."

"With Bob gone, I expect Jack was worried about what was going to happen to him."

He groans. "Oh, God, I didn't even think about that. He was about to get married. I guess I'll have to go tell her."

I feel like someone has shoved me backwards. "What are you talking about? Who was he going to marry?"

"That waitress down at the café. Lurleen Zachary. They'd been keeping company for a good while. She wouldn't marry him, said she liked things just the way they were. But when Jack's daddy passed, she changed her mind. Jack just told me a couple of days ago. It was going to be awhile before they could make it official. I guess Lurleen never bothered to get a divorce when she and her old man split up. So she had to file and wait for it to go through."

"I'll be damned."

Dunn stands and gestures toward my cup. "You want a warm up?"

While he's gone, I think about Lurleen's solicitous way with Jack down at the café last week. I don't remember her at Bob's funeral, though. But why would I? And then I think about Woody's plan to rescue Jack from his troubles. Jack getting married would have put a kink in that notion.

Dunn comes back and looks at the darkening sky. "We're about to get a storm. I guess I better get on down to Lurleen's. Do you know her?"

"Just from the café."

"How about if you come along?"

"Not on that cycle, I'm not, but I'll follow you."

Lurleen lives in a rusted out aluminum trailer on the other side of the railroad tracks directly east of the café. It's on a regular size lot, and looks like it has been there so long it has taken root. A makeshift wooden ramp leads up to the front door.

Dunn says, "The boys and I built that ramp."

There's no reason I should have known about the relationship. Jack and Lurleen are another generation entirely. Still, I like to keep up with the business of the town. I wonder if Loretta knows what was going on.

"They were real quiet about it so her ex-husband wouldn't find out and try to take the kids away."

Jack's disability check would have taken a financial strain off Lurleen. And it would have been nice for Jack to have a family. Whoever killed Jack took away hopes and dreams along with him.

When Lurleen opens the door, she's already dressed for work in her dull gold uniform. She's got a sweet, round face, with soft brown eyes.

The lines around her eyes are deep for a woman her age, a hint of the hard life she led before she kicked her husband out. Behind her I hear kids squabbling. She looks distracted and flustered. "Walter, what are you doing here?"

"Lurleen, why don't you step out here for a minute," Dunn says.

"I don't really have any time right now. And look at that sky. It's going to pour before too long." But then the gentleness of his voice registers with her. She looks at me and realizes something is wrong. Her hand goes up to her throat, a gesture women make when they sense bad news coming.

Her eyes widen. "Just a minute," she says. She pokes her head back inside. "You kids get ready for school. Right now. I mean *right now*." She closes the door behind her and stumbles a little.

Dunn reaches out and steadies her.

"Is this something about Jack?"

"It's bad news, Lurleen."

Her face closes up. "How bad? What happened?"

"He's gone."

She gives a little whimper. "Oh, Sweet Jesus, this can't be. What happened?"

Dunn glances at me to fill her in. "I'm sorry," I say. "Jack's nurse called me about three o'clock this morning and I went over there and . . ." I hesitate, not wanting to say the words. "It looks like somebody killed him."

Lurleen puts her hands to her face and her shoulders heave. "Killed him! What do you mean? Killed him how?"

"Lurleen, you don't need to know the details this minute. Just give it some time to sink in."

"Oh, this is just awful. Poor Jack." Her head comes back up and her eyes are wild. "Who did it? Who could have done it?"

The door opens and a little boy about six, still dressed in his pajamas, peeks out. "Mamma, Glory won't let me in the bathroom."

Lurleen seems not to have heard him. I move past her and take the boy by the hand. "Let's go see what we can do about this," I say.

He trots along inside with me. The interior of the trailer is as messy as three kids can make it. At the table sits a boy on the cusp of adolescence, long and skinny. He's pecking away at a computer, and scowls at me, being at the age where scowling is the only possible response. "Who are you?" he says.

I tell him. "Your mamma could use your help getting your brother and sister off to school."

"This is Saturday. We don't have school," the little one says, and busts out laughing.

"Don't be a goof," his big brother says.

I ask the little one his name. "Carlton. I'm six. And he's Will. He's twelve." The older boy glares at his brother as if he's just divulged a closely guarded secret.

"How old is Glory?"

"She's eight. Mamma says she's mean as a snake."

It's hard to keep my mouth from twitching in a smile, which provokes an answering grin in the older boy. "Carlton, you're never going to be much of a poker player," he says.

"Well, Carlton, I know you'd like it to be Saturday, but it's not. It's Wednesday. So let's see if we can't get Glory to give up the bathroom."

"What happened to your leg?" he says, pointing at my cane.

"Carlton, that is none of your nosy business," his brother says.

I tell him I don't mind being asked, and I tell Carlton about the cow knocking me down and stepping on it. He's pleased with the story and looks at me with admiration.

"Carlton, why aren't you dressed?" a prissy little voice says. I turn and see a pint-sized version of Lurleen, but bossy, with her hands on her hips and a smirk on her face.

"You wouldn't let me in the bathroom," the little one says with a hitch in his voice.

"Well now she's out, so scoot," I say.

"But . . ." He's ready to declare war.

"Go, go, go. This is your chance," I say.

"Who are you, and where's my mamma?" Glory says.

"You two," I say, including Will in my glance, "Your mamma has had some bad news, and maybe needs you to cut her a little slack."

Will stands up. He's taller than I would have thought. "What kind of bad news?"

"She'll tell you about it in her own good time."

CHAPTER 13

On the way home I stop by Loretta's. I've just reached her steps when another flash of lightning hits, and the rain turns on like a faucet. Loretta flings open the door. "I saw you drive up. Get on in here before you drown."

She gives me a towel to dry off as best I can.

"Come on into the kitchen. What brings you out here so early?"

The news about Jack shakes her up. She's got a son who's not much older. "I swear I never heard of such a terrible thing. What is this world coming to?"

I don't have an answer for her on that one.

"You had any breakfast?" Her solution for most things is to ply people with food.

"Just coffee."

She cracks a couple of eggs into a pan, warms up some coffee cake in her little toaster oven and opens a jar of peach jam. When she sets the plate down in front of me, she sits down to watch me eat and asks about the particulars of Jack's death. I tell her as much as I think she can stomach.

"We could all be murdered in our beds." She echoes what every woman of a certain age in Jarrett Creek will say. It's more a comment about the uncertainty of life than about really being afraid she'll be murdered.

"I suspect this isn't a random killing," I say.

"You mean somebody had it in for Jack? What kind of threat could he be, all lame like he is, not to mention with his eyesight gone?"

"You've asked the right question. Either he was a threat or somebody was after revenge."

"Or his money. I understand he had a good bit put away. That brother of his . . ." Her voice trails away. Loretta doesn't think people are evil—just misguided.

"Let's not go off speculating. That's the job of the police."

"If Rodell has it in him to investigate properly," she mutters darkly.

I finish up my breakfast and carry my plate to the sink.

"Leave that," she says.

I obey, knowing how particular she is about the way chores get done in her kitchen. I pour myself another cup of coffee and sit back down.

"I guess it's up to Curtis and Marybeth to see to the house," she says.

"I was just waiting for a decent hour this morning to call Curtis, and then I'll drive over to College Station and break the news to Marybeth."

"Yes. You can't leave it to Rodell. Or his deputies." She purses her lips.

When the rain lets up, I head back to Jack's place. It's harder to locate Curtis than I expected. The phone number on the list in the Harbin kitchen has been disconnected. Information tells me his number is now unlisted. If I were still with the police department, I could demand the number, but the bored little operator isn't interested that Curtis's brother has died. I dig around in a kitchen drawer that holds pieces of paper with various scribbles on them, and finally come across one with a number for "The True Marcus Ministry."

A man answer brusquely, "Marcus Ministry."

"I'm looking for Curtis Harbin."

"He's in Dallas."

"Who am I speaking with?"

"This is Brother Kittredge. And who might you be?" He has a belligerent tone that aggravates me, but I need to stay cool since I need him to cooperate.

I tell him my name. "I'm wondering if there's any way I can reach him."

"He's at a gun show."

I wait for more, since this doesn't tell me how I can get in touch with Curtis, but silence prevails. "Well, there's a problem. His brother has died, and I need to get in touch with him right away."

"Uh-huh." He pauses. "You're talking about his blood brother, not a church brother."

"That's right. Do you know where Curtis is staying?"

"Hold on a minute."

After a long while he comes back and tells me if I'll leave my number, they'll contact Curtis and have him get back to me.

I stand at the sliding glass door and watch the rain slash down. I'm thinking it could take a while for Curtis to call back, and I should have left my home number, so I could have waited at my own house. But it isn't ten minutes before Curtis calls.

"What's going on? Did I hear this right? Is Jack dead?"

"I'm sorry, Curtis. Somebody killed him."

"What do you mean killed him?" He sounds more annoyed than upset.

"He was stabbed to death in his bed." I normally wouldn't be so blunt, but Curtis and his church brother have rubbed me the wrong way.

"Do they know who did it?"

"Whoever it was didn't leave a calling card."

He sighs. "I guess I'll have to come back down there."

"There's no hurry," I say. "They'll have to get a medical examiner from Houston to do an autopsy, and it may be a few days before they will release Jack's body."

"No, there can't be an autopsy. My church doesn't believe in desecrating a body."

"That's between you and the police." I don't see that it matters much. It's pretty clear what killed Jack. But Curtis won't have any say in the matter, regardless.

"I'll be there as soon as I can. Has anybody called Mother?"

"I'm going over there to tell her in person."

"I don't envy you that. Jack was her favorite. She'll probably go nuts."

After this unsettling conversation, I'm at loose ends. Where the hell is Rodell? Is he going to investigate Jack's murder, or just hope whoever did it strolls into the station and confesses?

I don't have long to wonder because just then Rodell stomps into the kitchen looking like hell. His eyes are bloodshot and that's just for starters. Despite his long affair with the bottle, he's usually pretty particular about the way he dresses, but today he looks like he slept in his clothes—in a barn. And there's dried blood on the side of his face.

I step up closer and peer at the blood. He's got a nasty cut. "Rodell, what the hell happened to you? Looks like you might need stitches."

"When did you get your medical license? And what are you doing at a crime scene?" A wave of stale alcohol fumes pours out of him. His ire brings on a coughing fit so hard he doubles over.

"Get over here and sit down." I lead him over to a kitchen chair and he sprawls into it, almost falling off.

He moans and buries his face in his hands. "I'm a sick man," he says hoarsely.

"You're a drunk man." But in Rodell's case, both are true. A few months back Doc Taggart told Rodell if he didn't stop drinking he was going to do major damage to his liver. And for a while Rodell slowed down considerably. But he's an alcoholic. Slowing down isn't good enough, and stopping doesn't seem to be an option. "Where's James Harley?" I ask.

"I don't know." Rodell moans again. Suddenly he lurches up and staggers over to the sink and starts retching. The sight and sound of it calls up memories of my father, who had a long and unsatisfactory relationship with alcohol. That's probably why I don't have much patience with Rodell.

I get Rodell to sit back down and then call down to the station, but there's no answer. Some police department. I call James Harley's place and get an earful from his wife about the nerve I have disturbing a man who has just come off duty. But she tells me that Bill Odum is the deputy on duty today. Eventually I reach him down at the café and tell him to come get Rodell, that he's not fit for duty.

CHAPTER 14

I'm about ready to leave to go tell Marybeth about Jack's death when I stop in my tracks at the front door. A plan has popped into my head. Since Taylor visited me last week, I've been thinking about her worries over her sister. Suddenly I see an opportunity has opened up to help Taylor find out what's going on at True Marcus Ministries.

I call Taylor's mamma for Taylor's phone number. I don't tell her mamma about Jack, because if I get her started, I'll never get off the phone. She'll hear the information through the grapevine soon enough.

Taylor isn't home, but she answers her cell phone. I hear people talking in the background. She says she's at a spa outside of Dallas.

When I tell her about Jack, she starts to cry and says she'll call me back in a few minutes. When she gets back to me, I tell her as much as I think she needs to hear, and she cries off and on.

"Listen, this may not be the best time, but I've been thinking about your sister." I tell her my plan.

She's quiet for several seconds. "You're right. This would be a good time. I can arrange to get away. I'll call you back."

"I'm on my way to give Marybeth the news about Jack."

"I'm sure she'll get some good drama out of it," she says bitterly. "That woman is a piece of work. Always was."

"Now Taylor, not everybody has as much strength as you."

I arrive at Marybeth's apartment at five o'clock, thinking Marybeth probably gets off work sometime after four. I'm surprised when she comes to the door in her bathrobe. She blinks nervously. Her movements are jerky, as if she's perpetually startled.

"Samuel, what a nice surprise. I'm afraid I'm not dressed for company." She clutches the robe closed. "I wasn't feeling good, so I took the day off."

"I'm sorry to disturb you."

"It's okay. I can't seem to get myself back on track since Bob died."

And I'm about to throw her even farther off the track. "I need to talk to you Marybeth."

Even though I try to put a warning in my voice, she doesn't catch it. She swings the door wide. "Come on in. I'll just go put some clothes on." She flits away before I can stop her.

I've been in her apartment before. It's the tiniest place I've ever seen, one small room that's a combined living room, kitchen and dining area, and an even smaller, closet-size bedroom. There's one window that looks out onto the parking lot. It's in a building where a lot of students live, close to the Texas A&M University campus. Marybeth works there as a secretary in the research park.

I get over to Bryan–College Station often, usually to consult somebody at the vet school about one of my cows. So I take Marybeth to lunch or dinner every couple of months. It's barely an hour's drive.

My wife, Jeanne, and Marybeth were not particularly good friends, but Jeanne felt bad about whatever demons drove Marybeth to leave her husband and son. Jeanne thought people should make the effort to be kind to her.

While Marybeth gets dressed, I wander around her front room, longing for a cup of coffee. But I remember that she doesn't drink it, so I'm out of luck. She has lived here for many years, but she could easily move out tomorrow without any fuss. She's not an accumulator. The furniture is strictly utilitarian: a glass-top table with two iron chairs near the kitchen, a boxy sofa, and two matching armchairs facing the world's smallest TV. I wonder what drives Marybeth to take up as little room as possible in the world.

She has a small bookcase that holds stacks of old *People* magazines and a few romance novels. A vase with some pale plastic flowers sits on top of the bookcase. She has a few pictures on the walls; the kind you can purchase at Walmart—unfocused pictures of Paris and some generic landscapes.

Finally she emerges from her bedroom, wearing a dress that hangs shapeless on her tiny frame. Her hair, a quiet brown streaked with gray, is pushed back with a hair band. "What can I get you?" she says, skittering to the kitchen area. "I'm just going to have a cup of tea."

"Marybeth, come on over here and sit down."

"Just a cup of tea. I'll just . . ." She looks over at me, and my solemn face. "Okay, I'll get it later."

I sit down on one of the armchairs and she perches on the arm of the sofa, like a sparrow. Her smile twitches on and off. I wonder, not for the first time, if she takes some kind of medication.

I tell her about Jack, and for a few minutes I'm not sure she's taking it in. She nods vigorously, chewing on the side of her mouth like a school child struggling with a perplexing math problem. People react in different ways to news of a death, but Marybeth doesn't seem to understand my words. Her eyes flit from me to the TV and back. Finally she jumps up and paces around the room, hugging herself. "Thank you for coming all this way to tell me." She stops in the kitchen long enough to set the kettle on to boil, then starts moving again. "Does Curtis know?"

"I reached him in Dallas. He said he'll be at the house sometime tomorrow."

"Curtis hates Jackie," she says, in an off-hand way, as if talking to herself. She takes shuddering breaths.

"I doubt that."

"Oh, he does. He hates me, too. He's not a very nice man." Suddenly she stops in front of me. She has peculiar look on her face. Defiant? That's a first. "And you know what? I never liked Curtis. That's a horrible thing for a mother to say, but from the minute he came out, I didn't like him."

I'm jolted by a flash of anger at Marybeth. I think about how my brother, Horace, could never do anything right in our mamma's eyes. She had no patience for boys or men in general. But she singled out Horace for her wrath. Horace and my daddy took to the bottle to soothe the hurts she inflicted. Being the younger son, I was cushioned a bit.

Maybe Marybeth did the right thing by leaving Bob and Jack. Maybe my brother and I and our daddy might have been better off if my mother had realized that she wasn't suited to the job and left.

"Listen, you don't need to open those old wounds."

It's like she didn't hear me. "Jack made me feel the opposite. The second he was born, I said, 'He's mine.' That's why I had to leave after he was hurt in that war. My heart just plain cracked in two every time I looked at him." She paces back to the window. "It was selfish, I know that. But better than me there crying all day, every day. And I knew Bob could handle it. He was like a mule. You put him in a harness and he just plodded along getting the job done. Me? I'm . . ." She stands wringing her hands. "Oh Samuel, how could someone have hurt my sweet boy?"

I feel trapped in her tiny place. "Let's go get something to eat." I walk over and turn off the kettle.

"Eat?" As if it's a foreign concept. "Yes, that would be okay."

We go to a cafe and I order a hamburger. Sitting there with Marybeth is a hard slog, with her picking at a salad and starting sentences she doesn't finish. But what little food she gets inside her brings some color back to her face, and she sits a little quieter.

"Marybeth, somebody needs to go over to the house and figure out what to do with Jack's and Bob's things, find out if there's a will, and make funeral arrangements."

She puts her fork down and shrinks back in her seat. "Curtis will do all that."

"Isn't there anything you'd like to have from the house? Photos? Anything?"

She chews her lip. "There might be pictures of Jackie, from before. I might like those."

"If you want, I can take you over there. The house probably belongs to you now."

She puts a hand to her mouth and starts to shake. "I think I have to go back to my apartment."

When we get to her apartment, she goes into the bathroom and I hear pills rattle from a plastic container and water running. When she comes out, she sinks onto the sofa and stares at the wall. Eventually she rouses herself. "I want to ask you something. Do you think Curtis could have killed Jack?"

That's exactly what I think, but I don't need to go into it with her. "Marybeth, what would make you say such a thing?"

She moves forward to the edge of the sofa. "Curtis was always out for what he could get. He never had any interest in other people."

"I don't know what he'd get out of it. Seems like you're the one who would inherit the house and anything Jack left."

Marybeth shakes her head. "I signed over the house to Bob when I left. I told him I didn't want anything. If he left a will, I expect he left everything to the boys. Which means with Jack dead, Curtis will get it all."

"Do you know if Bob left a will?

She shakes her head. "After the funeral, I got out of there."

"Did you talk to Jack?"

Her lips are trembling, and there's such longing on her face that I can't look at her. "I didn't know what to say to him. What do you say when you've abandoned your son? If I'd been a good person, I'd have told him that I'd come back home and take over where Bob left off."

"Marybeth, I'm sure he didn't expect that of you. He knows you've struggled." Would things have been better if she had stayed in Jarrett

Creek? I expect Bob would have ended up with two people to take care of.

"Still, I should have told him I'd try."

I wish like anything that Jeanne were with me. She'd know what to say. All I can think of is practical details. "You and Bob never got a divorce, am I right?"

"I never thought about it, and I guess Bob didn't either."

I'm wondering if Bob left a will. Not that it is any of my business, but things get talked about in a small town, and Loretta surely would have told me if she'd heard.

"I know a lawyer you can talk to about legal matters."

"Oh, legal matters." She waves a hand. "I'm not going to fight with Curtis."

"Still, it would be good for you to talk to my friend Jenny Sandstone. Besides being a good lawyer, she has a lot of sense. There may be things you have to do legally, even if you want to turn everything over to Curtis. Jenny can help you with that." I write down Jenny's phone number and lay it on the coffee table. Then I stand up.

"Marybeth, do you have a friend who could come over here and spend some time with you?"

She shakes her head. "I don't want anybody around right now." She looks up at me. "Oh, Samuel, you don't need to worry about me. I don't have the courage to kill myself. If I did, I would have done it a long time ago."

I pat her shoulder. "Listen, don't dwell on Curtis. I'll grant you, he's a different kind of person, but there's no reason to think he killed Jack. You should leave all that to the authorities." Even as I say it, I'm damned sure if it were my son who had been murdered I wouldn't leave it to Rodell to investigate.

"If Curtis killed Jack, they'll never figure it out anyway. He's smooth." She pushes herself off the sofa gingerly, like she's afraid she'll break if she moves too fast. "I guess you're right. Maybe I should go over and take a look at the house. Even though everybody will think I'm a vulture."

"Marybeth, it doesn't matter what anybody thinks. It's nobody's business but yours."

Marybeth says she'll drive over tomorrow. "You think Curtis is going to be there?"

"I don't know." I'm hoping he'll show up in Jarrett Creek tomorrow, but for my own reasons.

CHAPTER 15

I'm in Waco by ten o'clock and manage to find the Starbucks Taylor suggested we meet at. We don't have anything like it in Jarrett Creek. But I've been to a Starbucks in Houston, and I like it fine, even though I'm the only person in line who orders plain old coffee.

Taylor rushes in a half hour late. "I'm sorry. The woman who usually stays with my girls was late. Do I have time to get a cappuccino?" She's dressed conservatively in a dark skirt that covers her knees, low heels, and a white blouse buttoned all the way up. I took care with my own clothes this morning, copying what I've seen Curtis wear, although I feel like I'm ready for a game of golf rather than a foray into enemy territory.

"Sure, you have time. We need to strategize, so get your coffee."

When she comes back with her foamy drink and a muffin, I see that her make-up can't hide her swollen eyes or the dark circles under them.

"I still can't wrap my head around Jack being dead," she says. "I knew him from the time we were babies." Her eyes well up. "I called Woody after I talked to you. He hadn't heard about it, and he was all torn up."

"He told you about his plans to have Jack come and live with them?"

"I already knew about it from Laurel. She wanted me to talk to Woody. I told her I was the last person he'd listen to."

"Turns out it wouldn't have come to anything anyway."

"What do you mean?"

"You know Lurleen, the waitress down at Town Café?"

She nods. "Couple of years behind me in school."

"She and Jack were going to get married."

"Really?" She gives me a rueful smile. "Well, that's good. He had something to look forward to. I'll go by and see Lurleen. This is going to be hard on her." Then she frowns. "When did they decide to get married?"

"Walter Dunn told me he found out a couple of days before Jack died. Apparently Lurleen had never gotten a divorce from her first husband, and she liked things the way they were, so she and Jack had no plans to marry. But when Jack's dad died, she changed her mind."

"Oh." She nods her head slowly. "That makes sense."

"What does?"

"Mmm, something Jack said." She gets up abruptly and dumps her muffin and empty coffee cup in the wastebasket. When she sits back down, she says, "We should talk about what we're doing here. Have you found out where this cult is located?"

"No, I thought we'd drop by the police department. They usually keep tabs on cults, and the Waco police aren't strangers to that kind of thing."

The cop behind the front desk has a long, bony face and steel gray hair. He leans on his forearms and nods when we tell him what we're looking for. "The True Marcus Ministry," he says with a sigh. "That's what they call it, but it's just an excuse to hide out and collect guns. Ever since that David Koresh firestorm, this town has been a magnet for nutty groups. Gives us a lot of trouble."

"Can you tell me how to get out to their place?"

He looks us over. "I wouldn't waste my time. They're not going to give you any satisfaction."

"You don't even know what we're after," Taylor says.

His smile is patronizing. "I know they're going to take one look at you and think you're not welcome there. Their women wear those long dresses like something out of *Little House on the Prairie*. Hair long, no make-up. Not to be disrespectful of you, ma'am."

Taylor sighs. "I'm trying to see my sister."

"Oh, it's like that," he says sympathetically. He stands up straight. "Let me get somebody to drive you out there. They don't want to get crossways with the law, so they usually cooperate with us to a certain extent."

Officer Redmond, who is barely dry behind the ears, drives us out in a squad car. "Let me do the talking," he says. "They probably won't let us go inside, but maybe they'll bring your sister to you."

We drive northeast for about thirty minutes through increasingly dense woods. Taylor is quiet, but there's no need for either of us to say much because Redmond is a one-man advertisement for the wonders of Waco. He tells us he was born here, went to school at Baylor, and the only time he's spent outside the area was in the Texas Department of Public Safety training. And there is not a better place in the great state of Texas. In other circumstances I might argue the matter with him, but I need him on our side.

Eventually the trees give way to high, dense scrub brush. Everything is hot and dusty and forlorn. We turn onto an unpaved road. Dust rises behind us as we barrel along parallel with a high chain link fence that looks like it means business. At the end of the road, we stop in front of a little shed next to a gate. A large man carrying a rifle in his left hand steps out to greet us. He's dressed in khaki pants and shirt with an emblem of crossed guns with an eye in the middle of it. He introduces himself as Brother Dan. He's wearing sunglasses, so I can't see his eyes.

I wondered if Redmond was old enough and trained enough to deal with the Marcus Ministry folks, but he eases my doubts right away. He gets out of the car to talk to Brother Dan. His voice projects authority, yet he maintains a relaxed stance.

"In the car here I have Samuel Craddock and Taylor Venable. Mrs. Venable says her sister is married to one of your members, and she's having trouble getting in touch with her. She's a little worried. I imagine you can sympathize with that. She'd like a chance to talk to her sister if you can arrange it."

"What's Craddock's interest in this?"

"He's a lawman from Jarrett Creek. Mrs. Venable asked him to accompany her."

Brother Dan slaps at a mosquito on his arm. If he's sympathetic to Taylor's situation, he sure doesn't show it. "I'm sorry she's having trouble, but we don't keep people from talking to their families. If they want to, that is. A lot of our members prefer not to be involved with their former family members."

"Mmm, mmm. That may be, but Mrs. Venable would like to see firsthand if that's the case. It would set her mind at ease, and it would go a long way to keeping your ministry's relationship with our department on friendly terms."

The man takes off his sunglasses. His blue eyes are hard as ice. "I see no reason for threats. We haven't broken any laws."

"I'm sorry if you thought that's what I was implying. What I meant to say was, the chief gets nervous if an outsider, somebody who doesn't understand how things work in Waco, gets upset and thinks the police don't run a tight ship." Redmond has been standing at attention, but now he leans back against his car and folds his arms as if they're discussing the price of land in the area.

"There's no need for the lady to be upset. We treat our women just fine."

"I'm sure you do. But I hope you understand Chief Kolecek's position. He wouldn't like somebody like Mrs. Venable here, a perfectly nice, respectable woman, to complain to state authorities that we're letting a group keep officers from carrying out their duties properly. Our job is to keep citizens safe and sound, and sometimes we need to assure ourselves that we're doing the job right." If he sounded any friendlier, he'd be wagging his tail.

Brother Dan's expression is patient, but I notice his fist clenching and unclenching. "Just a minute," he says. He goes inside his hut. I don't see any wires, so he must have a walkie-talkie of some kind. After a few seconds, he comes out. "What's the sister's name?"

"Sarah. Sarah Harbin." Taylor's voice quivers.

Brother Dan disappears back inside. The temperature inside the car has become unbearable. Taylor unbuttons the top button of her blouse and fans herself with a brochure she dug out of her purse. I feel sweat trickling down my back.

It's a good ten minutes before Brother Dan comes back to the car. He avoids making eye contact with Taylor, but speaks loud enough for us to hear him. "Brother Kittredge will bring Sister Sarah here. He consulted with her and she said she'd be willing to show herself. You should be appreciative. Not everyone wants contact with outsiders."

At the word "outsider," Taylor's cheeks flush and she grabs my hand, but she just nods.

"Thank you kindly," Redmond says. "It really helps when you folks are so forthcoming." I guess it's partly the heat that makes me want to say a few choice words on the matter. But that would probably mean the end of Taylor's chance to see her sister.

A golf cart with two people in it comes into view, bumping along the rutted road through the brush. Taylor sits forward and says, "Officer Redmond, would it be all right if I got out of the car?"

He sticks his head inside and says quietly. "Wait until your sister gets close, then step out. But keep your distance unless she makes a move."

"I hate this," Taylor breathes to me.

I hate it as much as she does. Jarrett Creek has several churches, but they're all some version of regular religious establishments: Baptists and Methodists, Catholics and Lutherans and Church of Christ. I don't know that we even have any Mormons or Christian Scientists. About the most exotic congregation we have around there is a little nest of Seventh Day Adventists out near Bobtail.

Waco is a whole different story. Since the Branch Davidians had their disastrous run-in with the federal government near Waco back in the nineties, the area around Waco has become a magnet for fanatic religious sects. The groups are run by men who thrive on fear and suspicion and who assert their power by treating their wives and children like property. I remember Curtis's coldness when he talked about his wife. How does a man get to where he doesn't feel safe or powerful unless he has a gun and an iron grip on his family's every move?

Brother Kittredge gets out of the cart and says something to Sarah. She nods and he goes around and helps her out. He takes her arm, as if she's unable to trust her own feet, or he wants to make sure she doesn't bolt. Her pale blue dress is a little long, and it's an old style, like something from the fifties, but it's not as old-fashioned as the cop at the station described. Her sleeves come only to her elbows, and the neck of her dress is open at the top button in deference to the heat. Her hair, dark like Taylor's, is long, but worn simply, held back by barrettes. Her face is flushed, and she keeps her eyes on the road in front of her until they get to the gate. Brother Dan fiddles with the elaborate lock and opens the gate enough for them to step through. Only then does Sarah lift her eyes to the police car. Her eyes are as watchful as a dog used to being hit at random.

When she's a few feet away, Taylor gets out of the car. "Sarah!"

Both Brother Dan and Brother Kittredge react as if Taylor has rushed at them. They quickly move in close on either side of Sarah, and Brother Dan puts his arm up as if to ward off a blow. "She doesn't want physical contact," he says.

"Sarah is that true?" Taylor says defiantly.

Sarah nods. Although her clothes are strange, she looks healthy, and her dress is clean and pressed.

"But . . ." Taylor starts to protest, but stops when Brother Kittredge seizes Sarah's arm.

"If you can't abide by Sister Sarah's wishes, we'll have to ask you to leave," Brother Dan says.

"I understand. I'll do what you say." Taylor's voice shakes.

Brother Dan nods, and they lead Sarah a little closer.

Sarah's expression is calm. "It's good to see you, Taylor. Thank you for coming. As you can see, I'm fine. I'm very happy. Tell Mother I'm fine." Is it my imagination, or does her voice wobble a little at these words? "Are you well?"

"Yes, but I've been worried about you. I thought I'd get to see you at the funeral when your father-in-law died, but Curtis said one of the kids is sick. What's wrong?"

"She's better. It was just a cold. Are your children well? Who did you leave them with today?"

"They're great. I wish you could see them. My middle one reminds me so much of you. I couldn't bring them because they're in school. I have a wonderful woman staying with them."

"At Marcus Ministry we don't let strangers take care of our children." Sarah speaks as if she's reading from a script. But then she adds, "Send me a picture." She shoots a furtive sidelong glance at Brother Kittredge, as if she's said something out of line.

"I wish I could see your children, Sarah. I'm their aunt, and I would like to see them."

"Maybe sometime that can happen. Marcus Ministry doesn't keep us captive. We just want to do what's best for our families." She swallows and speaks louder. "I wouldn't lie to you."

Taylor gasps.

Sarah turns to Brother Kittredge and whispers something to him. He says, "Sister Sarah wants to go now. Thank you for your visit. We always want to assure our members' families that they are happy with their spiritual choice."

"Sarah!" Taylor calls out. But they keep up a steady pace away from us and Sarah doesn't look back. They climb into the golf cart and scoot away. Taylor stares after them until they disappear into the thicket. Brother Dan locks the gate and goes back inside his little hut without acknowledging us further.

Redmond takes Taylor's arm and says, "We'd better go now. That's all you're going to get."

He turns the car around and we drive away. By the time we reach the main road, Taylor is sobbing.

"Ma'am, she looked okay to me," Redmond says. "You should see some of them. They look like they've been drugged."

"She's not okay," Taylor says.

"Your sister looked well-cared-for, and she seemed content enough," Redmond says. "There's a lot of people who would be satisfied with that."

Taylor clutches my hand so hard that it hurts. Her lips are set in a thin line.

When we are back in the parking lot of the police station, and Redmond has left us, Taylor explodes. "What a horrible farce!"

"Now calm down. It's not as bad as all that."

"Yes it is! You don't know. Something she said—I know she's not okay."

"What did she say?"

"She said, 'I wouldn't lie to you.'"

My heart begins to thud. "That means something to you?"

She nods. Tears are slipping down her cheeks. "When we were children, we played a game with my cousins, a lying game, where we had to guess who was telling the truth. Sarah and I cheated." Her voice is high with tension. "Those are the words we used to signal each other if we weren't telling the truth."

She puts a hand to her forehead and her shoulders heave.

"Let's get out of here. We need some food."

We find a cafe, and over lunch Taylor tells me it's the phrase "well-cared-for" that made her want to hit Redmond. "Like a prize heifer!"

She's all for storming the place. She talks wildly about hiring men to use heavy equipment to ram the gate and race to her sister's rescue.

"You've been watching too many movies. We're going to have to think of something a little more subtle than that."

"Oh, subtle. As if those people understand anything but force."

"Nevertheless, I'd like to give it some thought. Let's think of force as a last resort, not the first choice."

Eventually I talk her down. She tells me she is driving down to Jarrett Creek today. "I'm going to stay until Jack's funeral is over."

"I wouldn't rush down. The funeral may not be for a few days. They haven't even released the body yet."

"I'm too wound up to go home. I've made arrangements for somebody to stay with the girls. I hate to do that, but I'm no good to anybody."

"I'm sure they'll be fine."

"My husband will come down for the funeral. He might have some ideas about what to do about Sarah's situation. Although his ideas usually involve throwing money at a problem." She clamps her mouth into an angry line.

"Maybe that's not a bad solution, if it gets the job done."

Her eyes soften and I feel like she's really looking at me for the first time since we sat down. "You're right. I should look at the goal, and not fuss about the way it gets done."

"Exactly. I mean what you were proposing may be exciting, but it breaks the law and puts everybody at risk. Throwing money at a problem sidesteps the drama."

CHAPTER 16

I haven't been home five minutes when Loretta shows up at my door. "You've been making yourself mighty scarce."

"Come on in, and I'll tell you about it."

"It may be me telling you." She's all puffed up with news. "All heck broke loose around here this afternoon." Strong language for Loretta.

I brew us some coffee and we sit out on my porch. The air is fresh after yesterday's rain, and it's not so humid. "You go first," I say, and she doesn't hesitate.

"Marybeth came into town this afternoon, and they say she was at the house when Curtis got there. From what I hear, he tried to throw her out, but that big man, Jack's friend, was there, and he intervened. He and Curtis got into a fistfight."

I set my coffee down and stare at her. "You're kidding!"

"No, sir! A neighbor called Rodell, but apparently he was not available." She gives me raised eyebrows.

"I'm not surprised. He was coming off a binge when I saw him yesterday. Something has got to be done about that."

"Something has been done." She lowers her voice. "It's supposed to be a secret, but he's been hauled off to a facility near Austin to dry out."

"Oh, my Lord. How did that happen?"

"What I heard was that he got home yesterday morning and he'd been on a bender and his wife, Patty, had had all she could take. She called her kids and they came over and decided he had to go off to get some help."

"Who's in charge with him gone?"

"City council was meeting this afternoon to decide that. I expect they'll appoint James Harley. He's been with the department the longest." She waits, and when I don't say anything, she says, "Samuel, you know we might as well have a billy goat in charge as James Harley Krueger."

"What about that youngster they hired last year? I've talked to him once or twice and he seems smart enough."

Loretta sniffs. "You know as well as I do that smart has got nothing to do with it. It's all politics, and with James Harley's father being so well thought of, that's who they're going to choose. Unless . . ."

I don't like the sound of that. "Unless what?"

"A couple of people suggested maybe asking you to step in." She throws up her hands as she sees I'm going to protest. "Don't get all riled up. It would just be temporary, while Rodell is gone."

"I don't know that I'm ready to take on that responsibility. And you never know, James Harley might be one of those people who rise to the occasion."

Loretta snorts. "I'm surprised at you. I figured you'd want to help find out who killed that boy. If it hadn't been for you poking your nose and figuring out who killed Dora Lee Parjeter, they'd have the wrong person in jail right now."

I'm wondering if there's any way the city council can ask Bobtail's police chief to get involved, or if we can ask for assistance from the highway patrol, not that it's any of my business.

"Let's wait and see what happens," I say. I need to tell Loretta about the surgery, and how it will put a damper on my activities for a time, but I can't go into it right now. If I tell her, it will take on a life of its own. Before she can harass me anymore, I ask how things were left with Marybeth, Curtis, and Walter Dunn.

"Last I heard they were at a standoff. Who would have thought Marybeth had any spine? I guess when it comes down to money people find a way to get brave. Somebody said she called your little lawyer friend next door to sort out the inheritance."

"I'm not so sure it's Marybeth wanting money so much as wanting to keep it from Curtis." There's something odd rattling around in my brain from what Loretta said earlier, but I can't think what it was.

"She's a different kind of a person," Loretta says.

"I'll give you that."

My phone is ringing and I haul myself to my feet, wincing at the damned knee. It's Taylor, telling me she's at her mamma's house and wondering if I've had a chance to think further about how to approach Curtis. I tell her to come on over and we'll talk about it.

"You sure you aren't too tired? It's been a long day."

"I'll live. Get on over here."

"Good, because there's something else I need to tell you."

After I hang up, I go out and tell Loretta I have to check on the cows before it's full dark.

She gets up and sighs dramatically. "Well, okay, I'll be on my way. I guess you don't want to hear the rest that happened today."

"There's more?"

"Oh, I'm just getting started."

"Well, tell me."

"Boone Eldridge got beaten up."

"He what?" I groan. "What in the world has gotten into everybody?"

"He showed up at the café about noon with a black eye and his arm in a sling. He said he was walking up to his house last night and a couple of men jumped him and said they were paying him back for being stupid."

"It's about that goddamn football game."

"Samuel, there's no need to curse."

"Well, I mean it! I like football as much as the next person. But some people just get carried away. Now was this before or after Rodell got hauled off? And did Boone file a report?"

"I'm not privy to all the details. I'm just telling you what I heard."

For some reason, I think of the two strangers who were in the stands at Friday night's football game, and I feel uneasy. If they'd been scouts, they most likely would have checked in with the coach. I'll have to ask Boone about that.

"You're right. That's a lot going on." I shake my head. "Hard to believe it was just yesterday that Jack Harbin was killed. You said you were just getting started. What else happened?"

"You know Lurleen down at the café?"

I nod.

"She never showed up for work yesterday and when she came in this morning she told everybody that she and Jack Harbin had been engaged to get married!"

"That one I knew about."

"You what?" She flinches like a scalded cat. "How did you know?" Loretta hates for anyone to get a jump on her with regard to news, especially a man.

"Just settle down. I found out by accident. And I didn't tell you because I didn't think about it with all that was going on."

"Which was what exactly? Where have you been all day?"

I give her the short version and swear her to secrecy. I don't often do that because I know she likes to be the source of information, but when she pledges not to tell, I can trust her word.

"By now most likely somebody from Marcus Ministry has called Curtis and told him we showed up in Waco, so I think we can expect some aggravation from him pretty soon." I figure this is no surprise to Taylor, but I feel like I need to say something just to be sure she's prepared.

She and I are sitting in my kitchen with half-empty beers in front of us. It's dark outside, and we're both glum. I'm so tired I can hardly see straight, but I can tell there's something bothering Taylor that she hasn't come out with, so I'm letting her get to it in her own way.

"He doesn't scare me," Taylor says. "Not when he's here, and doesn't have somebody like that creepy Brother Dan to back him up."

"That may be, but you ought to be prepared. He's not going to be happy with either of us."

"Too bad it was Jack that was killed, and not Curtis."

She has been picking at the beer label, but suddenly pushes the bottle away. "There was a message from Laurel when I got to mamma's. I called her. She said she's never seen Woody so upset. Apparently he did talk to Jack about having Jack come and live with him and Laurel."

"Poor Woody. He was probably pretty surprised when Jack told him was getting married. He probably told Woody to go to hell."

"No, Woody told Laurel they had a civil conversation."

"I'm glad to hear that. If Jack had died with the two of them still not speaking, it would have been on Woody's mind forever."

"But that's what Woody's so upset about. He thought they would be on friendly terms again. Laurel said Woody came home all pumped up, saying everything was going to be okay. And then Jack . . ." She trails off with a sigh.

"So Woody's taking it hard."

"Yes, he is." Taylor picks up her beer and stares down into the mouth of it. She puts it back down. "I have something to tell you."

"Thought maybe you did."

"You know I told you that Jack called me after Bob's funeral and I went to see him?" Her voice is wobbly with emotion.

I nod.

"When I got there he was in a terrible state. He said his life was pure hell and he didn't want to live anymore."

"Taylor, he was probably drunk. And his dad had just died. It's no wonder he was in a bad state."

She lets her head drop forward. "You don't understand."

"Tell me."

"That night." She raises her head and wipes the back of her hand across her eyes. "Jack asked me to help him commit suicide."

"Oh, for heaven's sake." I get a terrible mental picture of Jack in his wheelchair, begging for relief from his life.

"I told him I couldn't do that, and that things would get better. But suppose he asked someone else and they took him up on it?"

The question hangs there in my quiet kitchen. All I can hear is the two of us breathing. Finally I pull together some thoughts. "I don't see it. Who would say yes to that?"

"One of those vets. I heard one of them say they'd do anything for each other."

"I haven't told you the details of how he died. Believe me, if somebody was going to do that—put him out of his misery—they would have chosen an easier way. They would have used an overdose of drugs, or shot him—some quick way. The way Jack went wasn't quick or easy."

She gets up and goes into the bathroom and I hear her blowing her nose. When she comes back she says, "Well, either way, he's gone now."

I feel a surge of unexpected anger toward Jack. How could he ask Taylor to do such a thing? "Maybe Jack was messing with you a little bit."

She sits back down. "What do you mean?"

"That afternoon when Woody was at the reception after Bob's funeral and Jack had him thrown out? You said to Jack that his condition was as much your fault as Woody's. Remember?"

She nods. Her expression is suddenly odd, almost scared.

"Maybe he believed that, too, and he asked you to help him commit suicide as a way of getting back at you. He didn't need anyone to help him, if he was serious. The boy wasn't a coward."

Taylor gets a funny look on her face. "I wouldn't say that."

"What do you mean? He couldn't have been such a good football player if he'd been a coward."

"Samuel, Jack struggled with fear more than anybody I've ever known. It took everything he had to go out on that field every week. I remember sitting in the stands with him one afternoon after practice and he was just shaking. He said he was always scared, and had to work himself up to go out there."

"Then why did he do it?"

"Because Woody did." She sighs. "I hate to say it, but in some ways I'm glad Jack died. Not the way he did, but he just carried so much baggage."

I remember what Dottie Gant said about coming across patients who were in worse shape than Jack who managed to live independent lives. "It's possible he never forgave you and Woody for getting married, with him going off to the Gulf."

"We never forgave ourselves either. Poor Woody." She gives herself a little shake. "I don't know why I say that, he's got a good wife and family. I think he's really happy."

"And Jack would have been happy with Lurleen, too. I really believe that."

"You're right. At least he had something to look forward to. But poor Lurleen!" She has a funny smile on her face. "What in the world could she have been thinking, trying to raise her kids around Jack?"

I tell her about the gentle way Lurleen had with Jack and how well he responded. "Might have been good for Jack. He might have enjoyed the kids. 'Course, there's no need to ponder that now."

Taylor sets her beer down with a thump. "Samuel, do you think Curtis knew Jack was thinking of getting married?"

I get her drift right away. "I know what you're thinking. That he killed Jack for his money. But Curtis was supposedly at a gun show in Dallas when Jack was killed."

"Supposedly. But what if he was lying? What if he snuck into town and killed Jack?"

"It should be easy enough to find out if he was really at the show, the way he claims."

Taylor groans. "It would make things so easy if he killed Jack. Then I'd have a reason to get Sarah and her kids out of that place."

After Taylor leaves, I sit for a time at the table. Something Taylor said about Jack and Lurleen jiggled something in my mind that doesn't seem quite right, but I can't put my finger on it.

I wonder if Jack asked anyone else to help him kill himself—Lurleen or Walter Dunn, for example. Or Woody. I only have Woody's word for it that he and Jack made up. I come back to the horrible sight of Jack's body after his struggle with his killer. I told Taylor I didn't think someone who cared about Jack would have chosen that way to kill him. But people don't know how much someone who's in danger of death fights to live—even if they think they want to die. Whoever stabbed Jack might have thought stabbing would be easy.

CHAPTER 17

I should have been expecting it after what Loretta said, but I'm surprised the next morning when I get a call from the mayor, Alton Coldwater. He says he and a couple of the city council members want to come by and talk to me.

While I wait for them I try to figure out how I'm going to refuse the job of temporary chief of police.

I needn't have worried. When we are seated around my kitchen table, Coldwater, who looks like somebody puffed him up with a bicycle pump, says, "We've appointed James Harley Krueger as temporary chief."

"Sounds like a good plan," I say cautiously. If they've appointed James Harley, what do they want with me?

"There was a good bit of opposition to the idea, but we decided it was the best way to go about it."

"Alton, stop beating around the bush," Chuck Rathbone says. He's president of the chamber of commerce, a large, red-faced man who lives down the street from me and keeps a dog that barks pretty much nonstop. "We decided making James Harley temporary chief was the best way to keep him busy and out of trouble. But somebody has got to figure out who killed Jack Harbin, and we'd like you to take that on."

Coldwater is staring off into a corner, which tells me he probably was okay with James Harley being temporary chief, but not so okay with asking for my help.

"It's not official, mind you," Coldwater says sternly. "We don't have any authority to offer you money, or give you a badge, but we're asking for you to put your mind to it."

"I don't mind helping out," I say. Luke Schoppe said budget cuts made it likely that any investigation by the state is going to take some time. The longer it takes, the more likely the case will die. "I think somebody ought get on it before the evidence gets cold. But without official standing, I'm not sure how effective I can be."

"That's what I said!" Coldwater sets his coffee mug down with a thump. His pudgy fingers straighten his string tie. "And we can't give you any official standing. That's up to the sheriff in Bobtail."

Conner Middleton, the youngest of the three, is a meek man who wears thick glasses and always looks alarmed. "We're not asking for an arrest or anything. Just that you see what you can find out. I just don't think James Harley Krueger is likely to get anywhere with this."

We wrestle around for some time, but I find myself unwilling to put up the kind of protest I had planned. I feel a certain stirring in my brain, a desire to investigate what happened to Jack. They're right; James Harley isn't up to the job. And what have I got to lose? I don't have to worry about blame or credit. If I don't find out who killed Jack, it's not like I've lost anything but a little pride. And if I do find out, I have the satisfaction of bringing Jack's killer to justice.

"Look, I'll do what I can. But if push comes to shove, I need to have something official-sounding so people don't tell me to go to hell when I start asking questions."

Coldwater blinks a few times. "How about if James Harley deputizes you?"

"Or we could get the sheriff in Bobtail to give you a title. Special investigator, or something." Conner surveys the men around the table.

"That's not going to work," Coldwater says. "If that damned sheriff gets pulled into it, there'd have to be a meeting and a consultation and a special dispensation."

I laugh. For once I'm in agreement with Coldwater. Bobtail is the county seat, and anytime you get the powers-that-be in Bobtail involved in anything, it starts to take on bureaucratic steam. It would be a year before they'd agree to my being official, if they ever did.

"Why don't I just say I'm a special investigator to the mayor's office? That gives me something to tell people, without Bobtail having to know about it."

Coldwater looks pleased, as I knew he would. A mayor who has a "special investigator" is a mayor of some importance.

When my wife, Jeanne, died, I thought I was at a dead end. On top of that, several months later my knee got bunged up, and I thought I was ready to be put out to pasture. But then my old friend Dora Lee Parjeter was murdered and I took it on myself to find out who did it, believing that Rodell Skinner was fixing to arrest the wrong man. The whole time I was investigating I worried that I didn't have what it took any more to get it right. When I managed to figure out who killed Dora Lee, I felt like my life kicked back into gear.

This time it's different. In a lot of ways Jack's investigation is harder, since I didn't know Jack well and don't have access to his personal records the way I did with Dora Lee. But I know now that my mind is still sharp and chances are I'll be as successful as anybody else trying to find out who did it.

The only problem is, I worry that I might not like finding out who murdered Jack. Too many of the possible suspects are people that I've known and cared about in my life. But I'll have to put that worry aside and deal with it when and if it happens.

I'm not sure exactly where to start looking for Jack's killer, so it's time to take stock. While I strategize, I set about rearranging the pictures in my house. Jeanne taught me that if art hangs in one place too long, you stop seeing it. Since she died, I've kept up the habit of moving pictures around every few months. But today I have a hard time keeping my mind on it.

I'm wondering: Jack's death came so soon after Bob's, was there something about Bob that kept Jack safe? Something that Bob knew—sort of a reverse blackmail? Or someone whose respect for Bob kept them from killing Jack? And how am I going to find that out?

As Taylor said, the easy suspect is Curtis. His motive is strong and his alibi weak. I can find out if he bought tickets to the gun show in Dallas, but that doesn't mean he actually went.

But I have to consider Woody and Laurel as suspects, too. I don't want to think of someone like Laurel killing Jack, but women will go to great lengths to protect their families. Given how stubborn Woody was, and how alarmed Laurel was that she'd end up with Jack in her care, I can imagine her going to talk to Jack and angry words being exchanged between them. Maybe even killing him. They say the majority of women who murder do so with a knife. But I can't picture Laurel wrestling with Jack and stabbing him again and again.

Woody said he and Jack made up, but I wonder if anyone was present when the two of them talked. Maybe Woody had reason to lie about it.

And then there are the vets, their wives, and any number of people Jack had run-ins with over the years. I saw how the wives of his vet friends looked at Jack. I doubt they're going to lose much sleep over his dying.

I find myself standing in a trance, holding my Wolf Kahn in my hand. I hang it back where it was, my interest in rearranging things gone.

CHAPTER 18

"I heard Curtis and Walter Dunn got into a fight." I'm standing in the living room of Jack's house with Marybeth.

She gives a nervous squeak. "You know how people exaggerate. It wasn't a fight. They just shoved each other a little bit."

Dressed in jeans and a sleeveless blouse, Marybeth looks younger and more bright-eyed than I've seen her in a long time. You'd think with her favorite son dead, she'd be ravaged. But then I realize her eyes are too bright—glassy, in fact. I expect there are drugs involved in keeping her going.

"Did Curtis actually try to throw you out?"

"He grabbed me by the arm. Left a bruise right here." She encircles her left bicep with her right fingers, and I can see the faint bruise where he grabbed her. "I'm lucky Walter showed up when he did."

Lucky, yes, but why had Dunn been here? He stuck awfully close to Jack after Bob died, and I assumed he was protecting Jack. But if that was the case, why was he still hanging around? "Marybeth, Did Dunn say what he was doing here?"

Marybeth frowns. "I didn't ask. I was just grateful he showed up."

"Was he already in the house?"

She shakes her head. "He came up to the back door. It was open, so he could see what was happening. He's a big man. I have no doubt Curtis would have made me leave if Walter hadn't intervened."

"Who did you tell about this?"

"Nobody. I stayed over at the motel last night, and I didn't see anybody I knew."

"I wonder how people knew about it, then."

"One of them must have told somebody, because I sure didn't."

She flits over to the sofa. She has pulled out a couple of picture albums and they lie open on the coffee table. "Look at these pictures." I sit down beside her on the sofa. Her hand flutters over one of the open pages. "I love looking at these old photographs. Remember what a football hero Jack was?"

She points to a picture of Jack cocking the football. It's a candid shot, not one of those posed for a newspaper article. Jack has a goofy grin on his face. Standing nearby, Woody and Taylor are laughing at him.

"That was a quite a threesome."

Marybeth sits back abruptly, fingers tracing her lips as if she's not sure what words will come out. "Jack always felt like a fifth wheel with the two of them. I think that's why he wanted to go off to the army, because he knew they were going to get married."

"Really? The way I heard it, the two boys signed up together. I thought Woody and Taylor only decided to get married after Jack went into the service and Woody was rejected."

Marybeth frowns. "That's what they told everybody. But Jack thought they'd been planning to get married for a while. I never did trust Taylor Brenner. Everybody thought she was the cutest little thing, sweet and generous. I thought she was sneaky."

I've been around enough to know that mothers often resent the girls their sons are partial to. "Sneaky how?"

"Let me show you something."

Marybeth flips back a couple of pages and stabs her forefinger at another picture of the threesome. "See how she's looking at Jack?"

In the picture Jack and Woody are clowning for the camera. Taylor is off to one side and doesn't seem to realize the camera is including her in the shot. She's looking straight at Jack, and I have to admit that her expression is unfriendly. One could even call it calculating, as if she's measuring him and finding him wanting.

"Maybe they'd had an argument and she was mad at him."

"Hmph. She showed that face all the time when she thought no one was looking. But I saw it. Of course when she was the center of attention, she was little miss darling girl."

"Do you know who took this picture?"

Marybeth shakes her head. "Could have been any of their friends. You know what high school kids are like, they have to take a picture of every move." She touches the picture. "But I'm glad they did. It helps me remember Jackie in those good days."

Curtis comes in the front door with an armload of groceries. "Oh, it's you," he says. He continues into the kitchen.

Marybeth jumps up from the couch. "I'll be right back," she says, panic in her voice. She scurries to the bathroom and slams the door after her.

I go into the kitchen. I figure Curtis is going to have something to say to me, and I might as well get it over with.

"I understand you and Taylor took a little trip yesterday." He's done unloading the groceries and wads up the sack. From the dark look he gives me, you'd think I'd killed his dog.

"Taylor was worried about her sister. Seems natural she'd want to go by and see her. She asked me to meet her there."

"Quite a coincidence that she picked yesterday, since you both knew I'd be here."

"I doubt she keeps up with your business," I say. "And I sure don't. For all I knew you wouldn't be coming right away, knowing it would take some time for the state to release your brother's body."

He steps in a little close to me. If I were inclined to be a fearful person, I might be intimidated. "My wife would be a lot better off if Taylor would stop badgering her."

"Wanting to see her sister isn't badgering."

"It is if Sarah doesn't want to talk to her. Which she doesn't. And if I think anybody is threatening my wife in any way, I'll do what I have to do to protect my family."

"That sounds like a threat."

"I'm just saying Taylor needs to leave Sarah alone. She's not Taylor's sister anymore, she's my wife."

Marybeth is hovering in the doorway. "What about Sarah?"

"Nothing." Curtis says. "I'm going over to the funeral home. Are you coming?"

Marybeth shakes her head without looking at Curtis.

He makes a dismissive noise like a snarl and stalks out, shutting the door behind him harder than need be. Marybeth shudders, staring after him. "What was that about Sarah?" she asks.

We go back in the living room and sit down, and I tell Marybeth about going with Taylor to visit her sister. Marybeth chews her lip while I talk, but doesn't make any comment. I imagine it's hard for her to decide whose side to be on—the son she can't stand, or the girl she never liked.

I don't mention to Marybeth that Taylor's sister signaled that things at the compound were not as good as she claimed out loud that they were. I wouldn't be at all surprised if Marybeth and Curtis reconcile. If she told Curtis about the signal, Sarah might suffer as a consequence.

"How do things stand between you and Curtis now?" I ask.

"We're being nice to each other. Barely. We didn't find a will, so according to your lawyer friend everything Jack left is half mine, half Curtis's. Curtis told me I ought to sign everything over to him because I abandoned Jackie."

"He didn't exactly stick around himself."

She gives me a faint smile. "That's what Jenny said, but Curtis said I'm Jack's mother and that makes it different."

I'm thinking that Curtis seems awfully eager to get his hands on Jack's money, even if it means cutting his mother off. "I hope you'll take Jenny's advice, or at the least don't make a decision right away."

She rubs her arms, her expression uneasy. "That'll be hard. I want to get it over with. Curtis makes me nervous. He wants to sell this place right away, says he doesn't want it to stand empty."

"Would you think about coming back here to live?"

"Oh no, oh no." She shakes her head vigorously. "I couldn't live here." Her eyes dart around the room as if she's scared something is going to pounce on her. But then she lifts her chin in a show of defiance. "But since it's half mine, Curtis has to be nice to me. He'll need me to go along with selling it."

Marybeth asks me if I'll stay a little longer while she goes through some of Jack's things. "I'll feel better if somebody is here."

"You mind if I take a look around?" I don't feel the need to tell her just yet that I'm investigating Jack's death.

"Do whatever you want," she says.

I go in and make coffee and start looking through the kitchen drawers. Like me, Bob had a drawer where he kept business cards. Unlike me, he has most of them in a neat stack held together with a rubber band. I set aside a card for a doctor at the VA hospital in Temple, in case I need to find out more about Jack's condition. I make note that Bob and Jack's bank is the same one I use in Bobtail, and Hitch Montgomery is their banker. I keep considerable amounts of money in my accounts, having married a woman with more money than I ever thought I'd see. Because I bank with Hitch, he and I have a very cordial relationship. That might come in handy, should I need to know something about Jack's bank account.

Marybeth staggers in carrying a cardboard box. "Wait, let me get that," I say. I grab it from her and set it on the kitchen table.

"This is stuff Jackie brought back from the army." She fishes out a fistful of papers clipped together that look like official documents. "His discharge papers. Bob had to use these to get Jack's disability payments. It was a nightmare." She sets them down on the table, shaking her head. "You'd think the government would fall all over themselves to help out somebody who was injured in the service of his country. But no. They made it really hard. It was like he was trying to cheat somebody."

She opens a manila envelope, spilling photographs out onto the table. "Photos he couldn't even see." Her hand lingers over them for a moment, like a benediction. She sits down and begins to shuffle through them slowly. "I remember seeing pictures from when my daddy was in World War II. The pictures looked the same as these." She hands them to me. She's right. Young men with rifles mugging for the camera, one with them posing on a Humvee, looking like they are ready to go out on the town.

I pause at one of the pictures. It's a picture of three boys, arms around each other, grinning. One of them is Jack, and what has me puzzled is that I recognize one of the other two. Even though in the picture he's twenty years younger, I'm sure it's Walter Dunn, wearing a medical corps T-shirt. He still wears his hair in a buzz cut like in the picture. The thing is, Dunn told me he met Jack at a vet meeting in Bryan. But obviously he knew him in Kuwait.

"You mind if I make a copy of this?"

"Go ahead. It's a good one, isn't it? Jackie looks like he's happy."

I mumble assent, although that's not why I want it. I tuck the picture into my shirt pocket.

Marybeth puts the photos aside and stands up so she can finish going through the box. She brings out a bunch of brochures, frowning. "I wonder where all this came from . . ."

The brochures are from California—San Francisco, to be exact. There's one with a cable car on the front, another with the Golden Gate Bridge. Some ticket stubs fall out of them onto the table. She picks them up and frowns at them. "This is so strange. As far as I know, Jackie was never in California. Why does he have these?"

I'm suddenly reminded of an incident that happened right after Jack was wounded. I was chief of police at the time, and one day Bob came to see me, saying he needed my help. "I can't find Jack," he said.

"What do you mean, you can't find him?" Everybody knew by then that Jack had been gravely injured and was in a VA hospital in Washington, DC. Bob had flown up there to see him as soon as Jack arrived at the hospital from overseas and had come back in despair. They had told him it would be a few weeks before Jack would be ready to come home.

"I called to find out when they were going to release him so I could go bring him home, and they said he had already gone."

"Did they say who picked him up?"

"Some guy I never heard of. And they didn't know where he'd gone. I'm wondering if maybe, you being a lawman, you could find out more for me. They weren't particularly forthcoming, if you know what I mean."

There was nothing I could do, and I suggested he call the local VFW in Bobtail. I never heard another thing about it. And eventually Jack came home. Now I'm wondering if Jack had somehow made his way to California. But if so, what did he do there, and why had he never talked about it? I wonder if Marybeth knows anything about it and am thinking how to pose the question, when suddenly she cries out.

"Oh, no!" Her face crumples. Until now she has been calm, even weirdly cheerful going through Jack's belongings. But now she pulls Jack's uniform from the bottom of the box and buries her face in it and sobs.

I put my arm around her and sit her down in a chair. In a way it's a relief to see the dam finally break. Marybeth has held herself aloof from this horror for too long. She keens over the uniform, the symbol of the promise her son had as a boy.

Eventually she stands up and throws the uniform back in the box with as much violence as I've ever seen from her. "I've got to get out of here. What's the use of crying? The Jackie I knew was gone a long time ago."

I don't know why I haven't thought of it before, but I wonder if Marybeth knew Jack was going to marry Lurleen. "Sit down a minute longer. I have something to talk to you about." And I tell her about Jack and Lurleen.

"Who is this girl? This waitress! Somebody who wanted a meal ticket?"

"Now hold on a minute. If that's what she had in mind, she would have agreed to marry Jack a long time ago. He asked her, but she wanted to take things slow. But when Bob died, she knew Jack would need somebody to take care of him. I saw the two of them together. She really cared for Jack. She made him happy."

Marybeth is quiet for several minutes and I keep still, letting her absorb this new information. When she finally does speak, she says something I don't expect. "Did Curtis know about this?"

"Somehow I can't see Jack telling him, and I don't know how else he would have known. They only decided after Bob died."

Marybeth goes over to the sink and splashes water on her face. She leans against the counter as she mops her face with a paper towel, and when she speaks it's as if she's talking to herself. "I wonder how it would be if I talked to her?"

"I think you'd like her. She's a sweet girl. She has three kids. Good kids."

Marybeth nods. "I'll have to think about whether I should meet her."

She finds a paper sack to hold the few things she wants to take with her—photos and a signed football and other mementos from Jack's childhood. She doesn't even glance at the box with the uniform or the papers on the table. After she's gone, I find a plastic bag and place the uniform in it. She may want it later. I put the papers in with the uniform to take the whole lot home with me. I suspect if I left it to Curtis, he'd pitch them in the trash.

I take another look around Jack's bedroom. Even though Marybeth has been through Jack's things, I won't feel like I'm off to a steady start on the investigation until I go back to the beginning, where Jack died.

I try to lock all the doors so that I can hear Curtis when he comes in and I won't be surprised, but the back door leading from the kitchen into the backyard won't lock. The mechanism is jammed. I wonder if whoever killed Jack jimmied the lock to make sure he'd be able to get in, or if it's been that way a long time. I remember Dottie Gant saying Jack never locked up after Bob died. But I wonder if they did before. If so, then it must have been broken since then.

Jack's bed has a cover thrown over it to hide the stains. His clothes have been taken out of the closet and piled onto the bed. My guess is that's Curtis's doing. There isn't much in the way of clothing. I rummage through the pockets for oddities, but they're all cleaned out.

The smell in the room is a sickening blend of stale cigarette smoke, rancid blood, and bleach. Unless some realtor has sense enough to get rid of the bed and air the place out, Curtis may find it harder than he thinks to sell the house.

The closet is bare. The pills have disappeared from the bedside stand. I peek into a big plastic bag sitting next to the clothes, and the vials of pills are there. The top drawer of the bedside stand is empty. Curtis hasn't wasted any time.

But he hasn't gotten to the chest of drawers yet. The big drawers yield nothing but T-shirts and underwear. The clothes are so neatly arranged that I figure Jack probably never opened them. He wouldn't be able to see the things anyway. I feel around under the clothes for anything that would yield a clue, but come up empty.

I don't know a man who doesn't keep oddities in the top drawer of his chest, and Jack is no exception. There's a cracked old leather wallet, empty, a hard leather case containing medals, and a collection of items that look to be from his teenage years, before he went off to the army. This includes a number of yellowing articles clipped together from the weekly Jarrett Creek newspaper that was alive and well back then, but has since folded. The articles are all about the football games Jack was in. I'm surprised Marybeth didn't take them. I lay them on the bed to take home with the other things she left. Finally I come to a zippered pouch. Inside there's a rabbit's foot, a faded photo of Taylor from high school, Jack's army dog tags, and a cross on a silver chain.

I almost neglect to look in the bottom drawer of the bedside table. The knob is missing from it, and it looks like a false front. Inside, there's another wallet. It contains Jack's military ID, his social security card, a long-expired credit card, and a photo of Taylor and Woody in their wedding regalia. Inside, where money would be carried, is a newspaper clipping two paragraphs long about a homeless man found dead in a dumpster—in San Francisco. The bizarre thing is that someone has drawn a smiley face in the upper right hand corner of the clipping.

I check Bob's bedroom, but one look tells me that Curtis has been thorough in ridding the room of all vestiges of his dad. Drawers and closets are all empty. A single suitcase sits on a chair. Curtis's suitcase. I expect if I looked in it, I'd find at least one gun, but I don't look.

What interests me most is what I don't find—like any of Bob's or Jack's financial papers. No stack of bills paid or outstanding, no medical or insurance records, no bank statements. I look everywhere, but they aren't to be found.

CHAPTER 19

Tonight's football game would be away, but the opponent's town is so small they can't afford a stadium. The players' parents carpool to bring the team because they don't have a school bus. But they're a scrappy bunch that always gives a good game, even if they don't win often, so a crowd has shown up.

I've brought Jenny with me. She's not big on football, but says she's had a hell of a week and needs some diversion. She's from Bobtail, but she's got sense enough to wear a Jarrett Creek Panthers T-shirt, the one with Gabe LoPresto's advertising on the back. I don't get a chance to pay much attention to the game because she bends my ear about a woman client who is driving her crazy. She can't name names, but I know exactly who she's talking about and I get a kick out of her description of the problems that the woman has brought on herself by her stinginess and sharp tongue.

At halftime, there's a hastily arranged memorial tribute for Jack. They trot out Jack's old coach, who now has a cushy job at Blinn Junior College. It's clear that he doesn't remember much about Jack, but he does his best with platitudes. Coach Eldridge also speaks, talking about Jack's love for the game and his special place as a booster for the team. He gets emotional, which strikes me as crocodile tears, since he was never Jack's coach and they had some differences of opinion about the way the team ought to be run.

The event wouldn't be complete without Gabe LoPresto horning in, but at least he keeps his remarks short.

I see Taylor in the stands with her mother and a few of her friends, so I go over to say hello. When I start back to my seat, Taylor says, "I'll walk over with you."

I introduce her to Jenny, who is friendly enough, but suddenly reserved. "I'll be right back," she says. "You want anything?" She includes Taylor in her question.

As soon as she leaves, Taylor says, "Curtis called me this morning."

"How did that go?"

"I wish you could have heard him. He couldn't have been sweeter." She rolls her eyes. "He apologized for snapping at me at Bob's reception. He said he hadn't realized how worried I was about Sarah until he found out you and I went to the compound." She narrows her eyes. "He could have charmed the wings off a butterfly—a stupid butterfly."

"So you're not buying the apology?"

"Hell, no! Listen to this. He said as soon as Jack's funeral is over, he'll see to it that I get to spend an afternoon with Sarah and the girls." Her voice is prissy.

I laugh. "I'm guessing you acted like you were going along with it."

"I can charm the wings off a butterfly as well as he can."

"Did he say whether Sarah was coming down for Jack's funeral?"

"He said he'd have to see about that."

I expect it will be a cold day in hell before Curtis lets his wife and children see Taylor.

"I know what he's thinking," Taylor says. "He probably thinks that if he sweet-talks me, I'll sit around and wait for him to arrange a meeting, and then I'll forget about it."

"If that's what he's thinking, he doesn't know you."

Jenny is back with popcorn. She eases past us and I suddenly have an idea.

"Taylor, Jenny and I are going to have a glass of wine at my place after the game. Why don't you come by? Jenny's a lawyer. Maybe she has some thoughts about how to help your sister."

Jenny gives me the dead eye, but Taylor jumps up and grabs Jenny's hand. "Oh, it would be so great if you could help. Do you mind? I don't want to butt in." She shoots a glance between Jenny and me.

"I don't know that I have any advice, but I'll be glad to talk to you." Taylor doesn't know that Jenny has her formal voice on.

Taylor leans down and kisses my cheek. "I have to go back to Mamma. I'll take her home after the game and then come over to your place."

After the second half of the game starts, and we've got a comfortable lead, LoPresto finds me. He's heard that I'm investigating Jack's murder, and he wants in on the action. Or, at least, he wants to give me instructions on how I ought to proceed. I wiggle the conversation around so that it seems like I'm asking his advice, which he is only too happy to oblige with.

"Seems to me you're looking for somebody with a grudge against Jack."

"I expect you're right." It doesn't take a genius to figure that out. "You talked to Jack a lot. You ever hear anything I ought to look into?"

"Well, there's Woody. I hear he and Jack got together last week. Maybe Jack said something he didn't like."

"I don't know what that might have been. It's hard for me to see Woody killing Jack."

"Well, you know best." We pause while the crowd hollers about a touchdown that seals the game. After things have quieted down, he says, "Maybe it's somebody from way back when, like somebody he played football against who's still mad because they lost the game."

That's the silliest idea I can imagine. Jenny pokes me and makes a small, strangled sound. I have to force myself to keep a straight face. "If that were the case, why now?"

"Well, I don't know," LoPresto says in a testy voice. "That's what you need to find out."

"I do have a question for you, Gabe. You remember last week those two fellows I pointed out to you at the game? The ones you said might be scouts?"

LoPresto nods, and his expression brightens. "I never heard any more about that. Maybe you ought to ask Boone Eldridge. If they weren't scouts, it'd be good to know what those strangers were doing here."

Like me, LoPresto would love to pin Jack's death on somebody we don't know.

I'm glad Taylor won't be at my house right away. It gives me time to settle Jenny down. "I knew I wouldn't like her," she says.

"You haven't said three words to her. Give her a chance. Anyway, you don't have to like her. But she does have a sticky problem and it would be nice if you could at least listen to her."

"Well, that won't kill me," she grumbles.

"I'll sweeten the deal for you. I was going to drag this out on a special occasion, but maybe now is a good time." I go into the cabinet and bring out a good bottle of Cabernet that I bought last time I was in Houston. Jenny and I have a friendly competition about who buys the best wine without spending too much.

"You're at least singing the right song," she says.

I didn't eat before the game, so I bring out sausage and cheese and crackers and the good wine glasses.

By the time we sit down, I hear Taylor's footsteps coming up to the door. I notice the way Taylor breezes in as if she lives here.

I jump up to greet her. "Would you rather have a beer or some wine?"

"Oh, fancy," she says. She grins at Jenny. "This has to be your influence."

"Samuel isn't lacking some of the graces," Jenny says dryly.

I'm embarrassed because Taylor assumes something is going on between Jenny and me, but I don't know any good way to set her straight.

"I hope this wine is as good as the man who sold it to me said it was." I pour the wine, and notice I'm bustling around like a nervous hen so I sit down abruptly and take a sip.

"This is nice," Jenny says, sipping the wine. I guess it makes her feel magnanimous because she says to Taylor, "Why don't you tell me what you two have gotten yourselves into."

Taylor describes our foray to the Marcus compound. When Taylor says she wants a court order to see her sister privately, Jenny gives a regretful shake of her head. "I wish I could be more encouraging, but the courts haven't been too inclined to rein in folks like them. The law is on their side. Unless you have proof that your sister is being held against her will or that she or the children are being physically or sexually abused, there isn't much you can do."

"My sister used our old signal to let me know things aren't right there." Taylor beats her fist into her palm. "I know she meant it. Why can't she and her children at least be given protective custody while the police figure it out?"

Jenny shakes her head. "It's all about religion. Most courts bend over backwards to give them the benefit of the doubt. You remember the Yearning for Zion thing from a while back?"

"Yes," Taylor perks up. "That place out in west Texas. Several of those people got convicted."

"Hold on," I say, "Remind me what this was."

Both of them look at me like I've been living in the back woods for ten years. "Don't you remember all those poor women and children being bused in from west Texas?" Jenny says.

"This was how long ago?"

"Two years? Three? Something like that," Jenny says.

I'm not surprised I don't remember the details, although I do remember seeing pictures on TV of the women stepping off the buses.

Taylor is watching me. "That's when Jeanne got sick, isn't it?"

"I see." Jenny looks embarrassed. Emotions always seem hard for her. She clears her throat. "Let me tell you what happened. Some poor sixteen-year-old girl from the Yearning for Zion group managed to phone local police and tell them she was being forced into marriage. Authorities had known for years that something was wrong, but they couldn't do anything until this girl said she'd testify."

Taylor has a fist to her mouth and she's looking like she could be sick to her stomach.

"Turned out those old men were marrying girls as young as fourteen. Several of the men went to jail. Most of the women went right back to the ranch so they could be reunited with their kids, but a few of them took the opportunity to leave the cult. Warren Jeffs, their leader, was convicted of rape in Utah."

"Good! Those men are so disgusting," Taylor says.

Jenny waves away Taylor's comment. "Hold on. His conviction was overturned in Utah."

Taylor is so agitated that she jumps up. "Those damned Mormons!"

"You can't really blame the Mormons. The Mormon Church disavowed him. The reason he got off is because he's rich. And money talks. At least, it did in Utah." Jenny's eyes are lit up. She's enjoying this story.

"Wait a minute. Didn't a guy named Jeffs get convicted here in Texas a while back?" I ask.

"That's the one," Jenny says. "The state of Texas extradited Jeffs so he could stand trial here. Some of the crimes he committed were in west Texas. We may not be the last word in justice, but Jeffs isn't as well connected here as he is in Utah. So he was convicted, and this time it stuck."

Taylor stops in front of Jenny, hand cocked on one hip. "That's good news. But I don't see how that's going to help Sarah."

"I'll tell you how. Jeffs's conviction brought up all this cult stuff again. People here are religious, but they don't like that kind of sex stuff with young girls. I'll have to talk to some lawyers who know more about it. Maybe they can come up with a way to get your sister some protection."

Taylor is shaking her head. "It won't matter unless we can get her children out, too. She'll never say a word as long as she's afraid she'll lose them."

Jenny rises. "I understand. Let me poke into it a little bit. I'm no expert, but I know how to ask the right questions."

When I finally get to bed, it takes me a while to fall sleep. I can't forget what Jenny said about those children being married off so young. Neither Taylor nor Jenny brought it up, but I wonder if the same thing is going on out at True Marcus Ministry. And if so, how would Curtis feel if his daughter was one of those girls?

CHAPTER 20

It's going to be hard on Lurleen to have to answer questions so soon after Jack's death, but she probably knows more about him than anybody else, so I have to push it. She has Saturday afternoon off, but she declares that there's no way we can have a reasonable conversation at her place with her three kids hanging around. I pick her up from her trailer and we drive out to the lake to talk. A vicious Indian summer has taken hold after the rain, and the air is so hot and thick you could choke on it. At least at the lake there's a little breeze.

We sit at a picnic table drinking sodas. I ask her how long she and Jack had been dating.

She grimaces. "There wasn't much dating about it. We spent some time talking in the afternoons after I got off work. Every few weeks I'd pick him up and we'd drive down here to the lake and have a picnic."

"You had good times together?"

She nods and wipes her eyes. "He had a wicked sense of humor. Lord, he could make me laugh."

"But you didn't decide to get married until Bob died?"

"My kids take up a lot of my time, and there wasn't any hurry. It isn't like we were going to run off to a tropical island, or have a whole batch of kids or anything like that. But after Jack's daddy died, he needed somebody to do things for him—otherwise he was going to have to move to a VA facility. So we decided it would be good for all of us."

"Your kids, too?"

She nods and can't speak for a minute. "Bless their hearts, Jack's death has been hard on them. He got along with them real well. I didn't know how my kids were going to take finding out that we would be moving in with Jack, but when we told them, they were really happy about it."

"Even your oldest?"

"Especially him. But he's got it in for his daddy. Being close to Jack would be a way of getting back at Darrell."

"Does Darrell spend time with them?"

"No, sir. He's not much for kids."

"Lurleen, I'm trying to get a handle on who might have killed Jack. I was hoping you might help me with a little insight."

She crosses her arms on the table in front of her. Away from the frazzle of her job at the café, she looks younger. Her deep brown eyes are sad and soft. "Mr. Craddock, I've been thinking and thinking about it, and I don't know what to tell you. It was a cowardly deed. I know Jack could be cranky sometimes, but I don't know anyone who disliked him enough to do something like that."

"Did he ever talk about anybody in particular who he had problems with?"

"You know how Jack was. Everybody got under his skin at one time or another. And he surely annoyed more than one person himself."

A family with about a hundred kids pulls into the picnic area next to where we are sitting. They pile out of their big van like midgets out of a clown car in a circus and go barreling down to the lake. Lurleen watches them with a little smile on her face.

"How about those vet friends of Jack's? Any ongoing problems?"

"Oh, they argued about little things, football stuff mostly, but nothing serious."

The mother of the brood next to us hauls picnic goods out of the car while her husband fires up the grill. They're both hefty people, and there seems to be a lot of food involved. For some reason, it makes me think about how skinny Lurleen and her kids are. I wonder if Darrell leaves them to fend for themselves financially. "Darrell live around here?"

"Over in Burton with some floozy. That's why he moved out, he couldn't keep it in his pants. Excuse me, I know that's crude, but it's the truth."

"And he didn't want any custody of the kids?"

Her mouth twists. She gazes out across the water. "No, he didn't want them or me, but he didn't want anybody else to have us either. He would have kicked up a shit storm if he'd found out I was marrying Jack."

"Do you suppose he did find out?"

She shrugs, but then realizes what I'm getting at. She makes a sound like a bus releasing its brakes. "He wouldn't have it in him to fight for me, much less kill for me. He'd have just made my life miserable trying to get his support lessened—not that he pays it very often anyway. Or he would have made noise about taking the kids away, even if he didn't want them."

"Jack ever talk to you about Curtis?"

"Only after Bob's funeral. I never saw any two people more different. Makes you wonder, doesn't it? Why somebody brave and strong like Jack goes off to war and gets himself wounded, while his coward brother stays home and plays like a big man with his guns."

I remember what Taylor said about Jack being something of a coward. Lurleen had some romantic notion of Jack that escapes me, but I'm glad Jack had her to care about him and I tell her so.

"He never once raised his voice to me or my kids. We had nice times together. Could have had more."

"Lurleen, do you know if Jack made out a will?"

"We talked about it when we decided to get married. He said he'd want me to have everything if anything happened to him. But we hadn't gotten around to it. You know, we thought we had plenty of time."

We're both quiet for a minute, staring out over the lake. What a slippery thing life is. It can get away from you awfully fast. "Taylor said she was going to call you. Have you talked to her?"

She nods. "She was real nice. Always was. I remember when we were in school some kids teased me because I was so poor I only had one pair of shoes. Taylor put up a fuss and made them stop." She swallows. "She was real sad about Jack. But she said she liked knowing that at the end he was full of hope since we were going to get married."

I think about Jack asking Taylor to help him commit suicide. That must have been before he and Lurleen talked about marriage.

Lurleen props her chin on her hands, blinking back tears. She looks over at the neighboring campsite, where a couple of the kids have now come back, screeching for food like a couple of hawks. Their clamor doesn't faze the mother, who tells them to get on back down to the water; she'll call them when the food's ready.

"Did Jack tell Curtis or his mamma that you two were getting married?"

"I don't think so. We'd only just decided. And we knew it would take a while for my divorce to come through. Besides, Jack hardly talked to either one of them." She wipes away a tear with an impatient gesture. "Well, crying won't do me any good." She stands up. "I better get on back. Damn! I wish they'd release Jack's body so we could get the funeral over with. I'm hoping I'll feel better after that."

CHAPTER 21

Saturday afternoon I talk to Jack's neighbors to find out if they saw or heard anything suspicious the night Jack was killed. Becky Geisenslaw, next door, goes on about her insomnia, and says she's pretty sure she heard somebody sneaking into Jack's house that night. But she admits that she didn't get out of bed, so she never saw anything. And neither did anybody else.

Curtis's truck isn't at Jack's place, which is just as well. I'd like to look around outside without having to mess with him. I walk all around the outside of the house, not checking for anything in particular, just making sure the guilty party didn't leave anything incriminating, like a nice, waterproof note saying, *I killed Jack.*

I poke around in Bob's work shed. When I first looked inside right after Bob died, it was full of toasters, blenders, lawn mowers, TVs, radios, and other small appliances. But apparently people have come and taken them away. There are just a couple of TVs and a few unidentifiable gadgets on the workbench, and one lonesome lawn mower that looks like it might have been the first one ever made.

As I emerge from the shed, Curtis steps out onto the back patio. He doesn't see me at first, and he puts his hands on his hips and looks around the yard with a critical eye, like he's master of all he surveys. But then my movement catches his eye. "What are you doing back there?"

I step onto the patio. "Sorry, I didn't know you were here. I didn't see your truck."

He walks over to me, his expression stern. "You didn't say what you're after back there." He nods toward the shed.

"Nothing in particular. Just looking around. I've been handed the job of investigating your brother's murder. I'd appreciate your cooperation."

"Handed the job? By who?"

"The mayor and city council." I give him the short version of Rodell's situation.

"So the Jarrett Creek City Council begs help from their famous lawman. I'll bet that makes you feel like something special."

"I'd like to help out." I can't do anything about the flush that creeps up the back of my neck.

He sneers. "Well, if you're going to investigate, you better step on it. Mamma and I are going to sell this place real fast."

"You mind if I ask you a few questions?"

"Be my guest." He spreads his legs wider and crosses his arms.

"Did your daddy ever say anything about having problems with anybody?"

"Daddy? What does that have to do with Jack?"

"Did he?"

"Couple of people fussed because they didn't think he'd repaired their appliances properly. He told me people could be pretty particular, especially if their stuff was worn out. Seems like a lot of poor people want a handout, if not from the government, then from anybody who makes an honest living. They don't take care of their things and then expect somebody to be a miracle worker."

I expect this is mostly Curtis's notion. Bob didn't strike me as a man who would blame people if their stuff was old and they were trying to make it last. "Anybody ever complain to him about interactions with Jack?"

He shrugs. "We didn't talk too much about Jack. He knew I didn't think he ought to be spending his life slaving over somebody who wouldn't do for himself."

"Did Bob ever consider putting Jack in a veteran's home?"

He snorts. "Oh, hell no! That would have made too much sense."

"I take it you're going through Jack's finances. You find anything unusual?"

He stares at me for a few seconds and then shakes his head.

"I'd like to go through his papers, if you don't mind."

"I do mind. Everything looks straightforward to me. I don't see that there's any reason for you to snoop into my business. I think we're done here." He heads toward the house.

I follow him, silently cursing my damn knee that holds me back. "It's Bob's and Jack's business I'm interested in, not yours."

He turns, barring the door to the house. "Well, it's mine now. And I don't take to government interference. You say you're a special investigator for the mayor's office, and by my reckoning, that makes you part of the government."

Oh, Lord, deliver me from paranoid citizens. "Curtis, what the hell do you think I'm going to do with the information? Sell it on the open market? Hand out copies of it to the neighbors? Try to steal your money? Besides, whatever there is, it's half Marybeth's. And she seems more interested in finding out who killed your brother than you are."

"I just don't see what Jack's finances have to do with . . ."

There's a flicker of confusion in his eyes. I believe he's run across something that he doesn't understand. I take the opportunity to press him. "You can be in the room with me while I look through things to make sure I don't sneak off with anything."

He hesitates, measuring his options.

"You know, I can get a court order. Judge Herrera will give it to me in no time. It's an integral part of the investigation." I don't know Judge Herrera from Adam, and have no idea if he'd give me a court order, but someone like Curtis, who fears the all-seeing, all-knowing government, will no doubt think I've got the judge in my pocket.

"Let me get the box."

We head into the house. Curtis goes into his room and comes back carrying a banker's box. I don't remember seeing it when I checked the room earlier. He must carry it around with him for safekeeping. He sets the box on the kitchen table, sits down, and folds his hands in front of him, his posture ramrod straight. "Go at it," he says.

Bob has kept tidy records. I pull out Jack's medical file and the bank statements and set them aside to concentrate on later. I quickly go through the records of car and house insurance and repairs. There is a folder for life insurance, but it appears that Bob cashed it out several years ago. There is also a file of papers pertaining to Bob's old construction job. I can't imagine why he kept them, but my personal papers wouldn't bear scrutiny either.

Finally I open the fat folder of Jack's medical affairs. By the date on the last form, I can see that Jack hasn't gone for a physical checkup for some time, so I suspect it won't be worthwhile for me to contact his doctor, but all things are on the table at this point.

Curtis gets himself a Coke and me a glass of water. He has begun to relax, but when I get to the bank statements, he sits forward like a hunting dog on point. I pause and look him in the eye. "Curtis, I'm going to tell you something that you can count on. No matter what these bank statements tell me, you'll never hear it spoken about anywhere. It's confidential information, and I'll treat it that way."

"Just see that you do." He's back to the rigid posture.

As soon as I get a look at the balance, I can see why he's worked up. Twenty years of veteran's benefits has added up to a significant sum. But it doesn't take me long to find something odd. A few months ago, $20,000 was taken out. A couple of weeks later, $10,000 of it was put back. I show it to Curtis. "You have any idea what this is about?"

"It's a mystery to me." For the first time, he looks at me with something like acceptance. He nods toward the file. "Look back through and you'll see some other ones."

Six months prior, I find another transaction, this for $8,000, the whole amount put back within a few weeks. There are others, going back two years, with varying amounts from $5,000 to $15,000.

"If the money was just taken out," I say, "I'd wonder if it was some kind of blackmail. But it's all been put back. All except that $10,000 at the end."

"It doesn't make any sense to me, either."

"Maybe Jack or your daddy had some kind of health emergency they needed money for. Maybe when the insurance money came in, they put it back."

"I didn't see anything like that in the medical record."

"Have you talked to Hitch Montgomery at the bank?"

His face reddens. "I didn't think of that. I'll do that first thing tomorrow."

"Let me take care of it."

He opens his mouth to protest, but I cut him off. "I do know Jack liked to gamble. He and his friends would go off to that casino in Louisiana—Coushatta. But $10,000 is a lot of money to gamble. Your daddy ever mention worrying about Jack spending too much money gambling?"

"Like I said, Daddy and I didn't talk much about Jack."

I put the files back into the box. "I won't take anything with me, but I may need to look at them again."

"We'll see." He's back to being suspicious. "Are we done here?"

"Just about. Let me ask you about something that goes back to when Jack got injured. I think you were still in high school."

"Okay, I wasn't around much then, but go ahead and ask."

"Do you remember how you found out about Jack's injuries?"

Curtis chews his lip, which is unusual. He works hard not to show any nerves. "How could I forget? Mamma just plain went to pieces, and Daddy was madder than I ever saw him. I don't know if you knew, but my daddy was against the war. He didn't speak out about it because he knew most people wouldn't like it. So he was double mad about what happened to Jack."

"It must have been hard to be a teenager and find out your brother was coming back from the war seriously injured."

He shrugs. "We weren't ever close."

"Did you and Jack ever talk after he got back?"

"Talk about what? If you mean a heart-to-heart talk, that wasn't our way." His voice is hard with disdain.

"Did he ever tell you if he was in California?"

"Jack? When would he have been there?"

I tell him that Bob came to see me about losing track of Jack and that I found California brochures in Jack's belongings.

He frowns, trying to remember. "I do remember Daddy saying he couldn't find Jack. I didn't know exactly what he meant." He gets up and paces the kitchen and then halts in front me. He points a finger at me. "Wait a minute. I never put it together, but one night I came home and Taylor was here. She and Daddy were in the kitchen and Taylor was crying. She always was one to stick her nose in where it didn't belong."

"You know what they were talking about?"

He sits back down. "No, but I heard Taylor say she'd do what she could. I don't know what she meant. Tell you the truth, I didn't care what they were talking about. I tried to stay out of the house as much as I could around that time. Seems like everybody was always either crying or yelling."

"Bottom line is, your daddy lost track of Jack for a while. You don't remember that?"

He shakes his head. His leg starts bouncing up and down, so I know he's impatient to get me out of here.

"Just a few more things. Did Jack tell you he was about to get married?"

"You're just full of information, aren't you? Yeah, I knew, but not until yesterday. Me and Walter Dunn got into it, and he told me Jack was planning to latch onto somebody else to take care of him like Daddy did."

At that, I can't contain myself any longer. "How come you're so spiteful about your brother?"

He gives me a hard look. Most bullies don't like to be confronted. "We were just too different. What kind of man would let his daddy take care of him like that?"

I bite my tongue to keep myself from asking him how come he didn't go into the service if he was so all-fired manly.

But he reads my mind, or at least my expression. "Fact is, I thought Jack was a fool to join the US Army. The military is nothing but a political tool. Republicans are just as bad as Democrats. All of them out for a buck. They don't care about America. They're willing to sell out to foreigners and bankers. Those of us who know anything about the real world have sense enough to organize so we can take care of ourselves."

His face reddens as he speaks, and in the end he brings his fist down hard on the table.

"Be that as it may, you're going to be coming into money that Jack saved from his disability payments. I imagine you won't say no to it, even if it did come from the government."

"Damn right, I won't." His face is fire red. "They take my money in unlawful taxation, and I'll get it back any way I can."

The phone rings. Curtis jumps up and answers it, his voice a snarl. He goes still, listening. "Okay, thank you. Yes, Landau's." When he puts the phone down, he rests his hand on the receiver for several seconds before turning back to me. His face is without expression. "They're releasing Jack's body. That means we can get on with the funeral."

I get up as casual as I can, having to use a cane. "If you need any help with funeral arrangements, you let me know."

His lip curls. "Why would I need your help?"

He truly has no feel for the usual kindness between people. "I thought you could use help letting people know when the funeral is, that kind of thing."

"I expect Landau's will do what it takes."

"I'm sure you're right. Thank you for your time."

"Good luck to you," he says, although he really means good riddance.

At the door I pause. "One more thing. Is there anybody who can verify where you were the night Jack died?"

It takes a second for the question to sink in. "You son of a bitch. Are you accusing me of killing my own brother?" He moves toward me so fast he almost trips over his feet, and grabs hold of a chair to right himself.

I hold up my hand to stop him. "I'm not accusing you of anything. In a murder investigation everybody is suspect until they can be ruled out. Seems to me you had a lot to gain from your brother's death. I'd be a fool not to question what you told me."

CHAPTER 22

Coach Eldridge's wife, Linda, comes to the door wiping her hands on her apron. She's got a friendly smile. "Hello, Samuel, what brings you over here?"

"I need to ask Boone about something."

"He's out in the garage. Let me call him in."

"I'll just go on out there. It won't take but a minute."

The garage has no room for a car. The floor is mostly taken up with sports equipment, some beyond repair. The rest of the area is crammed with cardboard boxes, broken furniture, and the usual house upkeep paraphernalia, like cans of leftover paint, a lawn mower, gardening tools, and sacks of cement and potting soil. There's a rusted out heap of a car sitting in the driveway. Eldridge will have another flashy car before long, though, now that he sold the Harley.

Eldridge is staring at a shelf of paint cans. His left hand is on his hip, his right arm in a sling.

Linda calls from the kitchen door. "Boone, Samuel Craddock is here to see you."

Eldridge turns around. Sporting a black eye, his face, mottled with purple and yellow bruises, is dripping with sweat. It's about a hundred degrees in here. Eldridge played football for SMU, and has the physique of a ballplayer gone to seed—big hands, tree stump legs, thick neck, and a big gut. His short brown hair is shot through with gray.

His wife is an accountant for a construction outfit over in Bobtail, which is good because the coach in a small town doesn't have much of a salary. Even with their two paychecks, there's something shabby about the house.

"Boone, I heard about those guys jumping you," I say. Since he can't shake hands, I clap my hand on his left shoulder. He winces, so that shoulder must be bruised as well. "If you can spare the time, I'd like to ask you a couple of things."

He looks surprised, but says, "Let's go inside. It's too hot out here." As we pass through the kitchen, he says, "Linda, I can't figure out which can has the trim paint in it. See if you can find the receipt. Maybe it'll tell what the color is."

Eldridge leads me into the family room. His teenage daughter is bent over the computer doing homework, and is happy to oblige him when he says she can leave it for later. I watch her leave, carrying the computer with her, and suddenly I remember what it was that I thought was off when I was at Lurleen's the day Jack died. I need an explanation for it, and hope the explanation is a good one. I stick it in the back of my mind to take up with her.

After Eldridge's daughter is gone, I point to his arm. "You have any idea who did that to you?"

He scratches his head with his free hand. "I didn't see a thing. I expect it has to do with losing to Bobtail."

"Has Jarrett Creek's finest made any move to find out who did it? It's an awful thing when a football game leads to violence like that."

"I told James Harley to leave it alone. It just stirs people up. Nothing was broken. I'll be okay. Now what can I do for you?"

I tell him I'm investigating Jack's death.

He nods, like he's impatient to get on with it. "I heard that. I don't know what you think I might help you with, but shoot."

I tell him about the two men I saw in the stands at the football game. "Somebody said they thought they could be scouting the team. You know anything about it?"

His expression is uneasy, and I wonder if something is going on under the radar with one of his players. "If that's who they were, they didn't come talk to me."

"Would that be unusual?"

"It's protocol for scouts to identify themselves to the coach, but it's not unheard of for colleges to send scouts around without letting on, especially this early in the season."

"You got any players you think are especially worth looking at?"

Eldridge keeps shifting in his seat. I expect his injuries still give him pain, despite his downplaying them. But people say he doesn't like being put on the spot, the way he was after the loss to Bobtail. "I don't like to say it; it's just a rumor. But Dilly Bolton's dad has been talking him up a good bit. Maybe he contacted somebody. That's illegal, but it doesn't keep people from sneaking behind my back and trying to get a leg up with the scouts."

Dilly Bolton is one of the team's two black players. He's a senior, and I've never noticed him being anything special, but his daddy, Jess, has high ambitions for him. Jess hangs out with Gabe LoPresto a good bit, so I expect if he'd talked a college into sending someone to take a look, Gabe would have known about it.

"It seemed to me they were concentrating on the team. But can you think of any other reason for those fellows to be there?"

"How would I know?"

Linda comes back in with the receipt, happy to tell Eldridge she has found the name of the paint. Eldridge, on the other hand, doesn't seem to be all that thrilled. I don't see how he's going to do much painting, anyway, until his arm gets better.

He sees me to the door. "By the way," I tell him, "the medical examiner has released Jack's body, so I expect the funeral will be early next week."

"Well, that'll be an end to it," Eldridge says.

"There won't be a real end to it until whoever killed him is brought to justice," I say.

Eldridge cocks his head. "You really think you're ever going to find out who did it?"

"I'm sure going to try."

In the evening I phone those who should know right away that Jack's body has been released, not trusting Curtis to have the common decency to call them. Lurleen and Walter Dunn are stoic at the news, but Marybeth and Taylor cry. I offer to go spend the evening with Marybeth, but she surprises me by saying she's going to come to Jarrett Creek and wait at the funeral home for the body's arrival.

"You know, they'll need to fix him up before you can see him."

"I know that. But I want to be there when he comes home."

When I call Woody, I mention what Marybeth plans to do, and he says he'll go sit with her.

CHAPTER 23

Loretta calls me Saturday night to remind me that we have plans to go to a fiddle contest in Georgetown tomorrow morning. It's one of the few things she'll miss church for. My wife, Jeanne, never cared for country music, but I don't mind it.

I'm up and out early. I walk to Loretta's place because we're going in her car instead of my pickup.

"You're wearing that ratty old hat?" She poses it as a question, but what she means is, "You're not wearing that ratty old hat!"

"It keeps the sun off."

She hears in my voice that my hat is not open for discussion and says no more, but makes do with a good, solid rolling of her eyes.

We make the drive in a couple of hours, arriving in plenty of time to grab good seats in the folding chairs set up in the American Legion Hall. By the time the fiddlers and their backup players start tuning up, just about every seat is taken.

We've been to a few fiddle contests this year. Loretta is prim in most ways, but she loves fiddle music, and she taps her foot and bobs her head along with the tunes. I believe if there was dancing, I wouldn't be able to keep her off the floor. But these contests are serious business. No dancing.

There's a sizable amount of money at stake for such a small town event, and the performers look as nervous as if they were on *American Idol*. Musicians have come here from as far away as Amarillo, and they're primed to do their best. I enjoy myself and the morning passes quickly.

For lunch, they've set up a barbecue pit, and there's potato salad and coleslaw and beans to go with ribs and chicken. The only problem is that after eating too much, Loretta and I have trouble staying awake. I go back for coffee a couple of times.

On the way home, Loretta and I have a lively argument about whether the right person won. I was taken with an old boy who looked to have played fiddle his whole life. But Loretta was on the side of a little girl about fifteen who swept the judges off their seats. And she won, so Loretta has that to bolster her argument.

When I walk back to my house about nine thirty, I'm surprised to see someone sitting on my front porch in the shadows. I am halfway up the walk to the house when he stands up.

"Who's there?" I call out.

"It's me, Mr. Craddock."

"Woody? What are you up to?"

"Just thought we could talk a little bit."

"Let me get the house open."

Sometimes I wish I was forty again, when I didn't have any trouble extending my day. Now I'd like to tell Woody that whatever he wants to talk about will keep until tomorrow. But when I get closer, I can smell alcohol coming off him, and I know now is the time to talk. His tongue will be loose, and by tomorrow he may think better of whatever he has to say tonight.

"I'll make us some coffee," I say. "And I've got a little brandy we can throw in."

We take our coffee and brandy back out on the porch and sit in the dark. I'd like to turn on the light so I can see Woody's face, but he asks me to leave it off.

In high school, Woody and Jack were undisputed kings of their class: handsome, athletic, and with just enough devilment in them to make them popular. Their names were spoken together, as if they were one unit. But now I'm wondering which was the leader and which the sidekick. I do recall a certain hesitation in Jack. When Woody got hurt on the football field, he'd bounce back up. Even if he was limping, no way he'd let the coach take him out of the game. Jack was different. He made more of a show of being hurt—dragging himself off the field, only to come back out to cheers a few plays later. What did that say about the two of them?

Although he said he wanted to talk, Woody is quiet at first, so I make some general comments about the fiddle contest. Finally I run out of small talk. "Did you go over to the funeral home and wait with Marybeth yesterday afternoon?"

"Yes, they brought the body in about five o'clock. Lurleen was there, too."

"So she and Marybeth had a chance to spend some time together."

"It was real good for the two of them." His chair creaks as he hunches forward. "I understand you're going to investigate who killed Jack."

"That's right."

"I want you to get that son of a bitch." His voice has a hitch in it.

"Maybe you know something that would help me out."

He sighs. "I wish I did."

"I understand you and Jack buried the hatchet."

"We made some headway in that direction."

"Tell me about it."

He takes something from his shirt pocket, and I hear the rustle of paper and realize he's taking a pinch of tobacco to put in his mouth. "Not much to tell. I went over to Walter Dunn's motorcycle shop and asked him to act as a go-between and he brought me over to Jack's. He talked to Jack for a while and eventually Jack said he'd give me a few minutes." Woody gets up and goes over to the edge of the porch and spits the tobacco juice over the side. He doesn't sit back down, just stands looking out at the dark. "Like he was granting me an audience."

"What was he so mad at you for?"

"He blamed me for him going into the army."

That same old line. "That's ridiculous. You both signed up at the same time. I doubt you held him down while he signed the papers."

I see a movement of his head. "You have to understand how it was. We had it in mind to be in the service together. Stupid. Now I know there's a good chance we might never have been deployed together. But we figured it would be like an extension of being on the football field. Having each other's backs."

"So when you weren't accepted, he was upset. But I still don't understand why he'd blame you all these years. It wasn't like you planned it."

"But I could have prevented it."

"I don't see how."

He comes over and pours himself more brandy and sits back down. "You remember when I shot him in the foot?"

"Of course I do. I thought . . ." I thought wrong. I had assumed there was some altercation having to do with Taylor. An easy assumption, and now I realize how wrong I was. There was never any reason for me to dig any deeper—until now.

"I was supposed to do enough damage so he'd be unfit for duty. I was supposed to shoot him in the ankle. Somewhere that it would be hard to fix. But I just couldn't do it. At the last second I pulled up and hit him in the foot."

I'd heard of people doing that during the Vietnam War, on both sides. Wounding themselves so they couldn't be drafted. "I should have guessed."

"You were with me when the nurse came out and said his foot was going to be fine."

"I remember."

"I had a premonition that I'd just about killed Jack."

I recall the look on Woody's face. Maybe he did think he was seeing the future. I can imagine Jack's bitterness at what happened to him in the war, after Woody couldn't go through with the plan. "Seems like he could have done it himself if he was so all-fired determined to keep himself out of the service."

"He was too scared to do it himself. When he asked me to do it, he cried. I think that's why he couldn't stand to be around me. He couldn't get over my seeing him that way."

Woody's right: it would have eaten at Jack for Woody to know that he wasn't a war hero. Just a guy who tried to get out of going to war.

"So what did you two talk about when he finally saw you?"

"I didn't mention the past. I just told him that I missed his friendship and that if he'd let me take care of him, I would."

"Was that before or after he and Lurleen decided to get married?"

"After. Surprised the hell out of me. I told him I was really happy for him, and that even if I couldn't take care of him, I'd like us to bury the hatchet. He said he'd think about it."

"And that's the last you saw of him?"

"Yes sir, the last time. Goddamn! All those years we wasted."

We're quiet for a few minutes. He pours more brandy, and I sip my coffee. "Let me ask you something. Jack went missing after he was injured. You ever hear anything about that?"

"Taylor's the one to ask about it." He sounds angry.

"Taylor? But you two were married then. You would have known, too."

"You need to ask her." He gets up and shoves his hands in his pockets. "I should go. I just came over here because I needed to talk to somebody. And you're the only person besides Taylor who knew I shot Jack. So you know how bad it all turned out."

"Taylor knew, too? The whole story?"

"Yeah." He heaves a deep sigh. "I wish to hell I'd done what Jack wanted me to do."

"It was a lot to ask."

"No!" The word explodes into the air. "We were like brothers. Better than brothers. I failed him. And I don't want anyone to fail him again. I want you to find out who killed him." He tosses back the last of his brandy and takes off down the steps.

I sit there for a while longer, and my thoughts are dark. Even if I find out who killed Jack, which I have every intention of doing, it isn't going to heal Woody's wounds. Those years are gone. I think about the void between Jack and his real brother, Curtis. Jack had a better brother in Woody, and he rejected him. You'd think Jack would have found comfort in old friends. It's terrible what the need to save face will do to people.

Finally I get up and stretch out my leg. It doesn't do any good to brood over it. My job is to find out who ended Jack's life. I can't fix any more than that.

CHAPTER 24

I never paid much attention to the motorcycle repair shop halfway between Jarrett Creek and Bryan–College Station. It's a big barn of a building set back from the highway. A snappy red, yellow, and black sign reads, *HIGH RIDE MOTORCYCLE REPAIR*. I pull up there at nine o'clock. A huge plate glass window displays on a pedestal a vintage motorcycle. A neat, hand-lettered sign says, *Indian*.

I wondered how a motorcycle repair shop could keep five veterans occupied, but I don't wonder anymore. There are at least 30 motorcycles parked out front, all types. There are long, skinny ones, big, round, beefy ones. Some look like they are meant for a leisurely Sunday drive, and others like you could go across the country on them. Signs in the window say they repair every type of hog from Harleys to Yamahas to Hondas. A plaque on the front door announces that the shop won some award from a motorcycle association.

Inside it's noisy, but cleaner than I expected. Motorcycles stand in individual work areas in various stages of disassembly. In the office, Walter Dunn sits behind a desk talking to a burly man with bristly gray hair. Dunn glances over and nods to me. I stand at the window and watch the work in progress while I wait for them to finish their business.

Eventually bristle-top leaves and Dunn comes out from behind the counter to shake my hand. "What brings you over here?"

"I need to have a talk with you if you've got a minute."

He says he'll make some time for me. "But let's go in the back, otherwise we'll be interrupted every two minutes." He pokes his head out and yells to Vic, the tattooed man I met at Jack's, to watch the front for a few minutes.

We step into a small back room set up with a tiny table and couple of chairs, a half-size refrigerator, and a coffee machine. Dunn pours us some coffee and we sit down.

I tell him about Rodell being out of commission for a while and my being corralled to find out who killed Jack.

"Sounds good to me. Jack said you were the best lawman they ever had in town."

"That's a good bit in the past, but I'll do my best."

"How can I help you out?"

I take the photo of him and Jack out of my pocket and set it on the table in front of him. He doesn't touch it, but his gremlin's face goes still. If you don't look at his eyes, he can look like a fierce man. "You told me you met Jack in Bryan at a veteran's meeting."

Finally he looks up and pushes the photo back across the table to me. "You're right. I misspoke."

"Misspoke, or lied?"

"Say it however you want."

"How come you didn't tell me you knew Jack in the war? Seems like a big omission."

"It's complicated. I'm not going to go into it, but I can tell you with absolute truth that it has nothing to do with Jack's murder."

"It have anything to do with California?"

I've hit a nerve. He sits back; suddenly tense. He rubs his thumb along his chin while he looks off into space. "I'm just going to repeat what I said. All that has nothing to do with Jack's murder."

I pick up the picture and look at it. I feel like I'm soothing a wild beast. "I'd like to leave the matter alone. I really would. But it occurred to me that something that happened back then might have come back into Jack's life."

He doesn't rush to say no. He thinks on it for several seconds, but then shakes his head again. "Can't be. It cannot be."

I pull out the article about the homeless man in the dumpster that

I found in Jack's wallet and push it over to Dunn. He blinks at it for a minute and then picks it up. He's smiling. "I can't believe Jackie kept this. I cut it out to read to him. Told him if he didn't get his act together he was going to end up like this guy—on the streets, homeless, begging for handouts."

"Who put the smiley face on it?"

"Beats me." He gets up, dumps the rest of his coffee in the sink and heads for the door. "I'm going to have to get back out there. Mondays are always busy. You let me know if there's anything else I can help you with."

"There is one thing," I say, rising.

He turns back around. "Say the word."

"You prevented Jack's brother from throwing his mother out of Jack's house the other day."

He snickers. "I don't know that it would have come to that, but I saw to it that their argument didn't go too far."

"Marybeth says you just showed up at the back door. What were you doing there?"

He smiles sadly. "I'll tell you what I was doing. I went to get my books and magazines. I brought them over to Jack's after his dad died to have something to read to him, keep him company, get his mind off things. And after Jack was killed, I got to thinking I could bring the magazines back here. Curtis would just throw them in the trash. I doubt he has the stomach for that kind of publication, being an upright Christian, and all that."

And with that, I have to be satisfied. Dunn says he'll see me at the funeral tomorrow. "The boys and I are planning a special tribute."

Talking to Dunn gets me thinking about Curtis. When I get back to my place, I fire up my computer and go to work finding out everything I can about the True Marcus Ministry. And what I find chills me.

"Marcus" is Marcus Longley, an ex-Southern Baptist from Kentucky, who claims to have seen his way to a new religion after a "series of crossroads" shook his faith. Poking around on the Internet doesn't yield what those "crossroads" might have been.

I get hold of an older cop in Marcus's hometown who remembers Marcus well. "His parents were drunks and when meth came into fashion, they took to it like ducks to water." He snorts. "I guess they didn't take too well to being parents. Marcus spent his formative years in a juvenile facility."

"What for?"

"Uh . . . just a minute. Let me see."

I hear paper rustling. "I wanted to get the wording right. Says here, 'inappropriate conduct with a six-year-old neighbor.' I remembered it was some kind of high-toned words."

"Gets the message across."

"That it does. Then after he got out, when he was eighteen, wasn't any time before it happened again, this time with a twelve-year-old girl."

"Did he go to jail?"

"Naw, we couldn't get enough evidence to charge him, but we asked him very nicely to leave town and not come back. This is the first I've heard of him since. Is he up to his old tricks?"

"I'm not sure, but I appreciate the information."

I wonder how Curtis came to be involved in the group. Poking around a little more on the Internet, I find an article about Marcus Ministry in an online magazine called *Religious Soldier*. It says that the mission of the ministry is "survival after the takeover. The ministry is armed and ready to fight back against the SHADOW GOVERN-MENT that is determined to deprive us of our right to worship in our own way." The way they choose to worship isn't specified in the article. But their weapons of choice are discussed in detail, from assault rifles to shotguns to close-range combat guns. Funny how these steadfast Americans prefer weapons manufactured in Russia or China.

As a boy, Curtis was always a little strange, going off in the woods like he did. But a lot of boys went through that phase. As chief of police, I didn't take them too seriously. Mostly it was about shooting possums and snakes. By the time they were old enough to be interested in girls, they either lost their interest in guns altogether or channeled it into hunting. Curtis took a different turn.

Until now, Taylor's concern for her sister seemed nothing more than a logistical problem. Now I'm worried that Sarah's daughters might be at risk. It makes me sick to my stomach. I'm betting that Curtis was so glad to find like-minded people in the True Marcus Ministry that he never bothered to find out about Marcus Longley's past. It's about time someone gave him that information.

Before I can get out of the house to go see Curtis, the phone rings. It's the medical examiner's office with preliminary results of Jack's autopsy. Once an autopsy is complete, it's public record, but the bureaucratic process can take as long as eight weeks. So I asked them to call me informally as soon as they completed the autopsy. Although I was pretty sure I knew what the cause of death was, you can't assume anything in a murder.

But there are no surprises in Jack's report. He died from the knife wounds. Like me, the medical examiner concluded that the attempted strangulation was not sufficiently forceful to kill Jack, just to suppress any noise he might have made. I thank them for the report. "While I have you on the phone, can you email me another autopsy report?"

Within the hour both Jack's and Bob's autopsy files arrive as PDFs. There's something about autopsy results that always shakes me up. I saw Jack dead of his wounds, saw the way he had struggled, the blood, the contortions of his body, and yet the clinical language of the autopsy report seems more final, more intimate even, than seeing it before my eyes.

I take a cup of coffee out onto the porch and sit picturing the vague form of someone creeping into Jack's house, into his bedroom, with the intent of killing him. I wonder where the knife is now, if it was cleaned and put away neatly in a drawer somewhere or thrown away where no one will ever find it.

CHAPTER 25

Hitch Montgomery would be a shoo-in for the role of banker in a Hollywood movie. He's a tidy man who wears neat suits with buttoned-up collars and his hair short in back with just enough to comb over in the front. As long as I've banked with him, I've never known him to make a joke nor to gossip. It's all business, all the time. Just what you want your banker to be.

When I sit down across from him the next morning, I tell him I'm investigating Jack's death and have a question for him. "If it violates confidentiality, just let me know and I'll get a court order."

He lays his hands flat on the desk in front of him. It's bare except for a pen and yellow pad and a discreet picture of his wife and children. "You know I can't let you see his records without the court approving."

"I've already seen them. Curtis let me go through them."

"Then what's your question?"

I ask him what he knows about the money taken out of Jack's account at intervals and then put back in.

He thinks for a time, then draws what I'd have to say is a cautious breath. "The good part is that I can tell you what I know about it. The bad part is, I don't know anything."

It's as close to humor as I've ever heard from him.

"What I mean is, I remember Bob came in and told me he wanted to take some money out of the account. Seemed like a lot. You know, we're not like one of those Wall Street banks, trying to stick it to everybody. We pride ourselves that we aren't just here to deposit your money, but to guide you. We need to be alert if somebody is investing unwisely."

When Jeanne and I first bought an expensive painting, Montgomery had a little chat with us about art not being such a sound investment. Turns out in a couple of cases he couldn't have been more wrong, but we were glad he took a personal interest.

"I can't tell people what to do with their money, but I can tell them if I think they're making a mistake. Sometimes they even listen."

"I'm guessing Bob didn't tell you what the money was for."

"Only that it was Jack's money and Jack wanted it for a friend."

"He didn't say who the friend was?"

"He didn't. I don't mind telling you, I was a little worried. You might think it's none of my business. But like I said, we take care of our own. When the money was put back, I stopped worrying about it."

"And it happened several times."

"That's right. Seemed odd to me, but it got to be a regular thing, so I figured it was just what he said—helping out a friend."

"Is there anybody else here at the bank who might have handled one of these transactions?"

He shakes his head. "I'm the one who handles his account. If anything happened while I was away, I would have been told."

"I do know Jack liked to go to Coushatta and gamble with some friends. I'm wondering if that's what it was about."

He laughs. "If he was gambling with the money, you can be sure he'd be taking more out than he was putting in."

If the money wasn't used for gambling, there's another thought I have about what happened to it. And I don't like where the idea takes me at all.

An hour later I use my talk with Montgomery as an opening with Curtis. We're sitting out on the patio. It's the first real fall day we've had, crisp and clear. "I had a talk with Hitch Montgomery and he said he doesn't know why big sums of money went in and out of Jack's account. You had any more thoughts about it?"

"There's still $10,000 missing. Of course I've thought about it. I figure one of those vet friends of his needed to be tided over."

"You have any particular reason for thinking that?"

Curtis is restless. He's hunched forward in his seat and his foot keeps bouncing when he's not talking. "No. But all you have to do is look at them, scruffy and driving those motorcycles. Probably not one of them with a steady job."

"You're wrong there." I tell him about the motorcycle shop. "They've got more business than they know what to do with." I'd bet the shop brings in a lot more money than what Curtis makes buying and selling guns, but what do I know about that?

"Still, could be that they need tiding over every now and then. But they're not going to have that tit to go back to anymore." He's stubborn; I'll give him that.

"Taylor told me you offered to let her see her sister."

He's instantly still and suspicious. "What of it?"

"Is that real?"

"I don't see where you come into it."

"I don't. But I do have a question. Have you ever looked into the background of the guy who heads Marcus Ministry?"

"I don't need to look into it. I know everything I need to know just talking to him."

"I doubt if he'd tell you if your daughters are at risk from a pedophile."

He jumps to his feet. "My wife is perfectly capable of taking care of my daughters, and she hasn't said a thing about it. I take good care of my family and I don't like your insinuations." Despite the cool air, his face is flushed. He starts toward the back door.

"Hold up! You might want to hear what I have to say. Then you can do what you please with the information."

He takes a step back toward me. "I doubt you have anything to say that will be of value."

"I found out a little more about your buddy Marcus. And he's not who you think he is."

His body is as tense as a coiled snake. "What are you talking about?"

"Seems like Marcus has a record of sexual interest in underage girls."

Curtis steps close enough so he's towering over me. "That's just a flat-out lie. I've known the man for ten years and never known him to take the slightest interest in a young girl. He's happily married to a fine woman who knows her duty."

I sit back and cross my ankle over my bad knee. I'll be damned if I'm going to look up at him, so I speak to the air in front of me. "I had a talk with the police department in the town where Marcus grew up."

Curtis sits back down in the lawn chair, perching on the edge. "So what?"

"They confirmed that Marcus was arrested twice for sexual assault on two underage girls."

Curtis draws the back of his hand across his mouth as if wiping off an unwanted kiss. He leaps up and stalks around the patio like a caged animal, and then wheels on me. "It's got to be a different man. Lots of people with the same name."

I hand him a photo the police in Mississippi faxed me. He looks at it for a long minute, and then wads it up and tosses it aside. "There's some mistake. I know this man. He's a good, law-abiding, god-fearing man."

I get up. "Maybe so. But if it were my daughter, I'd want to be damn sure."

CHAPTER 26

Jack's funeral is just about the strangest affair I've ever attended. TV stations from Houston and Austin have gotten wind of Jack's life story, from football hero to Gulf War veteran to murder victim, and they are camped out in front of the Methodist Church with reporters and film crews.

Some people coming for the funeral want nothing to do with this circus and others are thrilled. I'm not surprised to see Gabe LoPresto and the mayor holding forth. For the benefit of a sleek female reporter, LoPresto points out the principal people in Jack's life—Taylor, Woody, Curtis, and Marybeth. They are all interviewed in turn on the steps of the Methodist Church, and none of them look happy about it. Thank goodness the vets haven't arrived yet, or there might be blood on the church steps.

I try to slip by, but Gabe sics them on me. I tell the guy who shoves a microphone in my face that I have nothing to say. He says he heard I was the person the nurse called when she found Jack's body. "I understand you knew Jack Harbin his whole life."

"That may be true, but it doesn't mean I have a comment," I say.

"This man was gravely wounded in the service of his country, and you have no comment about his murder?" The reporter, who has mastered the art of looking outraged, moves a step closer.

"That's right. No comment. Now if you'll excuse me." I try to push past him, but a doe-eyed blonde dressed to show off her assets blocks my way. She speaks into her microphone. "I've just learned that Jarrett Creek's mayor has appointed you as special investigator in the murder. Is that true?"

"Yes ma'am."

"Have you got any leads in the case?"

"No ma'am."

Her eyes would freeze hell. "What are your credentials? Why did the mayor put *you* in charge of this investigation?"

"You'd have to ask him."

"How do you intend to proceed?"

"Cautiously."

And with that they both jerk away from me in search of fresh meat. It's not that I object to talking to the press, but not until I have something to say. I've heard too many lawmen blab to the press and live to regret it. It's that old thing about keeping your mouth shut and being thought a fool versus opening your mouth and removing all doubt. There will be plenty of time for me to strut myself in front of a microphone after I've gotten results.

I duck inside the church and see Taylor and a tall, distinguished looking man I take to be her husband talking to Curtis. Curtis is inclining his head as if he's truly interested in what the husband is saying. I wish I could hear the conversation.

The casket is open, and folks are filing by to take one last look. Marybeth stands to one side of the casket with a grim-faced man and woman. Marybeth told me her sister and brother-in-law would be here. The sister weighs twice as much as Marybeth, which isn't saying much— she's still thin. I join them and they seem relieved to have something to focus on besides Jack. They own a second-hand store in Bobtail, and they tell me more about furniture than I ever wanted to know.

Marybeth tenses up, and I see Lurleen standing uncertainly in the doorway. She's wearing a dark blue dress and looks pale. "Samuel, do you think she ought to sit with me?"

"That's up to you, but I'll bet she'd appreciate it."

"Will you go get her?"

When I get to Lurleen, she eyes me like I'm throwing a rope to someone clinging to a cliff. "Jack's mother would like you to come sit with her."

"I couldn't."

"Why not?"

She swallows. "I'll be too sad. I don't want to make it worse for her."

"It may be that sharing her grief will give her comfort."

She nods. As I escort her, I say, "You didn't bring your oldest boy with you?"

"I needed him to stay with the young ones. I don't think it's a great idea for a young boy to have to come to a funeral anyway."

I'm wishing the boy were here. It occurred to me that the questions I want to ask Lurleen could be laid to rest if I question him instead.

"Don't be nervous," I say as we draw up close to Marybeth. "You look pretty."

"I don't feel pretty. I wish I could have just stayed in bed today."

Marybeth hears her say this and she takes hold of Lurleen's arm. "I know just how you feel."

At that moment I hear the loud racket of motorcycles outside. The vets come in with their wives, which is a good thing, because dressed in their motorcycle leathers they might have been barred from coming into the service. They move into the second row, all except for Walter Dunn, who comes over and hugs Lurleen and shakes hands with Marybeth.

"I'd like to introduce you to some of Jack's friends," he says to her.

Although Marybeth's relatives are rigid with disapproval, Marybeth goes over to the vets and shakes their hands and thanks them for coming. Their wives have sat down, but the vets have remained standing.

I leave them and go sit back with the general public. Loretta scoots in beside me at the last minute, smelling of shampoo and perfume.

I wonder what the Methodist preacher, David Coogan, will say about Jack. I like Coogan. He's a dry person, but down to earth. What will he say about someone who made it clear that church held nothing for him? It was Marybeth who asked that the service be held in the Methodist Church. The Baptists probably would have said no way, but the Methodist Church in Jarrett Creek is not wound so tight.

Coogan doesn't beat around the bush. "Jack Harbin didn't find religion soothing to his spirit. But that doesn't mean the Lord didn't love him." He goes on in that vein, and I see some heads nodding. He's hit the right note.

"In some ways, Jack was the conscience of our community." Startled movements. "Like Job, his trials reminded us that life can be a bitter experience, whether or not we deserve it. I once visited with Jack to try to find a way to bring him to Jesus. And he told me that he found his solace in the friends who best understood him." He looks at the vets seated on the front rows. "It's not the traditional way of coming to God, but I believe that God spoke to Jack by giving him those friends to comfort him."

It's a short service, but to my mind it's satisfactory, giving everybody something to think about, and allowing Jack his status as an iconoclast.

The TV people have all gathered on the steps outside. I suppose they have only so much tolerance for small town wisdom, and that's what the preacher served up.

I'm climbing into Loretta's car to drive her and a couple of other ladies to the cemetery when a giant roar shatters the quiet.

"Oh, my Lord," Loretta says. "Will you look at that!"

There must be a hundred motorcycles gathered in a the high school gymnasium parking lot down the street from the church. Every year there's a big motorcycle rally out at the lake with hundreds of cyclists in attendance. Dunn and his vets must have called on them to give Jack a monumental send-off.

At the cemetery, everyone gathers around the gravesite, and it's clear that Reverend Coogan has given his okay to the tribute. Before he starts speaking, he nods and Dunn speaks into a walky-talky. Then the cyclists stream past on the paved road, all decked out in black leather and displaying American flags. I wouldn't have thought such a display could be moving, but it is.

When the last motorcycle has gone past, the silence is profound. Coogan asks for the American Legion detail to come forward. Three elderly veterans dressed in uniform salute Jack's coffin, present arms, and shoot off a three-round volley. Old George Clark, who is in his eighties, can still play taps on his bugle. Everyone at the gravesite is moved, except for Curtis, who stands stone-faced.

After Bob Harbin died, a wake was held at the Harbin place; but that was Jack's doing. Marybeth has arranged for a reception at the Methodist hall for Jack. The vets congregate in one corner, their wives huddled nearby. Jack's high school friends make another group. Gabe LoPresto and the football boosters make a third.

Most people, including Loretta, mill around Marybeth and Curtis, extending sympathy. They may not approve of Marybeth abandoning her family, but this is not the time or the place to raise that issue. Marybeth looks like she's barely holding up, and she clings to Lurleen's arm like a lifeline. You can tell who hasn't heard about Jack and Lurleen by their puzzled expressions when they see the two women together.

I go to the food table and fill my plate with sandwiches and Jell-O salad while I ponder what group to approach first. It's likely that somebody in this hall killed Jack, and I might as well take advantage of the opportunity to nose around.

Gabe LoPresto's group is gathered around Coach Boone Eldridge, whose black eye has turned to yellow and whose arm is out of the sling. These fellows may be mad at him for losing the game to Bobtail and may want him fired, but they don't like the idea that somebody took it out on him physically.

"It's not right what happened to you," LoPresto blusters. This is the same man who was all for tarring and feathering Eldridge after the loss. But since the team won the last two Friday nights, things have smoothed out. He turns to James Harley, who has chosen to wear his police uniform to the funeral service. "What have you done toward finding out who attacked Boone?"

"We're on it," James Harley says. Since Eldridge told me he asked the police to stay out of the situation, I know James Harley is just being defensive.

"On it how?" LoPresto's voice is testy. He knows, like everyone else, that James Harley is not just out of his range—he doesn't even have a range.

James Harley glares at LoPresto and touches the gun at his belt.

"You think it was youngsters who did it?" somebody asks the coach.

"I wish I could tell you," Eldridge says, hanging his head. "I'm so embarrassed to let myself get caught like that, I can hardly show my face in town."

"You know how many of them there were?" I ask.

James Harley shoots me a resentful look. "I meant to ask you that, Boone. How many were there?"

"Well, I don't know," Boone snaps. He takes out a handkerchief and wipes his red face. "They jumped me from behind. Could have been two, could have been three. If it'd just been one, I could have held my own."

"Where were you when you got jumped?" LoPresto says. There's something funny in his voice, and I realize he has some doubts about the matter. I wonder what that's all about.

"Sons of bitches attacked me right in front of my own home!"

"Must have made some racket. Your wife didn't hear it?"

"They dragged me into the thicket down the street from the house." Eldridge loosens the knot of his tie, as if he's struggling for air. "Tell you the truth, I'd just as soon let it drop. I'm on the mend, and I doubt anybody's ever going to figure out who it was." He avoids looking at James Harley.

"You're probably right," LoPresto says. "I understand you and Jack had a chance to mend fences after the loss to Bobtail."

Eldridge snorts. "Wasn't any fences to mend. You know Jack, he was always spouting off about something. Neither of us was one to hold a grudge."

"That may be," LoPresto says, "but Jack said you brought some tequila over to the house Sunday after the game to soothe things out."

"It never hurts to sow a little good will."

When they start talking about last Friday's win, I ease on off to talk to the vets. I'm surprised when Walter Dunn hugs me. I'm not much for hugging other men. "You were a good friend to Jack after Bob died, and I won't forget that," he says.

"Nobody could measure up to you fellows."

"We were just doing what we'd do for any one of us," Dunn says. "Band of brothers."

Everyone nods and toasts with their punch. Dunn slips a flask out of his pocket to see if I want a little spike in my punch, but I wave it away.

"How often did you all get together with him?" I ask.

"Not as often as I'd have liked," Dunn says. He tilts his head in the direction of the wives. "Them and the motorcycle shop keeps us busy."

"All of you work for the shop?"

"We own it." Dunn speaks with pride. "It's a co-op."

"You all from around here originally?"

"I'm from Hearne," one of them says, and another is from Nacogdoches. A sharp-faced boy with arms full of tattoos says, "I'm from California. I just came here after I met Dunn . . ."

"He figured he'd be better off in Texas," Dunn says, cutting him off. The guy from California turns red.

"One thing we all did every few months is go over to the casino in Coushatta," Dunn says. "Jack enjoyed that."

"Jack bet any big money?" I ask.

Dunn looks surprised. "Naw, Vic here is the only one of us spends big."

One of the others pipes up. "He's not married, so he has plenty of cash." They all laugh.

"But Jack enjoyed playing? What was his game?"

Walter grins ruefully. "He liked to play blackjack or craps, either one, and one of us would bet for him. Sometimes he'd listen so close when we played craps that I think he could hear what numbers came up on the dice."

The sharp-faced boy is staring at Walter, his expression still angry. "That last time wasn't so good, though. Remember how pissed off Jack was when we left?"

"Never did figure out what got him going," another one says.

Dunn tosses back the rest of his punch. "Well, we better gather up the ladies and head on out. I guess we'll see you around."

Taylor sees me coming toward the group of people she's with. She steps away and hugs me. "I want you to meet my husband." She pulls me over. "Alex, this is Samuel Craddock, the man who went to Waco with me."

Taylor's husband makes a good first impression. He's my height, about six feet, with broad shoulders and he meets my eyes directly. His dark hair is cut neatly. His suit is probably expensive, but it isn't ostentatious. If anything, he looks a bit stuffy.

"I appreciate your helping Taylor out, going to Waco. I've got my hands full at work."

"I didn't mind a bit."

Taylor's mother lunges toward us. Taylor tenses. She's always been a little allergic to her mother, who is well meaning, but doesn't always curb her tongue. "Samuel, I haven't seen you in a while. When you called me for Taylor's number the other day, why didn't you tell me what had happened to Jack? And what happened to your leg?"

"Mamma, don't badger Samuel."

I lean over and give Agatha a shoulder hug. "That's all right. Your mamma's right, we don't get a chance to visit much."

"I'm just so stirred up about what happened to Jack, I don't know that any of us is safe in our bed." She rattles on like that for a few minutes. I catch Loretta's eye and she cruises over and takes Agatha off our hands.

By the way Woody and Laurel aren't looking at each other, I expect they've had a fight. Seems like funerals either bring people together or shake them apart.

Some receptions go on all afternoon, but this one breaks up early. I wait for Loretta while she bustles around helping with cleanup. On our way out, she says, "That Curtis is awful close with a dollar. He argued with Annie Milton when she told him the usual donation to Methodist ladies' auxiliary is $100 for a reception. Annie told him to keep his money. Nicely, of course."

"He didn't take her up on it, did he?"

"Gave her $50."

"Just a minute." She waits while I go back inside.

I slip some money in the donation box. Annie is still there, and sees me. "You don't need to do that." She gives me a sharp look. "Loretta told you about Curtis, didn't she?"

"I know I don't have to contribute," I say, "But when it comes time for my funeral, you all better do it up right."

CHAPTER 27

I've just gotten out of my funeral clothes and back into my blue jeans, and am putting on a pot of coffee when I hear someone coming up the front steps. Through the screen door, I see Taylor and her husband.

"Are you busy?" Taylor says.

"Not a bit."

"With Mamma rattling on at the reception, Alex hardly got a chance to say hello."

Alex's smile is strained. He has put in his time and is ready to get back up to Dallas. Why has Taylor brought him here? I offer them something to drink, but both of them say they had plenty at the reception. There's an awkward moment.

"Funeral went off okay," I say.

"Those motorcycles," Taylor says, shaking her head.

"Alex, you must think this is a pretty rowdy little town," I say.

He doesn't reply, because he's staring at the Melinda Buie painting above the fireplace that I bought in Houston a few months ago. After a minute he moves onto my Wolf Kahn and then to each of the pictures around the room. Finally he turns his gaze to me. "Where in the world did you get these pieces?" He looks at Taylor. "This is why you wanted me to come here, isn't it?"

Taylor grins at him like a puppy who's done well. "Alex loves art. I thought he'd like to see your collection."

Alex looks at me as if I've just sprouted wings. I'm used to this response. When Jeanne was alive, we sometimes had tour groups come through. Even though I dressed up in my good duds, to them I was just some old country boy. Me having a prize art collection was a wonder to behold.

I tell Alex how I got interested in art through my wife. "We just kind of fell into buying at the right time."

I take him on a tour around the house, pleased to have somebody appreciate the works.

"I keep meaning to take a class on how to buy art," he says, when we're sitting in the living room drinking coffee. "But I just don't have the time."

"You don't need to take a class," I say. "Let me get you the name of a good dealer in Dallas who can guide you."

He thanks me and looks at his watch. "Baby, I have to get on the road."

"You staying here for a few days?" I ask Taylor.

"I don't know. I should get back. My girls need me."

"Take your time," Alex says. "They'll be fine with Martha. You need to get this thing with Sarah taken care of."

Some husbands wouldn't want their wife sticking their nose into a hornet's nest like Curtis's religious organization. But Alex probably knows that Taylor can't be held back, so he might as well get some points by giving his approval.

"We'll figure something out," I tell him.

Taylor has to have Alex drive her out to her mamma's so she can pick up her car.

"After that," I say, "if you have some time, how about coming back here and we can talk."

While I wait for her to come back, I read Bob's autopsy report again. Why would he have had Benadryl in his system? Jack told me he never took the stuff, and as far as he knew Bob didn't have a cold or allergies. The report says there wasn't enough Benadryl in his system to trigger a heart attack. But it *was* enough to put him into a sound sleep.

So Bob's death looks innocent enough. But I'm not ready to let it go at that. I call T. J. Sutter's office and leave a message for him to call back. I don't know if he'll be any help, since he most likely believes that Bob died of a heart attack, but it won't hurt to discuss my doubts with him.

When Taylor comes back, she has changed into jeans and a T-shirt. "Sorry it took so long," she says. "Mamma had a lot on her mind about the funeral." She sighs. "She never liked Jack, but that didn't keep her from criticizing the way his funeral went—everything from the motorcycle brigade to the quality of the punch."

I laugh, but I'm not feeling chatty. I didn't ask Taylor to come back here for small talk. I sit her down at the kitchen table with iced tea.

"I need some straight answers," I say.

She smiles uncertainly. "About Sarah?"

"About Jack."

"I don't understand."

"About California."

She puts her hands up as if to ward me off. "Oh, no. We're not going there."

"Yes, we are. I'm investigating Jack's murder. And anything people don't want to talk about is of interest to me. I've pieced together that somehow Jack got out to California after he was injured. I don't know the how or why of it, or how he got back here."

"Really, honestly. California has nothing to do with Jack's death."

"You're going to have to let me be the judge of that."

She squirms, looking at everything in the kitchen but me. "Have you talked to Walter Dunn? He can tell you everything you need to know."

"I did. And he stonewalled me the same way you're doing."

Fire flares in her eyes. "Right. So instead of pressing him, you figured since we know each other, I'd be easier to put pressure on."

"We do go back a long ways." I speak softly because there may be some truth in what she says. "But Dunn's not talking and Woody said you're the one to ask." I pour us more iced tea and let what I've said sink in. "Now listen to me. I don't know what happened out there. Can't even begin to guess. But I need to have a complete picture of

Jack's life. And this is one big gap. So whatever you know, I'd like you to tell me."

She starts to protest, but I stop her. "Taylor, you know you can trust me."

"And you can trust me! I'm telling you that what happened in California has nothing to do with Jack's death."

She picks up her tea, and her hand is shaking. What in the world is she so afraid of?

"I asked Curtis what he remembered about Jack being missing. He was a teenager at the time. He says he came in one night when you were talking to Bob. You were crying, and he heard you tell Bob you'd 'do what you could.' What did you mean by that?"

We sit silently, Taylor tracing the condensation running down her glass of tea, me watching emotions, from defiance to sadness, flick across her face.

"It makes me sick to my stomach to think about what happened."

"It's a long time to keep a secret."

More silence, but I'm ready to wait it out.

"You got anything stronger than beer in the house?"

I bring out the bottle of brandy Woody and I were sharing last night, and two glasses. You can't let a lady drink alone, especially if you've asked her to tell you things she doesn't want to talk about. Taylor throws back the first slug of brandy all in one gulp, and then shudders.

"We were so goddamn young." Her voice is hollow. "High school kids think the world will always stay the same. I loved Woody and Jack, and until senior year I thought the two of them and my girlfriends here at home were all I would ever need." She smiles wanly. "I remember sitting in this kitchen with Jeanne, her telling me I might change, and me saying no, that my situation was different, that I had the best friends in the best town in the best state, ever."

I picture Jeanne listening and smiling at Taylor's naïveté. A regret goes through me that I haven't had in a long while. Jeanne would have been a good mother.

"But Jeanne was right. In my senior year I started to get restless. Woody and Jack both seemed content to stay here in Jarrett Creek forever. I wanted more. I wanted to go to college and get out into the world. I suddenly felt like their big sister. They were like children that I would always love, and yet I wanted to move on." Her mouth is smiling at the memory, but her eyes are sad.

I get up and put together a plate of cheese and crackers. She's laying into the brandy pretty hard.

"That's why you talked them into going into the army? You felt guilty about leaving them behind, and figured the service would give them a new focus?"

She nods and picks up a cracker and nibbles it. "You remember, when they signed up no one had any idea there was going to be a war. And then by the time Jack had to leave, we all knew the war was coming. If I'd known . . ." She trails off, shaking her head. "But as it was I was tickled to death when Woody and Jack signed up. I had this idea that we would all go out into the world, me to college, them to the army and we'd all come back here better versions of ourselves."

"And then Woody got rejected by the army." I don't want to rush her, but I'm wondering what this has to do with California.

Her shoulders slump. "All of us were devastated. Woody was hurt the most, though. He felt like a failure. Not only did he hate getting rejected, but he also hated leaving Jack on his own. He had always been an upbeat guy and he went into a horrible funk. When he asked if I would marry him, I didn't feel like I had any choice." She throws her hands out in appeal. "I thought if I didn't marry him, he'd . . . what? Die of unhappiness?" She bolts up from her chair as if it has caught fire and paces to the window, leaning her forehead against it to stare out into the fading daylight.

"Taylor, did you talk to Jeanne about this?"

"She begged me not to marry Woody. She said she adored him and knew he was a good man, but she didn't think getting married would be good for either one of us. But I was in high school. I couldn't be told what to do. God, I wish I had listened to her." She turns back to face me. "Now do you see why I blame myself? I ruined Jack's life. And by marrying Woody, I almost ruined his."

"Give yourself a break. All of you were mighty young." I pour her another shot of brandy and take a sip of my mine.

She comes over and takes up the glass. "You can't imagine the fights Woody and I had."

"I'm still waiting to find out what this has to do with California."

She eases back down in her chair, flashing me a crooked grin. "I thought maybe you'd forget about that."

"It's a big piece of the puzzle."

Her words are beginning to slur. "By the time Jack got hurt, Woody and I already pretty much hated each other. But when we heard about his injuries, it brought us back together. And then one day I got a phone call from Bob, wanting to know if I'd heard from Jack. Said he'd called the VA to find out when he could bring Jack home, and Jack had checked out of the hospital, and no one knew where he had gone. I told Bob I didn't know anything about it."

She puts her head in her hands. I don't say a word. California is coming. Eventually she draws a deep breath, takes a sip of brandy and looks at me. "Then one night, really late, I got a phone call. It was from a guy who said Jack had asked him to call me." She closes her eyes and shakes her head. "I'll never forget his words. 'Jack said you'd come and help him out. And lady, let me tell you, he needs help.' I asked where Jack was, and he gave me an address in San Francisco. And then he hung up!"

"He didn't say who he was?"

"Nothing. I didn't know what to think. Whether it was some kind of joke, or what. I went straight over to Bob's and asked if he had heard from Jack. He said he hadn't. So I told him about the phone call. Bob was hurt that Jack had asked the guy to call me instead of him. Bob wanted to go out to California to look into things, but I thought it should be me. I didn't know why Jack had asked the guy to call me instead of Bob, but I figured he must have a reason."

"That must have been the night Curtis heard the two of you talking."

She nods. Tears are slipping down her cheeks.

"What did Woody have to say about all this?"

"He was fit to be tied. He didn't want me to go, thought it wasn't right for Jack to ask me."

"Did Woody think about going himself?"

She shakes her head. "Even if Woody had wanted to go, we couldn't afford it. He was working construction and he knew if he left, he'd lose his job. But he sure as hell didn't want me going out there. He thought Bob should be the one. And he couldn't understand why I insisted. By the time I left, Woody wasn't even speaking to me. I knew that if I went to California, my marriage was over. In a way it was almost a relief."

What she says troubles me. Could Woody have been carrying a grudge all these years? He said he and Jack buried the hatchet, but there's nobody to vouch for that. "Why do you suppose he was so dead set against your going?"

"Woody was always jealous of Jack. After the army rejected him, it got worse. Even after Jack was injured Woody couldn't get it out of his head that I loved Jack more than I loved him." Taylor looks at me with sad eyes. "That was never true. I loved both of them, just not in a marrying kind of way."

"How did you get the money to go to California?"

"Bob paid for it. Up to the last minute he wanted to go with me. You know Bob; he would have done anything to help Jack. But in the end, he was afraid that if he showed up, Jack would reject his help. He finally agreed with me that I'd be the best one to persuade Jack to come home."

The light is gone outside and it feels like we are alone in the world. I can imagine that Bob must have been terrified that if he made a misstep he'd lose his son forever. "So you went off to San Francisco."

"It was so hard. I was terrified. I'd barely ever been out of Texas. I can't even imagine who I was back then. The only thing I could hold onto was that Bob said if I needed anything at all, he'd fly out and help me in a second."

She goes to the sink and gets a glass of water. She still hasn't eaten anything and when she sits back down, I shove the plate of cheese and crackers toward her. She shakes her head.

"You managed to find Jack."

Her expression is deadly grim. "Sometimes I think what happened was nothing short of a nightmare. I found the address. It was in a terrible part of town. Bums everywhere, trash in the streets. The building was run down. And the apartment Jack was living in was in the basement." She shudders. "Jack was filthy. The place was filthy. There was a rat living in his apartment. I saw it!" She squeezes her eyes shut and shudders.

I reach out and put my hand over hers. She grabs it and holds on. "I wasn't a spoiled girl, Samuel, you know that. But nothing in my life had prepared me for having to deal with something like that. The smell. Jack had soiled himself and no one had cleaned him up. I wanted to run out of there and head right back home. But of course I couldn't leave him like that. I had to do something. Jack kept saying he wished they'd left him for dead in Kuwait."

"So what did you do?"

"Took it one thing at a time. First I had to get Jack cleaned up. God it was awful! He didn't have any clean clothes, so I wrapped him in a blanket. It was filthy, too, but the basement was so cold I had to keep him warm. He didn't have any money, and there was hardly anything in the place for him to eat, much less cleaning supplies.

"Bob had given me $100 extra, so I went out and found a little store and bought a few things. You have no idea how scared I was. People out on the street were all wigged out on drugs. People drinking right there in front of the liquor store. I was too scared to try to find a laundry, so I washed Jack's clothes by hand, what little he had. And right in the middle of it—I'd only been there a few hours—all of a sudden this man walked in. Didn't knock, nothing! Almost scared me to death."

"Who was it?"

"The man who put Jack there." Her voice goes dead. "Oh, he was so cool butter wouldn't melt in his mouth. He said he had just heard I was there to visit Jack and he'd come to make sure everything was okay. He said he was real sorry I had found Jack in such a bad state, and that he had a bunch of vets he took care of and he was so overworked that he'd neglected Jack."

If I've ever seen anyone hate somebody, Taylor hated this man. Still hates him. Her eyes are hard and cold. And I know now what knocked some of the pep out of her.

"That son of a bitch."

"Jack was terrified of him. He was literally shaking. I knew I had to get Jack out of there. And I knew the guy would never let me take him without a fight. So I sweet-talked that bastard. God! How I sweet-talked. I told him he was just a saint for helping all those vets, and that I was happy to help him get Jack cleaned up." Her voice is a sneer. "Eventually I managed to get him out of there. When he left, Jack broke down and cried."

I pour us both another healthy slug of brandy. I need it to help this sordid tale go down.

"Who all knows what happened?"

She shakes her head. "There's only one person left who knows the whole story besides me."

"Your husband?"

She laughs, a little hysterically. "Oh, goodness no! I can't even imagine what Alex would say if I told him."

"How about Woody?"

"He doesn't know any of the details. Just that I went to California."

"Oh." It seems clear to me now. "So it's Walter Dunn who knows all of it."

"That's right." She sighs.

"How does he fit into this?"

"Walter was a medic in Jack's company. He was from Bryan, but Jack didn't know him before the war. When they found out they both grew up around here, they became buddies. Then Jack got hurt. While Jack was in the hospital back east, Walter left the service. Before he headed home, he went to see Jack. Jack told him he didn't want to go home. He didn't want people to see him so damaged and feel sorry for him. Walter tried to talk sense to him, but Jack begged him to find somewhere he could go. Walter had heard of a guy in California who was taking in seriously wounded vets and seeing to their needs."

I put my head in my hands, knowing what's coming.

"You can guess what happened. That bastard took all these poor vets' money and barely kept them alive. They had no way to get in touch with anybody. There were no phones. Most of them were bedridden or in wheelchairs and there was no way to get out."

"How did Jack manage to get somebody to call you?"

"Pure luck. One day the city sent somebody by the apartment building because there was a problem with the sewer line. The guy had to get in the basement, and he knocked on Jack's door by mistake. Jack grabbed the chance to ask the guy to call me. We don't know who the guy was, but he saved Jack's life."

"So how did you get Jack out of there?"

"Jack told me how to get in touch with Walter in Bryan. I called Walter and told him what was going on. He was out there twelve hours later."

I'm picturing Dunn's craggy face. "I can imagine how that went over with him, to see Jack in such a mess."

"It was such a relief to have him there." Taylor stops for a moment, hand over her mouth, holding back sobs. "He was furious to find out he'd been duped and that Jack was being held in captivity."

"So what did he do? Did he confront the guy?"

She shakes her head. She's looking down at the table, so I can't see her eyes. "We brought Jack home. That's all."

I recall Jack's welcome home party. Nobody said a word about him being in California. So why was it kept secret? And why is Taylor lying to me now? I know there's more to the story. For one thing, Dunn wouldn't have left the rest of those vets there to rot when they brought Jack home. I still don't know if this has anything to do with Jack's death, but I don't think either one of us can take anymore tonight.

CHAPTER 28

I'm not expecting much from the medical examiner who performed Bob Harbin's autopsy. No one likes to do autopsies, and most MEs do just enough to satisfy the job requirements. This is especially true in Bob's case, where there's no reason to suspect that his heart attack was anything but a natural death.

The ME, Jim Hadley, makes it clear that he's only seeing me as a favor. He's a lean, agile man of forty. He wears a stethoscope around his neck just to make sure everybody knows he's a doctor. I assure him I won't take much of his time. He sits down behind a desk that takes up most of the room in the little box of an office, and waves me to a straight-backed chair across from him.

He flips through Bob's autopsy report. "My girl told me you had some questions about this. It looks pretty straightforward to me."

"Here's the thing. At the time Bob died, we assumed it was due to natural causes. But with his son being murdered so soon afterward, it brought up some questions. First, what was the condition of Bob's heart? Was he a likely candidate for a heart attack?"

Doctor Hadley takes his time reading the relevant section of the report. "A good question, but one that's almost impossible to answer. There's no evidence of past scarring, so he hadn't had any prior episodes; at least not anything major. And I didn't find any sign of blockage. But unfortunately, a fair percentage of people who die of ventricular tachycardia don't present any good reason for it. So in the absence of indications to the contrary, my conclusion was warranted."

"What about the Benadryl in his system? I understand that the dose was sufficient to put him into a sound sleep."

"That's right."

"Here's the problem. I talked to Jack right after he got the autopsy results and he swore his dad would never take anything that might make him sleep so soundly that he wouldn't hear Jack in the night. So I'd like you to set my mind at rest here. Could someone have drugged him with Benadryl and then done something to induce a heart attack?"

Hadley steeples his fingers and stares in my direction, but he's not seeing me. He's thinking hard. "Yes. It's something I wouldn't have looked for, of course. But somebody could have given him a shot of something like digitalis to bring on an arrhythmia." He gets up abruptly. "We keep some tissue samples for several months after an autopsy. Let me do a couple of tests, and I'll get back to you."

Just like that, I'm dismissed, but with more possible answers than I expected. I don't know what I'll do if my hunch is right. But having all the facts at my disposal is my first priority.

I stop for a quick sandwich, so it's almost two o'clock when I get to the motorcycle shop. But I'm in for a disappointment. Walter Dunn has gone off to San Antonio to deliver a motorcycle and won't be back until tomorrow.

I'm almost home when I decide on a detour to Woody's house. The kids are in school today, so there's not the uproar it was the last time I was here. Laurel is at work, and her mother opens the door. She's a fussy old woman, known to have a sharp mind and a sharp tongue. She's eaten up with curiosity about what I want with Woody, but I manage to sidestep her questions and find Woody out back, working.

He's sanding a big cupboard, and doesn't see me at first. When he stops the sander and sees me, he puts it down, and dusts his hands off.

He greets me flatly, in a voice that isn't like him. "What can I do for you?"

"Thought you might have a minute to visit."

He cocks his head at me. "'Visit.' A neighborly visit, or an official visit?"

"Somewhere in between."

I don't know what Taylor was lying about yesterday, but I intend to get to the bottom of it. I'm here to find out if Woody knows more about the California affair than Taylor let on.

We sit down at his little picnic table, this time with iced tea that he's fetched for us. He tucks tobacco under his lip and crosses his arms across his chest. "Okay, let's hear it."

"Taylor told me a little bit about her trip to California to bring Jack home. I was wondering if you had anything to add."

"Taylor said she brought Jack home? That's not true. She didn't bring him home. That big guy did, Walter Dunn." He spits onto the ground.

"I was wondering why you didn't go out there with her."

His look is not particularly friendly. "What did Taylor tell you?"

"I want to hear it from you."

"Couldn't afford it."

"Couldn't, or wouldn't?"

"Take your pick. Jack asked for Taylor, so he got Taylor."

"Sounds like you weren't too happy about it."

He spits again. "Samuel, that's a long time ago. And if you're thinking I held a grudge against Jack and killed him because Taylor went to California to see him, you've treed the wrong possum."

"What did Taylor tell you about Jack when she got back?"

He takes his time answering, "She said Jack had gotten himself into a bad situation and he needed help getting home. She said she straightened things out and she called Walter Dunn and he went out there and brought Jack back." He runs his thumb along his bottom lip. "I got the feeling she wasn't telling me everything. But by then we were fighting so much, my judgment wasn't as good as it could have been. She could have told me anything. I didn't really care what the truth was. I wanted to be done with both of them."

"If you were so mad at Jack, how come you changed your mind after Bob died?"

He shifts in his seat, picks up his tin of tobacco, changes his mind, and sets it back down. "Oh, I'd changed my mind a long time before Bob died, but Jack wasn't having any of it. I had burned my bridges. When Taylor went out there to California, I thought Jack was a threat to our marriage. She kept telling me it wasn't true. I knew he'd lost a leg and his eyes, but I was eaten up with jealousy." He opens the tobacco tin and slips a plug into his cheek. "When Jack got home I went storming over there to tell him to keep away from her. What was I thinking? When I saw him, I realized I'd been an idiot. Now I can see that I'd blamed all my problems with Taylor on Jack, thinking she wished she hadn't married me so she could marry him. I couldn't see the real truth, that she needed wider pastures than this town, and that's something I never could give her."

"But when you saw Jack, you couldn't let it alone, even though you saw how damaged he was, could you?"

He shakes his head, his face full of regret. "I was looking right at him, seeing him all bunged up like that, knowing there could never be anything between him and her, and I still told him he was a son of a bitch, and accused him of trying to take Taylor away from me." He gives a humorless laugh and spits a stream of tobacco. "When Taylor found out, she called me every name in the book. She said Jack had been through hell and I was only making things worse for him."

He spits one last time and takes a sip of tea. "That's what jealousy will do to you. Makes you into a maniac. If I was going to kill Jack, it would have been then. So I lost both of them. Wasn't a month later that Taylor put in divorce papers. And Jack never spoke to me until just before he died." He looks toward his house. "I got lucky. Laurel is a damn good wife for me." His voice is suddenly husky. "I might have lost my mind if it hadn't been for her." He wipes his eyes. "I look at those boys out there on the football field Friday nights, and I wish I could tell them that whatever they imagine their life is going to be, it'll be different from what they think."

"Tomorrow! Why didn't you tell me before? How am I supposed to get ready that fast? You think I can drop everything and go off with you?" Loretta is flustered because she doesn't like last minute arrangements. Still, she loves to gamble, if you use the word loosely. Her upper betting limit is quarter slot machines. Every so often the Mercantile Trust Bank in Bobtail sponsors trips for their senior depositors, one of them being a trip to Grand Coushatta in Louisiana. I've gone there with Loretta a time or two and seen her come home as much as ten dollars down.

"If you've got something to do, we'll go another time."

"Well why does it have to be tomorrow?"

The moment of reckoning has come. We're sitting in her kitchen in the late afternoon drinking coffee. I've put off telling her about my knee surgery, but now she's got to know. "I have a doctor's appointment at the orthopedic hospital in Houston tomorrow."

"A doctor's appointment." She glances down at my knee, then hastily away. "You must have known about it longer than today. And I thought we were going to Coushatta."

"We have to go right through Houston, and I'll stop off for my doctor's appointment."

"Samuel, you aren't making sense. Why didn't you tell me about this doctor's appointment before?"

She's right. I'm not making sense, because this knee thing has me nervous. "I didn't want anybody to know until I've seen the doctor in Houston, but I'm probably going to have an operation on this knee. And the idea about Coushatta just came to me this afternoon. I thought it would be a way to make the trip a little more fun."

She looks at me suspiciously, as she has every reason to do. The only reason I'm combining a trip to the doctor with an excursion to the casino is that my investigation of Jack's murder is taking me there.

"It's all right if you don't want to go," I say.

"No, you need somebody to go with you to the doctor anyway. Why men are so pig-headed about asking for help is beyond me. What time do we leave?"

CHAPTER 29

For some reason, the traffic in Houston is a lot worse than usual, as if they've let all the beginners out of driver's education early. I dodge SUVs and old, big-finned Cadillacs and little BMWs right and left. I wish we'd taken my pickup, which feels more substantial than Loretta's Chevy Malibu.

"Goddamn traffic," I snarl.

Usually she jumps on me about cursing, but now she wisely keeps her opinion to herself, although I can feel the disapproval simmering at my side. "You're just nervous about going to the doctor," she says. Then, as I swerve to avoid a bicycle, "Pay attention."

By the time we're parked at the orthopedic hospital, my palms are slick with sweat. Although I'm snappish with Loretta, she keeps her calm, and I'm glad she's with me.

Two hours later, we're headed out the east side of Houston, and I'm a new man. I liked Doctor Filbert right off, and he assured me that the surgery would make my knee right. "You'll be surprised," he said. "We have so many new surgical techniques these days that within a couple of months you'll wonder if your leg was ever injured." He also told me that like most people my age I've got traces of arthritis in my knees, but nothing to make a fuss over. "I'll clean that up while I'm at it."

Now that I've been sprung from the doctor, I'm actually looking forward to our excursion to the casino, and the closer we get the chattier Loretta becomes. We're spending the night, so she'll get a good twenty-four hours to indulge what she calls her "little vice."

It takes a few hours to get to the Coushatta Casino, just over the Louisiana border, and it's six o'clock by the time we check in to our rooms. We agree to meet for dinner in an hour, giving Loretta time to gamble and me time to strategize.

The place is packed, from a gaggle of cocky young men who can't possibly be twenty-one to one old man who walks with two canes and has trouble slipping coins into the slots.

I don't know how I thought I was going to get information from people working the tables. They are all completely absorbed in what they're doing. But then a blind man in a wheelchair is not your everyday gambler. One of the dealers just might remember Jack.

Walter Dunn told me that Jack liked to play craps and blackjack. "Because of the name, you know. Back in the service he had the nickname Blackjack, because he was pretty good at it. And you don't have to see to play either of those games. You just need somebody trustworthy standing by to tell you what comes up."

There are only a few people at the craps table. I don't really understand the game, but I pick out somebody to copy, and trust that the croupier will pay me when I win. I give up a few dollars and win them back. Just about the time I'm supposed to meet Loretta, somebody relieves the croupier and I figure I'll have a word with him.

He's not too keen on being approached, but I tell him who I am and what I'm after, and he says he'll talk to me, but that he's got to eat his dinner while we talk, as he only has a thirty minute break. He's about forty, tall and rangy, with hair slicked back and a wolfish look about him.

"Yeah, I remember those boys. They come in every now and then. Hard to forget a blind man playing craps." We're sitting in a cramped employee break room with a few plastic tables, where they can eat, and vending machines. The croupier, Felix, is eating a baloney sandwich. There are a few other people in the room, and he calls to one of them. "Harry, you remember that motorcycle group comes in here with the blind guy every so often?"

An older man with a potbelly hauls himself up from another table and joins us, bringing his can of Pepsi and bag of chips. "They have a good time," he says to me. "Why are you asking?"

I tell them what happened to Jack.

"That's a damn shame," Harry says. "What's your interest?"

"Our chief of police is swamped and I've been asked to help out in the investigation. I was chief a while back, and I told him I'd do what I could." Sort of sliding into the explanation, but it seems to work.

"I don't know what we can do for you," Felix says, his mouth full.

"Ever see any signs of problems between any of them? Arguments? People can get funny around money."

"Ha! Don't I know that! We had a couple in here last week came to blows. You hear about that, Harry? She was hitting him as hard as he hit her. Security had to pull them off each other." He gets up and asks if I want some coffee.

"I wouldn't mind a cup." It's past time to meet Loretta, but I'm not worried. She'll be glad of the extra time with her slots.

"Any of that kind of trouble with these men?"

Both of them shake their heads. Harry says, "They have a lot of laughs. I'm a vet myself, and I appreciate them looking out for the one in the chair."

I tell them what hotel room I'm staying in and ask them to mention Jack to their coworkers. "I'd appreciate a call to my room if anybody saw anything out of the ordinary."

Loretta was so busy at her Texas Tea slot machine that she didn't even realize what time it was. She's tickled because she has managed to win $50. Loretta and I have a reasonably good spaghetti dinner and when we go back to the gambling floor, it's much busier. Loretta goes back to her slots and I play a little blackjack and slip in a few questions to the dealers, but I come up empty. But I do manage to come away with a couple of hundred dollars in my pocket.

The next morning I talk to the manager of the casino, a guy who looks disconcertingly like an actor I can't place, with a smirk on his face and a lord-of-the-manor attitude. He assures me that if there had ever been any trouble with the vets, he would have known it. "Tell the truth,

I hope he took away more money than he dropped. I'm all for helping out someone who has sacrificed life and limb for his country."

In a way, I'm glad there were no problems among the vets who brought Jack here. It would be troublesome to find out they weren't as close-knit as it seems. Loretta and I are all checked out and ready to go after lunch. In the daytime there isn't so much action, and I sit down at a blackjack table I hadn't seen before, the only one in the house that requires a $20 bet. I'm up a couple of hundred dollars, so I figure I can get rid of it faster here.

The dealer, Elsie, is a big, bony woman with frizzy hair and a mouth full of teeth so white they look like they were just polished. I let a couple of hands slide by before I broach the subject of Jack and his friends.

"I remember them. You always remember good tippers. And then there's the wheelchair and all." Her voice has the silky undertone of someone who grew up speaking with a Cajun accent.

I tell her about Jack's death. For a split second she pauses, then glances up at the pit bosses' surveillance room and picks the pace back up. "I'm so sorry to hear about that." She deals the cards smartly. "Look at that. You've got twenty-one." She's got twenty and turns over a three.

"You ever see any problems among the guys?"

"Problems?" She shakes her head. "Not among them. But," she glances back up. "Listen I can't talk. It's against the rules. I'm off at one o'clock. How about if you meet me here and I'll tell you about something that did happen." After that she manages to win some of my money back for the house.

When we get back together, she takes me back to the break room I was in before. Elsie has been working here for ten years. "I've supported me and my boy pretty well on what I earn."

I take the hint. "Well, I'd be glad to pay you for your time, seeing as how I'm butting into your dinner." I take out a twenty, and when I see the little frown lines between her eyes, another twenty.

She smiles, and slips the money into her pocket. "I don't know if this is a big deal, or if it's what you're after, but it's something I remember. Your friend Jack was gambling with two of his friends. One of the guys glanced over toward the craps table and he says, 'Well I'll be damned. Jack, you've got a friend over there.' And Jack says, 'Who is it?' And the guy says, 'I don't know his name; I've just seen you talking to him at the café.' So Jack says, 'Let's go say hi.' So they cashed out and left the table." She's eating fruit salad with yogurt. Doesn't seem like much of a dinner.

"In a few minutes he and his friends came back by my station. They didn't stop to gamble, but I couldn't help overhearing them. Your friend Jack was all heated up and he was talking pretty loud. They had to calm him down because his language was a little ripe. You know, fuck him, screw this, screw that."

"Jack had a mouth on him."

Her mouth quirks up in a grin, showing those shiny teeth. "It's not like I haven't heard it before. But it's strange to hear a man in a wheelchair going on like that." She shrugs.

"I can see that."

"After they got him calmed down he said something like, 'He doesn't have any business being here.' And one of his friends said well he was entitled to do what he liked. But here's what was strange. Your friend Jack said, 'Not on my money, he's not.' Seemed like an odd thing to say, don't you think?"

"You sure that's what he said?"

"Hundred percent sure. They were standing in a little group near my table. Then they headed to another part of the casino. I figured they wanted to keep Jack clear of whoever had him fired up."

So that's why the money was missing from Jack's account. Somebody borrowed money to gamble, and Jack didn't know that's what the funds were going to be used for. Whoever it was managed to pay Jack back—except for that last time. But who is it? Gabe LoPresto? He and Jack got on pretty well and spent time together most every day at

Town Café. I can imagine LoPresto thinking he could get away with owing Jack money, and maybe after Bob died, Jack put the screws to him. But LoPresto has a pretty successful business. Why would he need to borrow money?

Maybe it's one of the football players' parents? Some of them cozied up to Jack in the stands during the games. Not that I'd ever thought of it as anything but kindness. But maybe one of them was using Jack as a banker on the side.

CHAPTER 30

Saturday morning doesn't start out to my liking. Checking on my cows is troublesome. My knee hurts like the devil from all the poking and prodding Thursday and from hustling around the casino. Plus, Loretta and I didn't get home until almost midnight last night.

But one thing is going my way. The motorcycle shop is open on Saturdays and when I call over there, Walter Dunn tells me he'll be working there all day. It's eleven o'clock before I get over to the shop. Dunn is working on one of the biggest cycles I've ever seen. The parts he's taken out are laid out next to him. His hands are on his hips and he's glaring at the cycle as if it's a child that's been misbehaving.

"I need a word," I say.

He gestures to the parts. "You can see I'm tied up."

"Sometimes if you walk away from a problem for a while, it's easier to deal with when you get back to it."

"Promised the guy I'd have it to him by four o'clock."

"I had a talk with Taylor, and now I need to talk to you."

He wipes his hands on a rag on his belt and takes his time doing it. "How much did she tell you?"

"Not quite enough." I put some steel in my voice to let him know I'm not in the mood to be put off any longer. "She said you'd know the rest."

He confers with a heavily tattooed mechanic, gesturing to the motorcycle he's promised to finish. The man eyes me and nods to Dunn. We walk out the front door. "Let's go down the road to Smoker's Barbecue. I'll bring back some lunch for the boys."

Smoker's is a wooden shack with picnic tables under a rickety wooden awning out back. It smells so good that I can't resist getting a plate of brisket, even though it's so early. Dunn does the same.

"Taylor tells me when she found Jack in trouble out in California, she called and you came right away."

His mouth is full and he nods. I wait while he swallows. "I blamed myself for not checking out this guy before I sent Jack to his facility. He sounded so dedicated that I never questioned whether he was telling the truth. You don't think somebody will try to make a buck off people who've gotten injured like those boys. I guess if something sounds too good to be true, it is."

"You don't want to believe the worst of people."

"I have to get me a beer. You want one?"

I decline. When he comes back, he's already drunk half the beer, and his face is grim. We sit quiet, and when it comes clear that he's going to wait for me to pull more out of him, I say, "How did you get Jack back here?"

He takes another pull on the beer. "By the time I got to Frisco, Taylor had cleaned up Jack and his apartment—if you can call it that. It was a big room, but just a basement really. Concrete walls and floors, bare bulb hanging from the ceiling for light. Not that Jack needed a light." He runs a beefy hand along his jaw. "I sent Taylor back home and told her I'd take care of getting Jack back to Texas. But first I knew I had to do something about this asshole who was making money off the misery of those vets."

"How many vets were in that place?"

"A dozen, give or take. Men who were in the same situation as Jack, except they didn't have somebody like Taylor to help them out. Filthy conditions. I hardly knew what to do. I was broke. We had just bought our shop and I'd put every penny into it. I called my daddy and told him what was going on. He didn't have much, but he got a little money together so I could at least get the place cleaned up. Had a crew come in. And spent the rest of it on food."

My head is bowed. I wish I'd known about this. I could have helped out with funds. "I was the chief of police, and thought I knew everything that went on in my little kingdom. You all kept this pretty quiet."

"Jack and I were ashamed for different reasons, and I think Taylor was so shocked . . ." He trails off, eyeing the past. Then he shakes his head to clear it. "Eventually it all got taken care of. All of the vets who were there were like Jack, not wanting to be a burden. Once I'd located their families, the relatives were grateful and pulled together the money to pay my dad what he'd lent me."

"You're a good man."

"No, I'm not. I should have checked out the place to begin with."

"If you had, Jack never would have gone there, and no telling how long those other vets would have suffered. Did you ever locate the son of a bitch who did it?"

"He was slippery. He got wind that somebody found out what he was up to and he laid low. But he wasn't as smart as he thought he was. He had used his own name to rent the place, and I tracked him down through the realtor." His smile is sardonic. "Had to put the fear of God into the realtor before he'd cough up the information, but once I told him I'd be calling the Veterans Administration about his part in it, he had a change of heart."

I wipe my mouth. "Anyway, you got those vets out of there, and put the guy out of business."

"Something like that." A shadow passes over his face. "I brought Jack home, that's the important part. In a way, I think he had to go through an experience like that so he could accept his family taking care of him. I had a lot of respect for Bob. He didn't get all teary-eyed. He reamed Jack out for not letting him know where he was."

Something about the way Dunn leaps onto this new subject and suddenly gets all chatty makes me wonder what he's left out. My mind flashes to the article I found in Jack's wallet about the homeless man found in the dumpster, and I bet I know who the man was.

"I expect you're not telling me the whole story."

He sips his beer, never taking his eyes off me. In effect, he stares me down, and I blink first.

"Makes you wonder how many times this happens," I say.

"The VA got an earful from me, but I doubt it made a lot of difference. They don't have the personnel to look into every situation. They're overwhelmed."

"Now I've got something else I need to spring on you." I tell him about my trip to Coushatta and about what the dealer told me.

"Yeah, that was a coincidence. I wasn't party to what went on. I was playing poker at the time. Vic can tell you about it. He was there."

Dunn tells me Vic isn't in today. He takes out his cell phone. "I'll see if Vic will come over to the shop and talk to you." But Vic doesn't answer his phone. "He's the only one of us not married, so it's a little harder to keep tabs on him. But he'll be in Monday."

Back at the shop, I watch Dunn tinker with the motorcycle he's working on and indulge myself in a fantasy of buying one. But then I remember my knee and figure it's not in my immediate future.

I'm surprised when Dunn follows me out to my car. Just before I get in, he says, "About the guy who scammed Jack. I know what you're thinking, and it probably didn't happen exactly the way you imagine. You find who killed Jackie, and I'll tell you the rest of it."

The remainder of the afternoon is a wash. I go by to talk to Curtis again, hoping I can drag something more out of him, but the place is locked up tight. He had that back door lock repaired.

I do some errands, and stop by the café about four o'clock for a cup of coffee. I'm surprised to see Lurleen on duty, since she usually has the weekend off. "I asked to work a shift this afternoon. My mamma has the kids, and I'm about to lose my mind being in the house by myself."

She looks terrible. "Have you had any luck finding out what happened to Jack?"

"I haven't sorted it out yet. But I'll get there."

Gabe LoPresto hollers at me to come over and talk to him and a couple of old boys. Their faces are so animated that I know they are rehashing last night's game, a squeaker of a win that spoiled Needleton's homecoming.

I ask Lurleen to bring me a cup of coffee and she talks me into a piece of fresh berry pie to go with it. LoPresto is happy to have me join them because I didn't go to the game last night. This gives him an opportunity to regale me with a play-by-play account of the drama that led to the win.

"Something has got to be done about Boone Eldridge," Jess Bolton says.

"He won, didn't he?" I say.

"Yeah, but the son of a bitch almost managed to lose again. Same as last time. He took Louis out for the whole last quarter."

"Why did he do that?"

"He's got a bug up his ass about something Louis is doing," LoPresto says. "But this time Collin had a surprise for him."

Collin is the second-string quarterback, a junior nobody has had much faith in. I ask what happened.

"It was Dilly's doing, so you tell it, Jess."

Jess Bolton doesn't even try to swallow his pride in his son. "Dilly has been putting in extra hours practicing with Collin, so this time when coach sent Collin in, he was ready. Surprised the hell out of everybody, including Eldridge." I'm glad for the boy, and a little surprised that Dilly Bolton bothered with Collin. Dilly is known to be pretty pleased with himself—ambitious, and not necessarily a team player. But I expect he realized it's better for his stats if the Panthers win. And if that means drilling Collin in secret, then so be it.

Eventually the game is hashed to death, so we all get up to leave.

My knee is so stiff I can hardly walk. LoPresto stops me. "Samuel, when the hell are you going to do something about that knee? You're hobbling around like an old man."

"As it happens, pretty soon." Somehow, telling Loretta about my surgery has loosened my tongue, so I tell them about my visit to the doctor Thursday.

As usual, since LoPresto knows someone who had knee surgery once, he knows more about knees than my doctor does. So I have to listen to his advice for a few minutes. But I find it comforting to hear that his friend came through with a knee that works as well as before.

After everyone trickles out of the café, I hang behind to talk to Lurleen. There's only one couple left, so when I tell Lurleen that I need to clear up something, she sits down with me.

"I've been going over Jack's finances and I'd like to know if he ever told you anything about lending somebody a chunk of money."

She shakes her head. She's brought a grilled cheese sandwich with her, but it's sitting there getting cold. She hasn't made a move to touch it. "We didn't talk about money much."

"Did he ever lend you money?"

Her expression hardens. "I may not be rich, but I can take care of my kids. I never needed to borrow anything from anybody."

"I didn't mean to offend you. I'm just trying to clean up some loose ends." I sit back and sip my coffee, giving her a chance to unruffle her feathers.

"What gave you the idea that I might have borrowed from Jack?"

It's the opportunity I need. "Well, I noticed when I was at your place the day Walter Dunn and I came to tell you about Jack that your son had a nice looking computer. I got the impression his daddy wouldn't spring for something like that."

She picks up her sandwich, looks at it like it's a dead rat and puts it back down. "All right, Jack did buy the computer for the kids. I didn't like it. He was at my place one day when Will was complaining about homework and said he wished he could have a computer. I told him no possible way, and next thing I know Jack buys them one. He had his daddy go over to Bobtail and buy it. And then Jack paid to have the Internet line put in and everything." She sighs. "I told Will that if he wants to keep that line now that Jack is gone, he's going to have to figure out a way to pay for it."

"And Jack never mentioned lending money out to anybody?"

She shakes her head. "I wish I could help you, but he never said a word."

When I get home, my telephone answering machine has been busy. I have three calls. One is from Jenny, asking me to come over for a glass of wine later, since we missed our usual date last week. The second is from my nephew, Tom, in Austin, wanting to catch up with me. It's unusual that we haven't talked in a couple of weeks. He's my late brother, Horace's, boy, and the best nephew anybody could have. I'll have to tell him about my knee. That will entail fending off his wife, Vicki. She'll want me to come to Austin after I get out of the hospital, so she can keep an eye on me while I get back on my feet. Not that I wouldn't love to take her up on it, but she's got her family and job to take care of. And I don't want to be a nuisance.

The third call is from Dr. Hadley in Bryan. I didn't know doctors worked on Saturday. "Mr. Craddock, I didn't have time Thursday and Friday to do the tests I promised I'd do, but your question about Bob Harbin's blood tests got under my skin, so I stayed late last night to run the tests. You were right. Harbin had a toxic level of digitalis in his system, and no reason on earth he should have been taking it. Looks like that's what you were after. If you have any more questions, call my office Monday."

I phone Jenny and ask for a postponement of our wine date, since I'm planning to turn in early tonight.

After the pie I ate at the café, I'm not particularly hungry, so I make do with a couple of tamales and some coleslaw that I think is still edible. I'm just washing up the dishes when the phone rings.

Linda Eldridge's voice is trembling. "Samuel, I don't know what to do. Boone left early this morning and he hasn't come home."

CHAPTER 31

"It wasn't even six o'clock this morning. He was all ready to go when I woke up. He said he had a couple of things to do and he'd see me later. And that's the last I heard from him."

We're sitting at the kitchen table in the Eldridge house. Linda's huge brown eyes are wild as a spooked horse. She's a pretty woman with a voluptuous figure. She gets her dusky complexion and black hair from her Mexican parents, who attend most of the football games. Linda said she called me because when she tried the police department, James Harley told her she was being foolish, that she should call him tomorrow morning if Boone hadn't shown up by then.

"Boone left at six? That's awfully early. Did he give you any idea what he was going to do?"

"I was still half asleep. I told him nothing was open at that time of the morning, but he said he had somebody he had to meet."

"Is it possible he went fishing?" Boone is known to spend a lot of time fishing, but it would be unusual during football season.

Linda thinks. "He wasn't dressed for fishing. Usually he wears this vest thing that smells to high heaven. And old pants. But this morning he was dressed in regular clothes."

"Has he ever done anything like this before?"

She's kneading her hands on the table. "I guess he has, but he usually tells me if he's going to be late. You know, Boone's job is different. It's not like he keeps regular hours. He teaches a few history classes, but being the coach he's got a lot of free time during the day because he works late after school with football practice." Nerves are making her chatter.

"I expect he practices with the team on weekends, too."

"He works with the boys all the time. Weekends are probably the worst, especially during football season. But if he's called a weekend practice, he'll always tell me in advance. And even if he forgot to tell me, he'd surely be home by now."

"He didn't say when to expect him?"

"No. And I asked my daughter if she'd heard from him—I went out grocery shopping and hoped he might have called while I was gone, but she says no."

"The boys won last night. Maybe he planned something special and didn't want anyone to know about it."

At the mention of last night's game, she frowns and her eyes dart away from me.

"Was there something about last night's game that bothered Boone? I understand it was a close one. Maybe he called a secret practice?" I'm thinking about Dilly working with Collin. I don't know Boone well, but coaches can be funny. Maybe he didn't like the idea that one of his players was training the backup quarterback without him knowing about it, and decided if the boys wanted extra practice, he'd give it to them.

Sweat is beaded on Linda's upper lip, and she swipes at it. "You could be right, I guess. But here's the thing. Boone is usually excited after we win. I tease him that he's just as bad as his boys, getting so worked up. But last night, he was quiet. I asked him if everything was okay. I thought maybe his stomach was bothering him—he has trouble with his stomach. But he said he was just tired."

"Have you talked to any of the boys?"

A hopeful smile lights up her pretty face. "I'm so stupid! No, I didn't. I should have called Waylon."

I wait while she calls Waylon Foster, the assistant coach. But I can tell from her responses that Waylon doesn't know Boone's whereabouts. When she hangs up, she says, "Waylon told me to call Louis. If Boone is with any of the boys, Louis will know."

A call to the quarterback yields the same results. And with that, I'm ready to get uneasy, too. I'm thinking about the attack on Boone. Nothing ever came of it, and everybody pretty much forgot about it after the boys won the next couple of games. "Do you think I could get a cup of coffee?"

She puts her hand to her mouth. "I'm so sorry, I should have asked if you'd like something."

When I've got coffee settled in front of me, and Linda has sat back down, I say, "I'd like to talk to you about the night Boone was attacked. Were you here when he got home?"

She shivers. "You think his being gone has something to do with that?"

"No way of knowing just yet, but it could."

"Yes, I was home that night. It scared me to death."

"Tell me exactly what happened."

"Well, Boone got a phone call and told me he had to go meet somebody."

"What time was that?"

"It was late, about ten o'clock. We were getting ready for bed. I asked him why it couldn't wait until morning."

"He didn't say who it was?"

She shakes her head. "I thought maybe it was one of the boys' parents. That happens, you know. Usually it's about grades, or if a parent thinks his son isn't getting enough playing time. But they don't usually call so late."

"How long was he gone?"

"Forty-five minutes, an hour."

"What did he tell you when he got home all banged up?"

"He looked terrible and I asked him where he'd been, but he said it didn't matter. We argued, because I said if one of the boys' dads attacked him, he had to tell the school. He said he'd taken care of it, and that was the end of it. I had to drive him to the clinic in Bobtail so

207

they could take X-rays of his arm and clean him up, and we dropped the subject."

Is it a coincidence that both the beating and Boone's disappearance happened after Louis was benched at the end of a ballgame? Even though this game turned out all right, maybe somebody didn't like Louis being taken out of the lineup. "Was Boone ever threatened by any of the parents?"

Linda's mouth twists and her voice is bitter. "Only all the time. I know I'm the coach's wife, and I shouldn't say anything. I like football, but people take it way too seriously, if you ask me. But the threats aren't about harming him physically. It's usually that they're going to see to it that Boone loses his job, or they're going to yank their boy off the team, or they're going to boycott. That kind of stuff."

"Was Boone ever worried about any of it?"

"Not that he told me. He tried to be polite, but once or twice he blew up."

"Anything recent?"

Linda hesitates. "After the loss to Bobtail, Louis's mom just about blew a gasket. Boone was pretty upset about that."

"His mom?"

"Yeah. Louis's dad is a hard man, but he's mostly hard on Louis. Louis's mom is after Boone all the time."

It sounds like I need to talk to Louis's family. It's also possible that the team wanted to teach the coach a lesson for taking Louis out of two games, so they cooked up some kind of prank. I get a mental image of Boone trudging back home after being left out in the country somewhere.

"Did he say whether Louis's mom was upset last night?"

"We didn't really talk about it. I was home before him. I always am. He comes back on the bus with the boys after an away game. And like I said, he was quiet when he got home."

She pauses, her eyes locked onto mine. "Usually when he comes in, he's hungry. I made chili for him, but he said he didn't want anything. Then he went into his office—he calls it an office, it's just our guest room with a desk there. And he shut the door."

"And that's not a regular thing?"

"He never does that. He hates paperwork, and only does it when he has to—and even then he usually leaves the door open. Last night he didn't come out of the office for a long time, and when I knocked on the door he told me to go on to bed, that he'd be a while."

"What time did he come to bed?"

"I don't know. I woke up, but I didn't look at the clock."

"Do you mind if I take a look in his office? I might spot something that would give us a clue to where he went."

"Please, please . . ." She gets up. "I'll show you."

We walk down the hallway. I say, "You know, it's still possible he's just running late. Does he usually call you when he's going to be late?"

"No, he's not very good about that. He loses track of time when he's at practice."

What strikes me first about the desk where Boone does his paperwork is how neat it is. I expected a coach to be messy. I tell Linda that, and she smiles. "He's fussy that way. Always likes everything neat. He says it's because high school boys are so messy that at home he needs things to be in their place." She's standing in the doorway with her arms crossed. I get the impression that she isn't there to keep an eye on me so much as so to have company.

It's strange going through another man's desk drawers. There's no point of reference to tell you if something is off, or if whatever looks unusual to you really is off, or if this is the way he always does things. Or if what looks normal to you is evidence of a problem.

Boone has a master calendar on the wall next to the desk, and he has made liberal use of it. Games are noted in pen, while extra practices, meetings, and appointments are in pencil. All the notations are clear. No baffling initials, no cryptic phrases to arouse suspicion. He had a doctor's appointment two weeks ago, right after he was attacked. There's a dentist's appointment coming up next month. Monday he's supposed to take his car in for service.

In one drawer I find a collection of newspaper cuttings describing the football games, large ones from the Jarrett Creek weekly newspaper, smaller ones from the San Antonio paper. On top of the cuttings is a memo sent out to all state coaches, reminding them to submit the names of players they deem worthy of all-star status.

On one corner of the desk there's a stack of papers. I look them over and see that they are history tests that Boone needs to grade. A small town coach always has to put in time teaching a couple of classes, and Boone teaches Texas history. Unlike some coaches, he's actually got a reputation for being a pretty good history teacher. Next to the tests is a tray containing bills. "You mind?" I ask Linda.

"Nothing to hide."

The bills are the regular expenses—water, electricity, gas, house payment, car insurance, and TV and Internet service. There's a second mortgage payment that appears to be a month overdue. And there's a small bill for payments for another house. "What is this?"

"Fishing shack." Her grimace is indulgent. "Nothing but a one-room cabin. The land is worth more than the house. It's over by the lake. Boone keeps a little motorboat there that he can hitch up to the car. He uses it to fish out on the lake. This time of year Boone never goes to the shack, but during the summer before school starts he likes to take his buddies out there. Sometimes we have barbecues."

"Could be he went out there with somebody and they had a little too much to drink . . ."

She shakes her head. "I drove out there right after dark, ready to give him hell. But it was closed up tight."

I look through the bills again. Something tugged my attention the first time, and I'm trying to remember what it was. I stop at the TV and Internet bill. "Where does Boone keep his computer?"

Linda straightens up and walks over to the desk. "It's usually right here. Maybe he took it into the den, or maybe one of the kids has it. They share another computer and sometimes one of them will take Boone's if they both want to use it at the same time."

We look in the den, then the living room, but don't find the computer. I sit on the sofa to wait while Linda goes off to ask her kids if they are using it. She comes back into the living room shaking her head. "They don't have it." Her daughter has followed her back down the hall. A young teenager, she's dressed in pajamas with a pattern of Scottie dogs. She's got her mother's eyes, but is taller and is all arms and legs.

"Mommy, what's going on?"

Linda puts her arm around her daughter's waist. "Nothing, sweetie. Mr. Craddock just had a question and I thought maybe Daddy would have the information on his computer."

"Where is Daddy?"

"He's going to be home late. Go on back to bed now."

The girl looks from her mother to me, and back. "You asked me earlier if I'd heard from Daddy. Why did you ask me if you knew he was going to be home late?"

Smart girl. Linda sighs. "Okay, Allie, I don't know where your papa is, but I'm sure he's fine."

"But how do you know?" Panic edges into the girl's voice. "Maybe those men who beat him up last time hurt him again."

"No, baby, I'm sure he's fine. He's just gotten busy—you know how busy he is—and he's just not home yet."

"Allie." I get up and walk over to the two of them. "You said 'those men who beat him up.' Do you know anything about them?"

The girl flushes and darts a glance at her mother. Linda frowns at her daughter. "Allie, do you know something you haven't told me?"

Allie glares at me. "I don't know anything."

Linda grabs her daughter's arm. "If you know who attacked your daddy, you have to tell!"

Allie wrenches her arm away and massages it. "I told you I don't know anything!"

Linda puts her hand to her heart. "I promise you won't get into trouble, but you need to tell me if you know more about it."

Allie backs away, a few steps down the hallway. "You say I won't get into trouble. But I will."

"Allie, I don't want to scare you, but it's possible your daddy is in trouble. You need to tell anything you know. Please." Linda has tears in her eyes. Her daughter's eyes widen at the sight.

"It's nothing, really." She glances over at me and I give her the stern eye. She bites her lower lip and makes a little whimpering noise. "I was just . . . all right, I'll tell you. The night Daddy got beaten up, I sneaked out with Liz." She swallows and can't look at her mother.

"Okay," Linda keeps her voice even. "Let's go sit down." She walks to the sofa and her daughter reluctantly follows. Linda pats the sofa next to her, but the girl shakes her head. Linda looks up at her. "I don't like that you sneaked out. You know that. But I promised I wouldn't get mad, and I won't. I won't ever mention it again. Just tell us what happened."

"We didn't do anything. Liz had a fight with her grandmother— she lives with Liz and her folks. Liz was really mad. We just walked around." She sits down in a chair facing her mother and nibbles at her thumbnail.

"It's okay, sweetie. I know you wanted to be a friend. Just . . . next time, please tell me. I promise I'll try to understand."

I sit down so I can see both of them. "You saw who attacked your dad?" I say.

Allie nods. Her voice is tearful. "I was so scared. I was a block away. Daddy got out of the car. I hid so he wouldn't see me." She puts her hand to her mouth and gives a little sob. "And then these two men got out of a car across the street. Daddy put his hands up, like he thought they were going to hit him. Like this." She throws her hands in front of her face. "They grabbed him, one on each side of him, and they all started walking down the street." The girl is sobbing now.

"Maybe you can get her some water?" I say to Linda.

Linda jumps up and kisses her daughter's forehead. "I'll be right back."

Allie pulls her legs up and wraps her arms around them as if to make herself as small as possible.

"Did you recognize the men?" I ask her.

She shakes her head.

"They weren't from around here?"

"No!"

Linda comes back with the water and sits down on the arm of the chair next to her daughter and puts her arm around her shoulders.

"Try to remember what they looked like," I say. "Were they taller or shorter than your dad?"

Allie looks up at Linda. "Mommy, are they going to hurt him again?"

"Sweetie, we don't even know that this has anything to do with where your daddy is right now, but please answer Mr. Craddock's question."

The girl sips her water. She shivers and nestles up next to her mother. "They were about the same height as Daddy, but not as fat. I don't mean fat," she glances hastily at her mother. "I mean, just not as big."

"Can you remember how they were dressed?"

"Just regular." She cocks her head. "But I remember thinking they looked like they were from the city."

"What made you think that?"

"They weren't dressed in jeans and T-shirts. They had like the kind of pants men wear to church."

"Khaki pants?" Linda interjects.

"That's it. And button shirts. Short sleeves, but buttoned up."

I smile at her. "You're very observant. That helps me a lot. Hair color? Length of hair?"

"I guess it was just regular, because I don't remember anything funny about either one."

"How about the car they got out of?"

She shrugs. "Just a car. A dark car."

"You're doing great, Allie. Now, tell me what happened when they walked away. Did you hear anybody say anything?"

"Only Daddy. He said, 'I did what you wanted.' But I didn't know what he meant."

"And the men didn't reply?"

"One of them laughed." She squeezes her eyes shut. "And then they took him down the street."

"When you say 'down the street,' what do you mean?"

Linda says, "The street ends about half a block down, and the lots there are overgrown."

Having to comfort her daughter seems to have given Linda strength. "I need to get Allie settled down. You don't have to stay." I get up and she walks with me to the door. "We'll be okay," she says. She thanks me for coming. "It helped me steady myself."

"Let's talk in the morning. And call me if he comes home, no matter what time it is."

I walk to my pickup, but I'm not ready to leave just yet. I drive to the end of the block, pull a flashlight out of my glove compartment and get out to look around. I don't see any immediate signs of disturbance, but I'll come back for a better look in the light of day.

CHAPTER 32

I n the morning, I go down to the pasture before daylight to take care of my cows. Linda didn't call last night, and I have a feeling I'm going to be working overtime. There's a nice nip in the air. It's just turned October, a time of year when we get some crisp, clear days.

At eight o'clock I phone Linda. She says there's still no word from Boone.

"It's time to get the highway patrol involved." She says Boone took her old Chevy and gives me a description. I tell her I'll be right over.

I stop on the way to tell Loretta what's going on and ask if she has some coffee cake or rolls I can take over to Linda. She's already been up baking this morning and cuts half a coffee cake for me to take.

"Should I keep this quiet?" she says.

"No need to. Somebody might know something. If you hear anything you think is important, call me out at Boone and Linda's."

I park in the Eldridges' driveway behind a brand new Taurus with dealer plates. Looks like Eldridge didn't waste any time replacing the motorcycle. The Taurus is a surprising choice for Boone, though, not as showy as his usual rides.

Dark circles under her eyes tell me Linda hasn't slept much. But she has made the effort to put on makeup and is dressed in a skirt and blouse. She's grateful for the coffee cake. "When Jimbo gets up, he'll be starving and I don't think I'm up to cooking this morning."

Allie comes into the kitchen, still in her pajamas, her eyes bleary with sleep. "Did Daddy come home?"

"No, and you need to get ready for church."

Allie screws her face up. "We can't go to church with Daddy missing."

"That's exactly why we need to go to church, to pray for him."

Her tone leaves no room for argument. Allie stomps out.

I tell Linda I'll be back later to look in on her. I've got a few people I want to call on before they go off to church. But first I go back down to the end of the street. In daylight, I see that the lots down here aren't deep, but they are overgrown. Ten minutes of poking around doesn't turn up anything that might tell me more about what happened when Eldridge was beaten up.

Despite what Allie said about the two men, I haven't abandoned the idea that Boone's disappearance might mean he's the victim of a nasty prank by football players who weren't happy with Boone taking the quarterback out for the fourth quarter.

I don't like having to confront Louis Cardoza's father, especially first thing on Sunday morning. Hector Cardoza is a hard-working man, but he's also a hardheaded man who takes everything personally. He owns the beer distributorship for the county, and he has gotten huffy with just about everybody he distributes to. Oscar Grant down at the Two Dog Bar got so aggravated with him that he stopped having Hector deliver his beer, and instead picks it up himself from a warehouse in Houston every month.

From the way Hector is dressed when he answers the door, in baggy shorts and a ripped T-shirt, I'm pretty sure he's not a church-going man. "Samuel, what can I do for you?" Suspicion hoods his eyes.

"I'm here to talk to Louis, if he's up."

"My boys are both up. I don't hold with kids sleeping half the day. But I need to know what this is about."

He keeps me standing on the porch. "I need to know if Louis and some of the players might have been involved in a prank having to do with Coach Eldridge."

"My boys don't do pranks."

"Hector, Louis is a leader on the team. Even if he wasn't personally involved, he might know something about it."

I'm hanging onto my temper by a thread. Cardoza sizes me up, trying to see how far he can go. Then he sticks his head back into his house. "Louis, get out here."

Louis is dressed in jeans and a bright, white T-shirt. His hands are stuck in his back pockets, but as he approaches us, he pulls them out and lets them hang by his side. He tries to read his daddy's expression, then hopes to find more in mine. "Yes sir?"

"Mr. Craddock needs to ask you a question. I don't need to tell you that I want the truth."

"No, sir. I mean, yes sir." His cheeks flare up red.

"Son, have you gotten wind of any prank involving Coach Eldridge?"

"Like what?"

His daddy's voice is like a whip. "Like anything!"

"No sir, not at all."

"What's this about?" Cardoza says.

"Coach is missing. Left yesterday morning and didn't come home."

"And you think my son has something to do with that?" His voice jumps a couple of decibels.

"Hector, I don't know your son. I only know he's the quarterback, and that a lot of people were upset when he was kept out of the game against Bobtail and again last Friday night. I thought maybe some kids decided to take Boone for a ride and make him walk home. Kid stuff."

Louis's face is bright red now. "No, sir. Nobody would do anything like that. I mean, if they did, I don't know anything about it."

"Can you think of anybody who might have been madder than anybody else about what coach did?"

"If I was you," Cardoza's voice cuts ice, "I'd look to that blowhard LoPresto and his gang. They're mighty quick to talk about retribution when the coach makes decisions they don't like."

"I'll talk to Gabe. Sorry to have disturbed you."

"Mr. Craddock?"

Cardoza frowns at his son.

"Yes, Louis?"

"Will you let me know if you find coach? He's the coach, and he's fair. If he kept me out, he had his reasons. I'm not mad." The boy's father would do well to take some lessons from his son.

As I haul myself into my truck, I hear sirens out on the highway. I have no reason to believe it has to do with Boone Eldridge, but it makes me nervous anyway.

By now I'll have to wait until church is over to talk to people, so I swing by the Eldridge place to see if Boone's car has shown up. When I get there, a highway patrolman is sitting in his car in front of the house. In his fifties, he's got his hat tipped way back on his head, and is listening to a country and western station on the radio.

He climbs out of his car to greet me. He's a bigger man than he looked sitting inside, with a paunch that looks like he's carrying a bowling ball inside his shirt. I introduce myself and tell him Linda called me last night when Eldridge didn't come home and I told her to call the highway patrol.

"Craddock." He sizes me up. "I remember you. Not that we know each other, but I remember hearing your name. You used to be chief of police here and made yourself a little reputation. I thought you'd retired a good while back. Why did the Eldridge woman call you?"

"Our current chief is having some medical problems, and I guess she thought I might be the right person to talk to."

He laughs. "I'm reading between the lines here, but I expect what you're not telling me is that whoever is in charge with the chief gone is two cards shy of a deck."

"He's okay; just green. You boys find Boone Eldridge's car?"

"Not yet. I thought I'd come by and ask the wife some questions. By the way, my name is John Ryder."

We lean against the car. "I've gotten some information from Linda Eldridge," I tell him, "but it won't hurt for you to ask again. Maybe she'll remember something she left out." I've been thinking about that missing computer, and I mention it to him.

"Uh, oh. That doesn't sound good. Sounds like maybe he took off under his own steam. Maybe afraid somebody would find something on the computer that he didn't want known. How well do you know him?"

I shake my head. "Just to see him coach."

"Any rumors about him being into porn? Anything he wouldn't want to have found out?"

"Never heard anything like that."

"Eldridge. Wait a minute. I'm remembering the team lost to Bobtail this year, didn't it?"

"You have to bring that up?"

He chuckles. "I know a couple of old boys who would have taken him out behind the woodshed after that game. They lost their shirts."

"They were gambling? On a high school game?"

"Hell yes. Some people will gamble on anything." He throws his hands up in denial. "Not me. I'm too close with a dollar. I'm about ready to retire and no way I'm risking one red cent."

"I'm with you on that." I straighten up. "Not much use me hanging around here. Would you ask Linda to call me if she needs anything?"

"I sure will."

I head to my truck, but what Ryder said about people gambling on the game sinks in. And my heart sinks with it. I walk back over to where Ryder has already climbed back into his car. He sticks his head out. "What's up?"

"Something I need to mention to you."

"Get in the car, here. Sun's about to kill me."

I tell him about the coach's beating at the hands of two strangers. And I tell him about the two men I saw in the stands that at the time I speculated were talent scouts from college.

"I don't like the sound of that," Ryder says. He thinks about it for a minute. "You say the daughter said Eldridge told them he'd done what they asked?"

"That's the way she remembered it."

"It's possible he threw that game."

I stare out the front window at Eldridge's house. "Lord, I don't want to think that. I can't even begin to imagine what the town would do if they thought the coach threw the game." And I'm thinking about how his poor wife would react if she knew. "I hope there's another explanation."

But it makes sense. Friday night Eldridge had kept Louis out of the game again. And Linda told me Boone didn't seem all that happy that the boys had won. Before I can get too far on this train of thought, Linda drives up with her two kids. When they get out of the car, Linda is scolding her son. "Your grandma is going to have a fit when she sees how you scuffed up her new car. Now go inside and get a rag and clean it off." I guess it's not Eldridge's car after all.

Ryder and I climb out of his car and approach the porch. The boy stops when he sees us, mesmerized by Ryder's gun.

"Scoot!" Linda says.

When they are inside, Linda turns to us. "The kids are driving me crazy. They're so upset." She puts her hand to her mouth as if to hold back the question she wants to ask. But then she blurts out, "Are you here with bad news?" Her eyes are wide with fear. "Have you found Boone?"

"No ma'am. Nothing like that." Ryder takes off his hat and introduces himself. "I just thought maybe you could help me with a few questions. Mr. Craddock here has filled me in on most of it."

About then, Ryder's cell phone starts up a racket. "Excuse me just a minute." He steps away and turns his back.

I walk up onto the porch next to Linda, worried because I hear Ryder's voice, urgent. He comes back holding his hat in his hand.

"Ma'am I'm sorry, but I'm going to have to come back later. We have an incident to deal with, and I'm going to have to help get things sorted out." He flicks his eyes in my direction, eyebrows raised, and I get the idea that he has something to say to me.

"But what about Boone?"

"You know, until he's been gone forty-eight hours, we don't really get too excited, and you shouldn't either." He meets my eyes and moves towards his car, but then he turns back. "There is one thing, though. Chief Craddock told me your husband was beaten up not too long ago?"

"You think that has something to do with it?"

I chime in. "Ryder told me that there have been people betting on the games and some people lost a lot of money on the game with Bobtail. So I need to ask you something straight out."

"Anything," she says.

"You won't like this, but it's got to be asked. Have you ever had the impression that Boone didn't do his best to win a game?"

Linda's eyes search mine, her expression turning furious as she understands what I'm implying. "You're right, I don't like it." She looks over at Ryder, hovering near the porch. "Are you two suggesting that Boone would deliberately throw a game?"

I let out a sigh. "You and Boone have any money problems?"

Her hands are on her hips now, her dark eyes hard as steel. "Not any more than anyone else." Her chin comes up. "Boone loves football, and he loves this team. He would never do anything like that. And I resent you saying so. It's like you're blaming Boone for disappearing."

"I'm just trying to figure out why those men beat up on Boone, and how it fits with what your daughter overheard Boone say to them."

"You keep my daughter out of this." She moves in my direction, pointing down the steps. "Matter of fact, I think I made a mistake calling you. I'd like you to leave now. Mr. Ryder, I'm assuming the highway patrol will keep up the search."

Ryder is fingering the rim of his hat. "Of course we will, but like I said it'll be forty-eight hours before we take it too seriously."

Linda makes a disgusted sound. "Just get out of my sight."

"Linda, I'm sorry to have upset you. But everything ought to be considered when you're thinking about why Boone left."

"I'll thank you to keep your considerations to yourself and not go spreading a rumor all over town," she says.

"No one will hear it from me." I clamp my hat on my head and slink down the steps.

When we reach his car, Ryder says, "Something tells me the lady protests too much. But now we've got bigger problems. I don't know what's going on in this little town, but you've got a couple men with guns threatening each other over on Third street."

"On Third? What's the address?"

"Not sure exactly. The cross street is Persimmon."

"Oh, for heaven's sake! That's Jack Harbin's place. He's the boy who got murdered."

CHAPTER 33

I pull up behind Ryder's car two blocks from the Harbin place. We can't park any closer because the street is cordoned off at the corner. An ambulance idles at the curb. The EMS team is standing on the sidewalk, arms crossed, looking up the street toward Jack Harbin's house. It takes about twenty minutes for an ambulance to get here from Bobtail, so this situation has been going on for a while. I remember the sirens I heard earlier as I was leaving Louis Cardoza's house.

Ryder and I duck under the tape. Two highway patrol cars are parked in front of the house along with the two Jarrett Creek squad cars. The patrolmen and cops are hunkered down behind their cars.

There's a black SUV parked on the lawn in front of Jack's house. A man is crouched behind it holding a nasty-looking weapon I don't recognize.

"What the hell?" Ryder and I duck low and make our way to the nearest highway patrol car, where one of the officers is sitting down smoking a cigarette. His shotgun lies across his legs.

"Elroy, what's happening?" Ryder says.

Startled, the patrolman tosses the cigarette onto the street, brings himself to a squat, and tips his hat. "Morning, Officer Ryder." He points toward the house. "A neighbor called us about an hour ago and said some guy had gone up to the house several times pounding on the door and screaming to be let in."

"I assume that's the guy behind the SUV?" Ryder says.

"Yes sir, that's what it looks like. The neighbor said the last time he went up there somebody inside opened the door and gunfire was exchanged.

"Anybody know who he is?"

"No, sir. We got here about twenty minutes ago and found the situation like this. He's been holding us off with his weapon and he and a man in the house have been yelling at each other back and forth."

"Anybody get shot?" I ask.

"We don't know if anybody inside the house was injured or killed. But the guy outside seems to be all right."

"Well why the hell isn't anybody challenging the guy behind the SUV?" Ryder says.

"We tried and he threatened us, too. Said he'd shoot anybody that comes near him."

"Well, I'll be damned," Ryder says.

The man positioned behind the SUV suddenly springs up and runs to the front door and starts pounding on it. I recognize him now from the police department flyer they sent me from Mississippi. It's Marcus, of Marcus Ministries. "Curtis, you let me in there," he yells. "I have rights, and you know it. God has put you under my . . ."

The door is yanked open and a hand pokes out holding a gun. "You go to hell!" It's Curtis's voice and he pops off a couple of shots.

Marcus hollers and goes down, holding his leg. "You've shot me!" he screams.

"I'll shoot you again if you don't get out of here!" Curtis slams the door.

Ryder's face is red from having to crouch down. I imagine that belly of his is giving him as much trouble as my knee is. I pull myself up using the handle of the car and reach out to help Ryder up.

"Are you crazy? You're going to get shot."

"Curtis isn't going to shoot anybody else."

"You sure?"

"I know a little something about this situation."

Ryder grabs the car handle like I did and hauls himself up. He nods toward the man on the porch who is writhing around on his back, moaning. We can see the blood on his pants now. "What are we going to do about him?"

"Let me take care of it. Curtis!" I holler. "This is Samuel Craddock. I'm going to get this man off the porch. I don't want you to shoot me."

Silence from the house.

I start to walk around the front of the patrol car, but Ryder grabs me. "I don't advise you to do anything until he acknowledges you."

I glance at the house and back at Ryder. "He's shot the only person he's after," I say.

"If you say so." Ryder joins me and we walk toward the porch.

One more time I yell, "Curtis, we're approaching your victim now. Just give us a minute."

Marcus is moaning. He's about forty and as big as Walter Dunn, with an oddly smooth face and collar-length hair. There's a spreading stain of blood along his left thigh, but it doesn't look too serious. If a major artery had been hit, blood would be gushing out. I stare down at him. "Your name Marcus?"

"It might be. I need an ambulance. I'm hurt bad. And you need to arrest the man who shot me."

"Can you walk if you're supported?"

"I surely don't think so."

I look at Ryder. "You think we can drag this man between us?"

"I suppose we don't have any choice. Those young ones aren't likely to put themselves in harm's way."

We each grab an arm and start dragging. Marcus yelps. "You're going to make it worse."

"Well then stand up," Ryder says. "You're not hurt that bad."

We manage to get Marcus to his feet and support him on each side. My knee protests all the way to the patrol car, where Marcus slumps to the ground.

Ryder says, "One of you boys get that ambulance over here."

"I need to know your full name," I say to the victim.

"Who are you?"

"Chief Samuel Craddock." It slips out without me thinking about it.

"I don't know why it's any of your business."

"All right, we'll do it your way." I reach down and feel his back pockets and drag out his wallet.

"Give that back!"

I fish out his driver's license, which confirms that he's Marcus Longley of Waco, Texas.

Suddenly James Harley charges over to me from where he's been hiding. "What the hell do you think you're doing here?" he says.

Ryder sizes up James Harley and says, "He's with me. You the police chief?"

"I sure am."

"So you'd be Rodell Skinner?"

James Harley flushes. "No, Chief Skinner is on medical leave. I'm acting chief while he's gone."

"I didn't get your name."

"James Harley Krueger." He sets his hand on his gun, as if to assure himself that he's got some power.

"Well, Chief Krueger, I'm Officer Ryder of the Texas Highway Patrol, and I'm the senior man here. Can you tell me who all is inside the house?"

James Harley darts a look at me. He could easily chew right through a two-inch nail. "It's Curtis Harbin, and we believe he has his family with him."

I'm struck by his use of the word "we." Maybe he thinks he's become royalty, but more likely he's worried that there may be some unknown blame to be apportioned and he wants to get a jump on sharing it.

"And what makes you believe that?" Ryder says.

"We talked to Becky Geisenslaw next door, and she said she heard a car get in late last night and she heard female voices. She looked outside and saw Curtis and a woman and some young children she didn't recognize."

"Has anybody tried to talk to Curtis?"

"We figured first things first. We had to worry about the man outside the house here."

"You mean the man who just got shot?"

"Yeah. They were both shooting. For all I know everybody inside is dead."

Ryder turns to me. You said you know something about these people?"

"The victim is Marcus Longley of the True Marcus Ministries," I say.

"True Marcus Ministries, huh? Never heard of it."

"It's one of those cults that descended on Waco in honor of that Branch Davidian FBI fiasco back in the nineties."

Ryder snorts. "And you know about this how?"

"It's complicated. I'll tell you about it over a beer sometime."

"I can't wait." He turns to James Harley. "Now that the ambulance is gone, maybe it's a good idea to try to talk to whoever is inside the house."

"Wait." I put up my hand. "James Harley, could you send some-body over to see if Taylor's still in town and bring her over here?"

"I know she's still in town," James Harley says. "Her mamma got sick and Taylor had to take her to the doctor on Friday. And the doctor told Taylor she ought not be left alone for a couple of days."

James Harley's wife is a nurse, and works for the town's only doctor, so she'd know.

"Good, then see if somebody can find her."

"But why do we need Taylor?" James Harley says.

"She's Curtis's sister-in-law. If Curtis has his wife in there, he might be persuaded to talk to Taylor."

"Well that may not be necessary." James Harley puffs out his chest. "I'll try and talk him out of there. Just give me a minute and I'll assign somebody to go get Taylor." He swaggers away.

Ryder smirks at me. "This little town hasn't seen this much excite-ment in a long time."

Suddenly I notice that the crowd has increased considerably, everyone dressed in their Sunday clothes. Driving home from church, they've stopped to get in on the action. Loretta is waving at me, so I step over to tell her what's going on.

"You want me to go around back and see if I can talk to them?" she says.

Loretta is not a brave person, so I'm taken aback by this sudden boldness. "Absolutely not! You stay away from there. That man is dangerous."

"Oh, don't be silly. Curtis is a coward, always has been. That's why he likes those guns."

"That may be, but a cowardly person is more likely to shoot somebody on a whim than a person with self-confidence is. Anyway, James Harley is going to see if he can't get Curtis to come out."

"We all know how well that's going to work." She looks toward the house and folds her arms in a stubborn pose. "By the way, have they found Boone yet?"

Her question wrenches me back to the problem of Boone Eldridge's whereabouts. "No, he's still missing."

"Maybe he was in a car wreck."

"Highway patrol would know about that and somebody would have notified Linda."

"Not if he wasn't on the main road. He might have been somewhere where nobody would notice if his car was off in a ditch."

"We'll have to check that out." James Harley is about to make his move, so I leave Loretta and go back to Ryder. He's lent James Harley a bulletproof vest. James Harley has a bullhorn in one hand and his firearm in the other. I want to tell him not to be too free with the use of the gun, but don't know how to say it without humiliating him.

Ryder apparently isn't worried about hurting James Harley's feelings. "Chief Krueger, you know how to use that gun?"

James Harley looks at the gun, a big Colt .45, as if he hadn't thought of that before. "Yes, sir, I've taken the gun safety course just like every-body else."

"Then you know not to be too quick to pull the trigger."

"I know that son of a bitch better not fire first," James Harley says.

His eyes and mouth tensed up with determination, James Harley walks over to the end of the sidewalk leading up to the Harbin house. When he puts the bullhorn up to his mouth, the onlookers get quiet. He pushes the button and the bullhorn gives a squawk. "Curtis, if you're in there, you need to let me know everybody is all right."

I'm surprised and impressed that James Harley has said the right thing, and that he spoke in a strong, confident voice. I had expected him to say something like, "Come out with your hands up," or some sort of TV talk. Maybe there is promise in him.

Silence. The house might as well be deserted for all the action James Harley's words elicit.

"Anybody in the house. I need to know people are all right. Just flick one of the shades open and closed, so I least know you're hearing me."

For several seconds there is no reply, but then there's a sharp cry from inside.

"At least somebody's in there," Ryder says. "And they're alive."

Ryder and I walk over to stand next to James Harley, who hands me the bullhorn and takes out a handkerchief to wipe his brow.

"Ask him if he'll send the women out," Ryder says.

"No," I say. "He's paranoid about his wife and girls. He won't take that well."

I hear a car door slam and someone running. I turn to see Taylor trotting toward us. "I can't believe this! That goddamn Curtis! Is Sarah in there?"

"Seems like she might be," I say. "I'm thinking you could let her know you're here, and maybe she can persuade Curtis to come out."

"He won't hurt them, will he?" She's trembling.

"There's no guarantees," Ryder says firmly. "But we'll do everything we can to defuse the situation."

He shows her how to use the bullhorn. "Just speak kindly, but firmly. Tell him you're concerned about your sister and just want a sign that she and the children are all right."

Taylor says just what Ryder told her to, and then adds, "Curtis, I know you love your family and don't want them to come to harm."

The door cracks open and then widens. A woman's voice, high and scared says, "Taylor, Curtis is hurt. We need help."

Taylor starts forward, but Ryder grabs her from behind. "No ma'am, this could be a trap. Her husband might be trying to lure you in there."

He puts the megaphone up to his mouth. "Ma'am, I see you at the door. Your sister is here, and we want to help you, but you need to show yourself."

The door opens wider, and Sarah steps outside, blinking in the bright light. She puts her hand up to shield her eyes. "Taylor?" She sways on her feet.

Taylor wrenches free and runs to her sister and grabs her as she slumps onto the porch.

CHAPTER 34

Ryder is the first one to reach the house. His Sig Sauer "Equalizer" drawn, he steps over the women and throws himself to one side of the door. He slowly peers inside and his shoulders relax. He lowers his gun to his side and gestures with a nod of his head for the rest of us to come inside.

Curtis is lying on the living room floor, his eyes closed, one hand clutched to a seeping wound in his side. Oddly, there is a rosy lump on his forehead. "Send in the EMS," Ryder hollers. "It's all clear here."

Three young girls in their early teens huddle together on the sofa, clutching each other's hands, all as pale as if they'd been in prison. Curtis and Sarah only have two daughters, so I'm wondering who the third girl is and where the boys are. It's unbearably hot in the house, which could account for Sarah fainting. I find that the thermostat is turned off. I flip it back on and hear the immediate whine of the air conditioner.

Then I go back to the girls and say to the one who looks oldest. "You three go into the kitchen." I nod in that direction. "Get yourselves some water." They get up, but they seem so uncertain about whether to obey me that I go with them, shooing them in front of me. I sit them down at the kitchen table and get water for them. "It should cool down in a minute. You all need something to eat?"

They stare at me mutely, and for a second I wonder if they are in their right minds. But then one of them, who looks to be about twelve, speaks up. "We haven't eaten since yesterday."

The older one grabs her arm. "Hush!"

I fling open the refrigerator. It's almost bare, but there is a jar of peanut butter and some jelly. In the cupboard I find a box of saltine crackers. I put them on the table with a knife. "Get some food in you."

When I go back in the front room the EMS team, a hefty young man and a tall blonde woman with muscular arms, are coming in with their equipment. They crouch down to take a look at Curtis, who is stirring. The man moves Curtis's arm away from his side. "This doesn't look too bad," he says.

The wound isn't in a strategic place, and isn't losing enough blood to account for Curtis being passed out on the floor. "You see this?" The woman points to the lump on Curtis's head.

"Somebody clocked him," the man says. They both rise and step away to make way for a couple of highway patrolmen who are taking pictures of the scene.

"Let us know when we can get him out of here," the woman says.

"Looks like he's waking up," I tell her. "And we'd like a couple of words with him. Shouldn't take long. You can go out and get your trolley so it'll be ready to go."

Taylor has helped Sarah to her feet and brings her inside, where it's starting to cool down. Sarah is leaning so heavily on her that Taylor staggers under the weight, so I get on the other side, and together we take Sarah into what was Bob's bedroom. Two boys, about ten or eleven, are already there, one lying on the bed, the other one pacing around. "Mamma!" the one pacing says, and throws himself at her.

Sarah musters strength to grab the boy to her. She closes her eyes and lays her cheek on the top of his head. The two of them cling to each other like shipwreck victims. The boy on the bed, who looks to be the older of the two, sits up, and I see that he has a bruised face. I have a feeling I know how he got his bruises and how Curtis got his lump, and anger surges up in me. I step to the bed and bend down to talk quietly to him. "What's your name, son?"

"Ben."

"What happened to you?"

He stares at me, his mouth tight in a way that tells me he has no intention of talking.

"It's all right, Ben. You can tell Mr. Craddock." Taylor sits down on the bed next to him. He shies away from her. Her eyes widen. "You don't know who I am, do you? I'm your aunt. Your mom's sister. I haven't seen you in a few years."

"Where are the girls?" Sarah is alert now and panicked.

"They're fine. I took them in the kitchen to get them out of the way and gave them something to eat. Now you sit down."

She sinks down next to Taylor.

"The girls said they hadn't eaten in a couple of days. Same with you?"

Sarah flushes. "They ought not to have told you that."

"I'm sorry, Mamma, I told Annie she shouldn't have said anything." The oldest girl is standing in the doorway with a plate of peanut butter and crackers. She holds it out to the younger boy.

"Thank you, sister," he says. There's a lofty tone to his voice, as if he feels like it was her duty to bring him food. I'm wondering what has been done to these kids.

I go back to the front room to find out what Curtis has to say for himself. When I get there I find EMS ready to wheel him out on the trolley. I could have saved myself the trouble of coming to hear Curtis talk, because it's clear from the grim set of the faces surrounding him that he's refusing to say anything.

I have no patience left for him. I step up close and say, "Curtis, enough is enough. What the hell do you think you're doing putting your family in danger? And having a fistfight with one of your sons. Not to mention having a goddamn shoot-out like you think you're in the Wild West. What the hell is wrong with you?"

He opens his mouth and I find I'm not quite done yet. "And don't you dare tell me it's none of my business. You've made enough of a screw-up. Somebody has got to talk some sense to you. Now what are you doing here, and why did that guy Marcus come gunning for you?"

I guess I'm saying what just about everyone is thinking, because nobody says a word or makes a move to stop me. Only the blonde EMS woman says anything. "Whoa," kind of an aside to her partner.

Curtis tries to sit up more, but he groans through gritted teeth. "All right, but I'll talk just to you," he says, looking at me. "I don't want anybody else in here."

"Okay, let's clear out," Ryder says.

"What the hell?" one of the troopers says. "Who is he?"

"I'm not leaving this man's side. He's in custody," James Harley says, glaring at me.

"Can I have a word?" Ryder takes James Harley's arm and pulls him aside.

He talks low to him, but I know he's telling James Harley that the Texas Highway Patrol has the upper jurisdiction and that I have permission from him to take a statement from Curtis. I'm glad Ryder didn't take James Harley to task in front of everyone.

When they are done talking, James Harley hollers, "Okay, everybody clear out!" Saving face.

"Talk to me," I say when Curtis and I are alone.

He runs a hand over his mouth. His eyes are full of fury. "You were right. That son of a bitch was looking to get his hands on my oldest daughter."

"And another girl, too, looks like."

He closes his eyes and his voice is a snarl. "We stole her. They're going to be after me, but she begged to go too. She and my girl had been set up in separate quarters. Both of them going to be married to so-called leaders." He opens his eyes again and they burn into mine. "My wife was trying to protect our girl by saying she was sick. But that could only go on so long." He clenches his mouth, and then spits out, "Why can't a man trust a soul in this world?"

"Why didn't Sarah tell you earlier what was going on?"

His face twists, and I'm pretty sure I'm seeing self-loathing in action. "She was scared to. Said she didn't think I'd believe her."

"Would you have?"

He lets out a tormented groan and thrashes his legs around. Curtis isn't a man who's likely to change much, but he's facing a future without the church support he thought was solid behind him and knowing he has made serious errors in judgment.

"Look, Curtis, you did the right thing getting your family out of there," I say. "Except for the shooting."

"He came after me. It was self-defense, pure and simple."

"Still, you could have called the police and let them handle it."

"Well, I didn't. I put my trust in myself. And I'm not sorry."

I'm figuring he will be sorry when he has to spend money he's so careful about to defend himself in court. But that's for another day.

I step to the door and call out for the EMS. "You all take him to the hospital and get him patched up."

"What about my family? When the Brother Elders hear about Marcus, somebody is likely to come after them."

"I'll see to it that your family is safe," I say.

When the EMS crew has taken Curtis away, with a trooper to guard him, I tell James Harley and John Ryder what Curtis told me.

"The chief of police in Waco is going to want to know about this," Ryder says. "And I'll alert the highway patrol center up there. Looks like that Marcus bunch is a nest that needs to be cleaned out."

I go in and get Taylor out of the kitchen and bring her up to date. "I have an idea about how to keep them safe, but you may have to persuade Sarah."

I tell her my idea. Taylor agrees that Sarah may make a fuss, but when we tell Sarah the plan she only puts up a token resistance. Before long, I hear the roar of a couple of motorcycles and I go out to meet Walter Dunn to introduce him to the people who need protecting.

It's another hour before I'm back home. As soon as I've poured myself a cup of coffee, I call Linda Eldridge, not knowing if my call will be welcome.

She tells me Boone still hasn't shown up. Her voice is subdued, like she's resigned herself to the worst.

"Mr. Craddock, I'm sorry I sent you away this morning. I know you're just trying to help."

I tell her there's no need to apologize, that I know that she's under a lot of strain. "Your kids okay?"

"It's getting harder to keep them from knowing something is wrong. And I haven't heard anything from the highway patrol. At least they haven't found Boone's car."

I tell her I'll come by first thing in the morning, and that she should try to get a good night's sleep.

I've never been so glad that Jenny and I have a wine-sipping date for this evening. I've got a lot to unload.

CHAPTER 35

I've just come back up to the house from seeing to my cows the next morning when the phone rings. It's Vic from the motorcycle shop. I'd almost forgotten about him in all the excitement.

"I hear you were looking for me Saturday. Sorry, I was down in Galveston for the weekend." He says he'll be working at High Ride all day, and I can come in anytime. He tells me that Curtis's two boys are being brought to the shop. "We're putting 'em to work. Walter says they need a little dose of the real world."

I call Ryder, and find out that the highway patrol had a quiet night, for once. "Still nothing on Coach Eldridge's car. But it's been forty-eight hours now, so we can put a little more manpower into it. But what I'm thinking is that it's going to be a local person who finds Eldridge, dead or alive."

Before I head for the motorcycle shop, I swing by to check on Linda Eldridge. I can tell when she opens the door that she's had a shock. Her face is dead white. "What's happened?"

Without a word, she walks over to the edge of the porch and vomits over the side. I hold onto her until she's done. She obviously hasn't eaten much; it's mostly bile that comes out.

When I get her sat down in the kitchen with a glass of water she says, "Just before you got here, two men came to the door. They said they were looking for Boone. They said they were expecting a call from Boone and they hadn't gotten it. I told them I hadn't seen him since Saturday morning." She starts to shiver.

"Did they say what they wanted?"

"They didn't have to. When I told them I didn't know where Boone was, they said I'd better not be lying, that if I was, they'd be back. They sounded so mean." She puts her head in her hands. "I think I'm beginning to figure out that Boone has done something bad. Probably what you were asking about."

She describes the two men as looking like the same ones her daughter saw the night Boone was beaten up. I don't like it one bit. I don't like strangers coming to town and threatening people. I don't like that Boone Eldridge has brought this on his family. First Curtis, and now Boone, each in his own way letting weakness drive their actions. And both of them brought low because of it. There's no doubt now that Boone Eldridge has gotten himself involved in trouble that he's not likely to be able to weasel out of.

"Well, at least we know they haven't killed him," I say. "It may be a matter of money. If Boone can manage to pay them off, he'll be okay."

"But if he threw that game . . ."

She doesn't have to finish. If Boone threw the game, he'll never coach football again, never hold his head up in this town. His kids will be tormented. It's a bleak prospect.

Suddenly Linda stands up and looks at her watch. Her expression has gone from fear to fury. "I'm not going to sit around and wait for Boone to show up. I'm going to work this morning. If Boone needs to reach me, he can call me there."

I get to my feet. "I think that's a good idea. It will keep you from worrying so much. There still might be a good explanation for what's happened."

Tears spring to her eyes and she draws a couple of deep breaths. "I wish I believed that, but meanwhile somebody has to bring some money in for this family."

When I arrive at the motorcycle shop, Vic is explaining to Curtis's wide-eyed teenage boys how he plans to repair the engine on a big

Harley-Davidson. You couldn't have taken those boys to Disneyland and entertained them any better.

Vic tells them to keep their hands off the parts lying around, but he gives them a manual and shows them the page that identifies the parts and tells them he's going to give them a quiz when he gets back. I'm curious why they gave Vic the job of working with these boys, seeing that he's the only one of them without a family. But he seems to do pretty well with them.

We step outside to enjoy the nippy weather. Vic lights up a cigarette. "Walter told me you were interested in the last time we went to Coushatta with Jack."

"That's right." I tell him what the blackjack dealer overheard. "Walter says you might have seen who Jack was talking to."

"I did. Jack and I were playing blackjack, and all of a sudden I see this man I know by sight, but don't know who he is. I tell Jack I think he's from Jarrett Creek, and Jack wants to go over there and say hello. I wheel him over to the craps table next to this guy and tell him Jack came to say hi. And then things get a little weird. The guy turns around, and his mouth falls open and he looks at me like he's seen a ghost. He doesn't say anything for a second and Jack says, 'Who am I talking to?' And the guy kind of laughs and says, 'It's Boone, Jack. How you doing?'"

"Boone? Are you sure that's who it was?" My heart drops to my stomach.

"Yeah, the high school coach. I didn't know him at the time, but I saw him again when I came to a game a couple of weeks ago with Walter."

"So did Jack and Boone talk to each other?"

"They did, but they both acted a little strange. Jack asked the coach what he was doing there. And the coach got all jolly and made a big fuss about how glad he was to see Jack, and what a coincidence it was. You know, clapped him on the shoulder, good buddy stuff. But he was looking at Jack like he'd seen the devil."

"What did Jack say to him?"

"Jack said he'd see the man back in Jarrett Creek and that they needed to talk and then Jack told me he wanted to go back and play some more blackjack. After that it happened pretty much the way the dealer told you. Jack was mighty pissed off. He said the coach shouldn't be gambling—especially with his money. We asked him what he meant, but he said that was between him and Boone. That was the end of it. He didn't want to talk about it anymore. We went off and had some drinks, and that was that."

On the way back to Jarrett Creek, I try every which way to put the best face on what I've heard. But there is no good way to get out of what I know. I thought the worst thing that could have happened was that Boone Eldridge had gotten himself into trouble as a gambler. But now I know he's done worse than that.

I feel like I need to talk to some regular people and try to figure out what to do next, so I stop by the café. The regulars are there, gathered around Gabe LoPresto. I remember what Louis Cardoza's dad said yesterday morning about asking LoPresto if he knew anything about where coach was. So I pull up a chair, wondering if I'm dealing with a whole gambling cartel I didn't even know existed. I listen for a few minutes while the men wrangle over a couple of plays that were called in the game Friday night.

Lurleen brings me coffee and leans down to ask me if I've found out anything about Jack's killer. I tell her I'm working on it and may have something soon.

When the squabble comes to an end, LoPresto says to me, "I hear you were in the thick of that shoot-out yesterday. That family has had more than its share of troubles."

"Curtis brought trouble on himself," I say.

"How so?" LoPresto is grinning like a fool.

I tell them about his involvement with the survivalist group in Waco.

One of the men leans in, his eyes narrowed. "Seems to me he was protecting his family. You can't charge him with anything."

"I'm in no position to charge him or not charge him. That's up to the law."

"By God, if it was me and my family, they'd have a court fight on their hands if they tried to tell me I couldn't use my lawful firearm to protect my wife and kids. So I don't see how you can say he brought it on himself, if someone came after him."

"I'm talking about his decision to throw in his lot with somebody without bothering to find out anything about his past. If he'd done his homework, he would have known this guy Marcus was a criminal and wasn't anybody he should be involved with."

"It's a matter of trust," the man says.

"You lie down with dogs, you get fleas," LoPresto crows. He likes a good argument. But his statement brings me to the reason I'm here.

"You all know Coach Eldridge is missing?" I say.

"I heard that, but I didn't take it seriously," LoPresto says. "Where would the man go? You think he's got somebody on the side?"

"You know his wife," one of the men pokes the man next to him. "He'd be crazy to look elsewhere."

"Anybody here ever gamble on the football games?"

They look at me uneasily. "Well sure," LoPresto says. "We have a pool down at the office, and anybody can get in on it. I don't think the law is too excited about that."

"I'm talking about big gambling. Like with a bookie."

"On a high school game?" Dilly Bolton's dad sneers.

"Hold on," LoPresto says, sizing me up. "I've heard something about that. You know my sister lives in Houston. Her husband likes to bet on college and pro games, and he told me once that somebody asked if he was interested in betting on high school games, too. My brother-in-law said he thought it was crazy, but the guy told him there was serious money to be made on Texas high school football."

241

"I'll be damned," somebody says. "If I'd known that, I could have been rich by now."

They all laugh. It's not serious to them, because it would never occur to them that their coach would be involved in something so sordid.

Only LoPresto realizes there's more to it. He acts like a buffoon half the time, but I know he's a shrewd businessman when it comes to his real estate business. "Why are you asking?"

"Those guys who beat up Eldridge a few weeks ago? There's some question that they might have something to do with gambling."

"What?" Bolton says. "I thought that was just somebody mad about the team losing to Bobtail."

Again, it's LoPresto who gets the connection. "You're not saying Eldridge gambled on the games, are you?"

"Anybody ever hear any rumors of that?" I say.

None of them have. "But if I find out that's what Eldridge has been up to, and he threw that game, I'm taking a horsewhip to him," the gun guy says. He's still riled up about our gun talk and looking for a target. He doesn't know I'm thinking that Eldridge's gambling problem took him a long way farther than just throwing a game.

LoPresto's face has grown fierce. "You're thinking he threw the game." I nod.

"Son of a bitch. So that's why he's skipped out of town?"

"Where would he go?" someone says.

"I'd look in Mexico," the gun guy says. "If he stays around here, he'd be in a hell of a fix."

"You think those boys who beat him up last time might have gotten hold of him and done worse?" LoPresto asks.

"I know they haven't gotten to him yet, because they called on Linda this morning."

"Serves Eldridge right if they find him," somebody says.

LoPresto shakes his head. "I imagine he's pretty desperate about now, trying to find some way to get them off his back."

And just like that, I know where Boone Eldridge has gone.

CHAPTER 36

Five hours later, I find Eldridge in the Coushatta Casino at the roulette table. He's doing pretty well, with a stack of chips in front of him. I slide in next to him. On a Monday afternoon, it's not busy, only five people at the table.

He looks to see who's crowding him, and his mouth goes slack when he sees me. But he puts on a front. "Well look who the cat dragged in."

"Boone, I thought I'd find you here."

"You a gambler?"

"Not especially. Why don't you cash out, now, and let's go somewhere we can talk."

Eldridge gestures expansively to the table. "I can't leave now. I'm on a roll."

"How much do you owe?"

He goes still, and when he looks at me, his grin is like a death head. "I guess you'd say it's gotten a little out of hand. I'm going to have to have a nice long streak of luck. And I've got a good start on it."

The croupier asks if Boone is in or out.

"Oh, in. For sure." He places a stack of twenty-dollar chips on red and another one on even.

We watch the ball hop around and land on twenty-two red. "See what I mean? I'm getting there."

I'm a patient man. I can wait until his luck changes, which it surely will before he thinks he's won enough. It takes about an hour. By then Boone has gotten reckless, so when he loses, he loses a big chunk.

He bows his head for a moment, and then shoves another bunch of chips out there, which he also loses. Still, he's up by more than he had when I got here.

"Maybe you could use a break," I say. "Looks like things have turned around for the time being."

I can see the sickness in him; see that it takes all his will to pick up what's left of his stash. "I'll be back in a little bit," he says to the croupier, and tips him three twenty-dollar chips. The croupier gives him a two-finger salute.

We go into the coffee shop. Boone is so restless he can't keep his eyes still. They dart around the room as if he's looking for something. I don't know if he's watching for the men who are after him, or if he's still thinking about getting back to the table. But I know that he doesn't recognize Texas Highway Patrolman John Ryder, sitting patiently at a table with a cup of coffee and a magazine in front of him.

Boone says he's not hungry, but I order us each a hamburger. I don't know when he'll get his next meal.

"Two men came by and threatened your wife this morning."

His face goes pale, and I see how slack the skin has gone around his jaws. A man losing control of himself. "What two men?"

"You know who."

He swallows. "I told them to leave her out of it."

"And you believed they'd listen to you?" I sigh. "Boone, how'd you ever get involved with people like that in the first place?"

Boone massages the back of his neck and moves his head back and forth. "College."

"You ever throw any games for them back then?"

He bares his teeth in what's supposed to be a smile. "I don't know what you're talking about. It's a little gambling that got out of hand, that's all. Nobody's talking about throwing any games."

"That night you got beaten up? Your daughter saw you and over-heard what you said."

Eldridge has managed to slough off everything else I've said, but the mention of his daughter cuts him. He puts his fist on the table. "Who all knows about this?"

He's a gambler, through and through, still laying odds that there's a way to weasel out of what he's done. And he's still thinking I don't know he killed Bob and Jack Harbin.

The waitress plops down the hamburgers. I pick up the top bun and peer at the gray piece of meat. I open the ketchup bottle and douse the meat with it, place the two pickle chips on it, and the single slice of tomato. Boone watches me. He's ordered a beer and he sips it, letting his hamburger lie there.

"How'd you get Jack Harbin to lend you money?" I say, before I bite into my burger.

He fakes a chuckle. "Did he tell you I lent him money?"

"You paid it back every time except the last time. Is that when you got out of control?"

"It wasn't a lot of money. Just a stake."

"Would seem like a lot to some folks. I'm guessing it seemed like a lot to Bob."

"Like you said, I always paid it back." He's desperate for me to believe him.

"And then when you couldn't pay it back last time, Bob got tough with you. He worked hard so that Jack would have enough money to live on if anything happened to him. So he leaned on you a little. You figured with him out of the way, you'd be able to manipulate Jack better."

"Hey, manipulate . . . that's a harsh word. I persuaded Jack to give me a little more time to pay him back."

I chew a bite of hamburger, taking my time. I'm thinking about the tequila that Boone brought to Jack and Bob as a peace offering the night before Bob's supposed heart attack. Either the bottle was spiked with Benadryl or Boone slipped it into Bob's drink.

"But Jack didn't buy into it, did he? Even with Bob gone, Jack insisted on getting his money back, and you couldn't get it for him. What did you tell him, that you and your wife had some extra expenses and you just needed a little help?"

Boone picks up a pickle chip, looks at it, puts it back down.

"But when Jack ran into you here at the casino, he knew what you'd been doing with the money. What happened? He tell you he was going to go to the school board and have you fired for gambling?"

Boone looks like he's going to put up a protest, but suddenly he looks up, and freezes like a rabbit in the sights of a shotgun. I turn my head and see two men walking toward us. I recognize them as the two men I originally took for college football scouts, and I stand up and wipe my mouth with my napkin. Out of the corner of my eye I see Ryder stand up, too.

"Boone, we've had trouble finding you." Up close, I see these are hard-looking men. The one who spoke has a scar across his cheek.

"You boys back off," I say. "Your business with Boone is done."

"Oh, really?" scar-face says. "And who are you to tell me when my business is done?"

"My name is Samuel Craddock. I've been given the responsibility of investigating the murder of two men in Jarrett Creek, Texas. And I'm here to bring Mr. Eldridge back on those charges."

"You and who else?" the other one says. They're smirking.

"Him and me," Ryder says. His hand is on his gun and he's smiling as friendly as if we'd all run into each other in the best of circumstances.

"You two are mighty cocky for a couple of old geezers," scar-face says.

"Oh, what is that old saying?" I look at the ceiling. "I guess I'm slipping, I can't remember. Something about old age and treachery."

Scar-face doesn't see the humor. He says to Ryder, "You're not about to pull your gun with all these innocent bystanders here. Eldridge, get up and come with us like a man."

Boone's face is pleading, but he gets up. "You don't mind, do you?" With a shaking hand, he picks up his beer and puts it to his mouth. But then he flicks the glass, throwing beer in scar-face's eyes.

The other one swings at Eldridge, but I bring my cane up to stop the blow. Meanwhile, Ryder slips his gun out and brings it level with his chest and walks over to join us.

The few people in the restaurant scramble out of their seats. I pick up a napkin and hand it to scar-face. "Clean yourself up. You think we're fools? That we came here by ourselves? You think this is the movies and we want to be heroes? Think again. You wouldn't have gotten two steps outside the casino before you were surrounded."

Ryder grins at me. He knows I'm lying.

"Now get on out of here." I gesture toward the door with my cane.

"Don't think Eldridge will live to go to trial," scar-face says. And the two of them stalk out.

Ryder puts his gun away and sighs. "I better go talk to security and make sure those boys get sent on their way."

"I don't understand." Boone is practically crying. "Couldn't you have them arrested?"

I pat his shoulder. "Boone, I could have if we actually had anybody waiting outside. As it is, Ryder here is going to have to call us up an escort."

"Jesus Christ." Boone sits down abruptly. Sweat is trickling down from his hairline. "You mean you were bluffing? You have no idea what those guys are like."

"Maybe not. But I don't see them here in front of us."

Ryder gestures toward Eldridge's hamburger. "You going to eat that?"

Boone shakes his head. "I thought you were going to talk to security?"

Ryder and I smile at each other. I say, "No need to go after security. Trust me, they will have heard about this little incident, and they'll be here any second."

CHAPTER 37

Except for Oscar Grant, the owner, Walter Dunn and I are alone in the Two Dog. It's the only place that passes for a bar in Jarrett Creek. At night people can convince themselves that it looks pretty good, but in the afternoon, like now, it's just a dive, pure and simple.

Dunn and I have things to discuss, but first we have to listen to Oscar complain that since Rodell Skinner was sent to dry out, his business has fallen off considerably. "I never thought I'd say it, but I miss having him around."

Eventually he goes off to do something else and Walter and I take the opportunity to move to one of the two tiny tables shoved up against one wall.

"I understand they've got the coach on a suicide watch," Dunn says. "That poor devil."

"That's what they're calling it, but the truth is he's being held in isolation to keep him from being murdered by the thugs he was in debt to."

Dunn sips his beer. "That gambling is a terrible sickness."

"I don't know what's worse, the gambling, or the need to save face."

"I don't know what you mean exactly."

I move my leg to ease it. Somehow since I've found out I'm going to have the surgery, it's been bothering me more. "If Eldridge had been willing to admit his gambling habit and get some help, it would have been hard, but not impossible. But he couldn't stand to lose his place in the community. He knew he'd lose his job and everybody's respect. So he killed two people on account of it."

Dunn looks away, scowling. "How's his family?"

"It's a mess. Linda can't stay here. Everybody's being nice to the family now, but eventually her kids will start being harassed. They're at an awful age."

Dunn kind of smiles and hunches forward in his chair. The chairs are so rickety that his squeaks in protest. "I guess you didn't ask me here to talk about Eldridge, though. Or to tip a few in Jack's honor."

"Although we could do that, too."

He salutes me with his beer and brings it up to his mouth.

"I'm here to satisfy my curiosity," I say. "You know what about."

Dunn stretches his neck, as if it's gotten stiff. "I suppose you've earned the right to know the rest, a little reward for finding out who killed Jack." He smiles. "You better be sure you want to hear it, though. It's not going to be easy on the ears."

"I have to hear it."

"All right, you asked for it." Still, he hesitates for several seconds as if he's plunging into cold water. "Back when I knew Jack in Kuwait, he told me he was scared to go into the army and that he had his buddy shoot him in the foot to get out of going. And when that didn't work, he decided that whatever happened, happened. But I don't figure he ever thought it could be as bad as it was."

"Maybe that's why he was so scared before he went in. Maybe he had some idea of how bad it could be."

He cocks his head at me. "Were you ever in the service?"

"Air force. But I never had to fight in a war."

"I went in the army because they said they'd give me an education. I thought I'd like to be a doctor. Couldn't begin to afford medical school. But I thought maybe I could be an EMT or something like that. Being a medic in the army cured me of all that."

I'm pretty sure he'll get around to the point sooner or later. He looks into his beer bottle. "You want another one?"

I'm not going to let him drink alone. I pull out my wallet. "I'll pay for it, but I'll let you run up there and get them." I pat my leg.

"Seems like more than a fair deal."

He comes back and settles in. "Did you know Jack died on the battlefield?"

"He told me he thought he'd have been better off if he had."

"I'm the one who saved him. Shocked his heart back. After that, I felt like I owed him my support. Seems like I never could do it right, though. He didn't want to come back here and be the object of pity and I thought I was doing him a favor finding him that place in California."

"That wasn't your fault. It was the fault of that sorry son of a bitch who scammed those guys."

"Right after I got out there, after Taylor called me, Jack tried to kill himself. Took an overdose of pills he'd managed to squirrel away. Here I came to the rescue again." His mouth twists in disgust.

"My daddy was a drunk," I say. I don't bring it up much, but Dunn has a right to hear it. "He had his reasons, but sometimes I felt like he was trying to drink himself to death. But he used to say, 'If you're born to hang, you're not going to die any other way.' You know what he meant?"

"Yeah, I've heard that my whole life, too. But it strikes me that's a kind of fatalist attitude. How could it be predecided that Jack was going to go through so much and then die in his bed at the hands of a two-bit gambler?"

I don't know why it strikes us funny, but we both laugh.

"You told me that things back in California didn't happen the way I thought they did. So you didn't kill that guy?"

He smiles. "Not exactly. What I did was give Jack the opportunity to kill him."

So now the real secret comes out. "How did you do it?"

"Well, it wasn't easy, as you can imagine. Jack was in a wheelchair and blind. But he said if he didn't kill that guy, the rest of his life would be pure torture. He figured if he could rid the world of that piece of shit, it would give him something to hold onto." Dunn's voice goes shaky, and I look away from him.

"So Taylor and I talked about how it could be done. And we came up with a scheme. She had already met the guy—his name was Phil. Next time Phil came around she sweet-talked him, rubbed him up every which way, told him he should come around again and she'd have sex with him."

"You're kidding."

"Girl should have been an actress. But maybe Phil just wanted to believe he was her dream man. Anyway, she told Phil she'd make sure Jack had some pills in him so he wouldn't know what was going on." Dunn pauses and squeezes his eyes shut. Then he takes a long drink of his beer. "You know what that son of a bitch said? He said, 'Oh, it might be fun if Jack got to hear us.'"

"Were you there for this?"

"Hell no, I would have killed the guy right then and there. Taylor said she wanted to do that, too. But she improvised. Told him that was a great idea, that she'd bet Jack would like it too."

"Dear God."

"So she and Phil set up a date. I bought Jack a gun and then we practiced so Jack and Taylor could get the timing right. It went down just like it was supposed to." He shakes his head, smiling a little. "Taylor told me it was easier than she had ever imagined. She thought being in on killing somebody would be the hardest thing she ever did. But she said helping Jack kill that guy didn't bother her one bit."

"How the hell did they manage it?"

"The plan was that she'd have the guy on the bed. We practiced, so Jack would know where to aim the gun. When she got him in position, Taylor planned to tell Phil to stay right where he was, that she was going to put on something sexy that would drive him wild. And she told him to talk to her while she changed. So while he was talking, Jack knew exactly where he was. He pulled out that gun and shot him. Shot him three times."

"Didn't anybody hear the shots?"

Dunn grimaces. "If anybody heard shots, they never said a word about it."

"And you got rid of the body in a dumpster."

"First I got Taylor out of there. She was all packed up and ready to go as soon as we took care of Phil. After she left, I went in and cleaned up. That night I took the body to a dumpster."

"You never told anybody else about this?"

He shakes his head. "Couple of the guys knew that something bad happened back in California—I guess Jack hinted around. But as far as I know, it was just hints. Sometimes the boys and my wife got a little impatient that I was devoted to Jack. But I just told them we'd been through things nobody needed to know about. And that pretty much took care of it."

And he's right. They went through things nobody should have to go through. We're quiet for a couple of long minutes. And then I ask how Curtis's family is faring.

"They're good, they're good. I expect Curtis is going to have to make some changes. Those boys of his are ready to bust out of the life he had them in. You ought to see Jack's mom with them. She's like a different person. Like she needed a mission, and they're it."

I'll be seeing Taylor this afternoon. She called to tell me she's headed back to Dallas and wanted to stop by to say goodbye. I'm remembering what Taylor said about Jack being a coward and about him begging her to kill him, and I wonder if Jack really did have the courage to pull the trigger on Phil. Or if in the end it was Taylor who did it. I'm not going to tell her about my conversation with Dunn and I'm not going to ask her if my hunch is right. She'd lie to me anyway, so I'd never know for sure. Some things are better left alone.

ACKNOWLEDGMENTS

My deep thanks to my mother and father, Adelle and Lloyd Klar, who made sure I was surrounded by books and music. They would have loved Samuel Craddock and the Jarrett Creek community.

I hear tales of editors who run roughshod over copy, publicists who underperform, and indifferent cover designers. Seventh Street Books decided not to go that direction. I am truly amazed at the professionalism, enthusiasm, and warmth of everyone on the team—Dan Mayer (editing magician), Meghan Quinn, Melissa Raé Shofner, Jill Maxick, Jade Zora Scibilia, Grace Zilsberger (love my covers), Cate Roberts-Abel, and Ian Birnbaum. These are my main contacts. I know there are others who work hard behind the scenes to make the books look and feel good, and my thanks extends to them as well.

A special salute to the generous, warm-hearted Carolyn Hart, author extraordinaire, whose support for other crime writers is legend. You're the best!

ABOUT THE AUTHOR

Terry Shames currently lives in Berkeley, CA, but her imagination is always stirred by the strange mix that makes up the vast landscape and human drama of Texas, where she grew up. Terry is a member of Mystery Writers of America and Sisters in Crime. Visit her website at www.Terrryshames.com.

ALSO BY TERRY SHAMES

A Killing at Cotton Hill